W9-AQW-346

DOROTHY SIMPSON

NO LAUGHING MATTER

WARNER BOOKS

A *Warner* Book

First published in Great Britain in 1983
by Michael Joseph Ltd

This edition published in Warner in 1994
Reprinted 1994, 1995 (three times), 1997, 1998

A CIP catalogue record for this book
is available from the British Library.

ISBN 0 7515 0153 0

Printed in England by Clays Ltd, St Ives plc

Warner Books
A Division of
Little, Brown and Company (UK)
Brettenham House
Lancaster Place
London WC2E 7EN

Dorothy Simpson worked first as a French teacher and then for many years as a marriage guidance counsellor before turning to writing full time. She is married with three children and lives near Maidstone in Kent, the background to the Thanet novels. *No Laughing Matter* is the twelfth in the series; the fifth, *Last Seen Alive*, won the Crime Writers' Association's Silver Dagger Award in 1985.

To Keith and Olwyn

I wish to express my gratitude to Stephen Skelton for allowing me to visit the award-winning vineyard at Tenterden, Kent, where he is winemaker, and especially to his assistant Chris Nicholas, who was so generous with his time and expertise at the busiest period of the year.

ONE

Thanet drummed his fingers on the steering wheel, scowling at the stationary line of tail-lights which curved away ahead of him. He glanced at the dashboard clock. Twenty to eight already. Bridget's train was due in ten minutes and he wanted to be there, waiting on the platform, when she arrived. He thought he had allowed plenty of time – at this hour of the evening the streets of Sturrenden were usually relatively deserted. There must have been an accident.

The approaching wail of an ambulance siren confirmed his guess. And yes, ahead of him, rhythmic pulses of blue light irradiated the sky, reflecting off the windows of the houses on the other side of the street, on the bend. Perhaps he should do a U-turn, make his way to the station by another route? Come *on*, he breathed. Move!

Miraculously, almost at once the furthest tail-lights disappeared around the curve in the road as the line of cars began to crawl past the scene of the accident. There was no time for Thanet to catch more than a glimpse of the Ford Cortina slewed across the road, the motorcycle half under its front wheels, the dazed figure sitting head on hands on the kerb and the stretcher already being loaded into the ambulance. Ben ought to be seeing this, thought Thanet grimly. Perhaps he'd stop nagging us to allow him a moped.

He arrived on the platform with a minute to spare, his mind now entirely focused on Bridget again. What was wrong? For the hundredth time their brief telephone conversation ran through his mind.

'Dad? Look, is it all right if I come home for a few days?'

'Yes, of course. But . . . Are you all right? Is anything wrong?'

'I'll be down on Friday evening, then.'

'What time? I'll meet you.'

'Lovely. I'll catch the 6.15. Thanks, Dad. See you then.'

And the phone had gone down, cutting off further inquiries.

It must be something to do with Alexander, thought Thanet. This was Bridget's wealthy, successful ex-public school boyfriend. She had been going out with him for over a year now and Thanet's initial misgivings over the difference in their backgrounds had gradually given way to acceptance. But he still had reservations. It was evident that Bridget was head over heels in love with Alexander but Thanet wasn't so sure of Alexander's feelings for her. He was fond of her, yes, but sufficiently fond to make a commitment? Thanet doubted it, and in one respect this was a good thing. At twenty Bridget was still very young. But if Alexander had broken it off . . . Thanet couldn't bear the thought of the heartache she would suffer. It was all very well to say that once your children were grown up they were no longer your responsibility and had to fend for themselves. They were still a part of you, always would be, and their joys and sorrows would always be yours, to a greater or lesser degree. And in

Bridget's case . . . Ah, here came the train. Thanet steeled himself. Yes, there she was. He walked briskly up the platform to meet her. She looked pinched and pale, he thought, diminished somehow, and in his opinion inadequately clad for a raw October evening in cotton trousers, T-shirt and thin cardigan.

She attempted a smile, kissed his cheek and handed over her psychedelic green and orange squashy bag.

'All right?' he said, trying to avoid too searching a scrutiny of her face.

Her eyes met his, briefly, then slid away as she nodded.

Well, he had no intention of pressing her. She could confide in them – if she chose to confide in them at all – in her own good time. They drove home in silence.

Joan heard the car and opened the front door to greet them. In response to the question in her eyes Thanet shook his head. *Nothing, yet.*

Joan gave Bridget a quick hug. 'Have you eaten?'

'I had a sandwich at Victoria.'

'Coffee, then?'

'Yes, lovely.'

They spent the next couple of hours watching television, trying to pretend that nothing was wrong, the air full of unspoken questions. When the ten o'clock news came on Bridget stretched and stood up. 'I think I'll go up, if you don't mind. It's been a pretty hectic week.'

Bridget, going to bed at ten p.m.? Unheard of! They concealed their dismay behind understanding nods and smiles.

'I think I'll burst if we don't find out soon,' said Joan as they listened to their daughter climb the stairs, her dragging footsteps a painful betrayal of her state of mind.

'The last thing she'll want is to be bombarded with questions.'

'Really, Luke, I meant no such thing. But a little parental concern . . .'

'She knows we're concerned! Give her time. She just needs a breathing space, that's all.'

The phone rang. Joan pulled a face. 'Must be for you, at this time of night. I'll make some tea.'

Thanet went to answer it reluctantly. He felt sluggish, depressed about Bridget, disinclined to do anything but have a hot, soothing drink and fall into bed.

As he picked up the phone Ben came in, slamming the front door behind him. At sixteen, already an inch taller than his father and with a physique to match, he seemed incapable of doing anything quietly.

'Sis home?'

Thanet pointed up the stairs and flapped his hand for silence, pressing the phone closer to his ear. 'Sorry, what did you say?'

'It's Pater, sir.'

Despite his lethargy of a moment ago, Thanet's scalp pricked. The Station Officer wouldn't bother him off duty unless it was important.

'Yes? Oh, hold on a moment, will you?' Thanet covered the receiver, exasperated. 'How d'you expect me to have a telephone conversation with all this noise going on?'

Joan had emerged from the kitchen. Ben was already halfway up the stairs and she was calling after him. 'She's tired. She's gone to bed.'

Ben looked astounded. 'At this hour? Anyway, I'm only going to say hi.' He took the rest of the stairs two at a time and they heard him knock on Bridget's door, the murmur of voices.

Joan shrugged and went back into the kitchen.

'Sorry, Pater,' said Thanet. 'Go on.'

'Patrol car responding to a 999 call has just radioed in for assistance. Suspicious death, sir. Could be murder.'

'Where?' Already the adrenalin was starting to flow.

'Sturrenden Vineyard. It's out on the –'

'I know where it is. Any more details?'

'Not yet, sir.'

'Right, I'm on my way. SOCOs notified?'

'Yes, sir. And Doc Mallard.'

'DS Lineham?'

'I'll ring him next, sir. And the rest of the team.'

Thanet put the phone down, went to the kitchen door.

Joan was screwing the top on to the Thermos flask. 'All right, I heard.' She handed him the flask. 'I wonder how many times I've done this.'

Thanet grinned and kissed her. 'I shouldn't start counting, it'll only depress you.'

Sturrenden Vineyard lay four miles west of the town, on the Maidstone road. As Thanet drove through the quiet streets he tried to recall what he knew about it. Very little, he realised, except that it was there and had become an increasingly thriving business. The Thanets drank very little and had never actually bought any wine there, nor had either of them gone on any of the vineyard walks or guided tours. Just as well, perhaps? He would be approaching the place with a completely open mind . . . No, not true, he realised. There was something he'd heard about the owner, what was his name? An odd name, but he couldn't recall it. Anyway, it was something unsavoury, he was sure . . . He frowned into the darkness. No, it was no good, the memory eluded him.

Ten minutes later the first notice appeared. 'STURREN-DEN VINEYARD 100 YDS ON R.' and shortly afterwards the illuminated sign came into view, a curved arch spanning the entrance. Thanet paused to look at it.

Details of opening times were given below in print too small to be legible at night. Bunches of grapes linked by vine leaves decorated each end of the board.

A car was approaching from behind as Thanet swung across the road and through the wide entrance gates. The car flashed its lights and followed suit. Lineham's Escort, Thanet realised. In the car park they pulled up side by side next to Mallard's old Rover. There were a number of other cars in the extensive parking area – a couple of police cars and several which presumably belonged to the vineyard.

'Nice white Mercedes over there,' said Lineham wistfully. 'This place is doing all right, by the look of it.' He and Thanet had worked together for so long that by now greetings were superfluous.

Thanet nodded. Lineham was right. The Mercedes aside, even by night all the signs of substantial reinvestment were there: fresh tarmac, new fencing and a general air of order and prosperity. Over to the right, set well back behind a tall, dense yew hedge, was a sizeable period farmhouse, lights blazing out their message of crisis from every window. Ahead, their roofs a looming darkness against the night sky, was a substantial cluster of farm buildings. Between two of the nearest barns there was a lorry-width gap in which stood a uniformed constable, clearly visible in the light streaming from the buildings on either side. As they drew closer Thanet could see that the one to the left had been converted into the vineyard shop, the one to the right the office.

'Evening, Tenby,' he said. 'Which way?'

The man half turned to the left and pointed. 'In that big building there, sir. The bottling plant. He's in the laboratory.' He paused, swallowed. 'It's a bit of a mess, sir.'

Thanet's heart sank. He always dreaded the first sight of the corpse. There was something so poignant about the newly dead, separated by so short a span of time from those who still lived and breathed. Although he had succeeded remarkably well in concealing this weakness from his colleagues Thanet always had consciously to armour himself against that first, awe-full moment. And if the death had been really violent, if there was a lot of blood and 'mess', as Tenby put it, the ordeal was ten times worse, Thanet's over-active imagination visualising those last agonising minutes before the victim was released to merciful unconsciousness. But forewarned was, to some extent, forearmed. 'In what way?' he said calmly.

'Looks as though the victim fell through a window, cutting his throat in the process. There's a lot of blood about. And glass everywhere.'

Bad, but it sounds as though I've seen far worse, thought Thanet. 'Do we know who he is yet?'

'Owner of the vineyard, sir. Chap called Randish.'

Of course! Randish, that was the name. And Thanet remembered now where he'd heard it. He wondered if Lineham would.

The sergeant had, of course. 'Randish,' repeated Lineham as they walked through the wide passageway into a big yard some sixty feet square, surrounded by buildings. 'That's the bloke I told you about, remember? A couple of years ago? Louise was worried about one of the mothers in Mandy's playgroup, she'd noticed bruises, usually in places where they weren't easily spotted, and she suspected the husband was knocking her about. She'd

7

tried to get the woman to open up, but she wouldn't and Louise wanted to know if there was any way we could help her.'

'Yes, I remember. And we said no, there wasn't. If the wife chose not to lay a complaint against her husband, there was absolutely nothing we could do about it.'

'So. Interesting,' said Lineham. 'Incidentally, what did Tenby mean, "laboratory", sir? What do you need a laboratory for, on a vineyard?'

Thanet shrugged. 'No idea.' He had come a halt and was looking around, trying to absorb the geography of the place. There was a lot to take in.

The whole of the right-hand side of the yard was taken up by the building PC Tenby had pointed out, the bottling plant. This was a relatively new construction, presumably purpose-built. Huge sliding doors stood open, spilling light into the yard. Thanet caught glimpses of tall stainless-steel vats, complicated machinery and, to the right, some of his men moving around near an open door to an inner room, the laboratory, presumably.

Straight ahead on the far side of the yard was an open-sided building. Harsh strip-lighting shone down upon a cylindrical stainless-steel structure some twelve feet long – a press, perhaps? – standing to one side, opposite a couple of trailers. A tractor, with a third trailer still attached, stood in between. Obviously the grapes were driven straight into this area from the vineyard beyond. Of course, at this time of the year they must be in the middle of the grape harvest, their busiest period. The floor glistened wet, as if newly hosed down.

Thanet became aware that Lineham was shifting from one foot to the other, trying to contain his impatience to get on and into the heart of the activity behind them. He was aware, too, that although he genuinely felt it important to take time to absorb his initial impressions of a place, part of the reason for this delay was his reluctance to proceed to the next stage. But it couldn't be put off for ever; he might as well get it over with. With a quick, comprehensive glance at the other buildings, at whose use he couldn't even begin to guess, he sighed and turned. 'All right, then, Mike. Come on.'

Lineham set off with alacrity, Thanet trailing behind.

Inside, the huge space was divided lengthwise by a plate glass wall, on the far side of which was the bottling plant, its tiled floor and walls spotless, the machinery of the plant itself gleaming hygienically. To the left of the double doors stood the row of vats which Thanet had glimpsed earlier, and two shorter rows of huge oak barrels supported by stout, crossed stretchers. The open door to the laboratory was in an inner wall to the right of the double doors and Thanet's stomach gave an uneasy heave as he noticed a pool of vomit nearby. A couple of SOCOs were talking to two patrolmen. As Thanet and Lineham approached a flash went off inside the laboratory.

'Bit tricky in there at the moment, sir,' said one of the SOCOs to Thanet. 'Never seen so much broken glass in my life. We took all the shots we needed of the body and then thought we'd finish taking the floor first so we could sweep up a bit.' He handed Thanet and Lineham some heavy-duty plastic overshoes.

They put them on.

'We'll be careful,' said Thanet. 'Just take a quick look.' He turned to the patrolmen. 'Who discovered the body?'

'Chap called Vintage. He's the assistant winemaker here.'

'Appropriate name,' said Lineham, with a grin.

Thanet shot him a quelling glance. *This is no laughing matter.* At once, he regretted it. He was being unreasonable.

9

Amongst policemen an apparently inappropriate levity was often a safety mechanism against the sordid reality of much of their work. He was too tense. The sooner the next few minutes were over, the better. 'Where is Vintage?'

'Down at the house, sir, with the victim's wife.'

'Right. Doc Mallard's still here, I gather?'

'Should be nearly finished by now.'

'Good.' He couldn't put it off any longer. Thanet took a deep breath and stepped inside, glass crunching beneath his feet. His brain photographed the scene, fixing it indelibly in his memory: an oblong room with high wall-benches swept virtually bare; and broken glass, everywhere, in chunks, shards and splinters, mostly colourless but with here and there a glint of green.

And blood.

Blood spattered on the floor, blood glistening on pieces of glass, blood smeared on the wall beneath the window, blood saturating the shirt-front of the man who lay in a half-seated position slumped against that wall, head at an awkward angle. Above him yawned a huge, jagged hole in the window. Despite the fresh air streaming in there was a slightly acrid underlying smell of fermenting grapes. The atmosphere seemed still to reverberate with echoes of the violent scene which had played itself out in this white, clinical room so short a time ago.

Behind him, Lineham whistled softly. 'Someone lost his temper here, all right.'

Lineham was right. Only a furious, ungovernable rage could have created this kind of wholesale destruction.

Mallard, crouched near the body, looked up. 'Bit of a mess, eh, Luke?'

Thanet nodded, bracing himself for a closer look, and

picked his way through the glass to stand beside the little police surgeon. And yes, there it was, that familiar twist in his gut, that painful pang of – what? Pity? Regret? Anger? Fear? Dread? A complex mixture, perhaps, of all of them. No one in the prime of life, as this man had been, should expect to die like this, in the familiar, apparent safety of his day-to-day working environment. Randish couldn't have been more than thirty-five, and looked tall, well-built and healthy. He had been good-looking, too; handsome, even, with thick dark curly hair and regular, well-formed features. Very attractive to women, probably, Thanet thought, and remembered Louise's suspicions. True or false? And, even if true, what were the circumstances which lay behind it all? Thanet knew that in the next days and weeks he would sooner or later find out; that Randish, until now no more to him than a stranger's name in a casual conversation, would come alive in a unique and extraordinary way. For, unlike the living, the dead have no means of safeguarding their secrets.

'What d'you think happened?' he asked Mallard, in no real expectation of an answer. Mallard invariably refused to be drawn on matters non-medical.

The little doctor peered up at Thanet over his half-moon spectacles, their gold rims glinting in the harsh bright light, and put out his hand. 'Give me a heave, will you? I couldn't kneel because of the glass and I think I've seized up.'

Thanet obliged.

'Thanks.' Mallard peered down at the body. 'You'll have to work that out for yourself. Not my province. But I can most certainly pronounce him dead and as you can see for yourself there's little doubt as to cause. The jugular vein was severed and there's so much blood about it's almost certain that the carotid artery was, too. I'll stick my neck out and say he bled to death. It would have been very quick, a matter of minutes. We won't be able to confirm until the PM, of course, but I'd say it was most unlikely to be anything else.'

'Look as though someone used him as an Aunt Sally,' said Lineham, 'chucked everything he could lay his hands on at him. Randish backs towards the window, probably holding up his arms to protect his face, then he treads on something – a bottle, perhaps – which makes him lose his balance. He falls backwards, twisting sideways, and goes through the window, slicing through that artery in the process. Then he gradually collapses, the weight of his body dragging him down into a sitting position.'

'Quite feasible,' said Mallard.

'How long ago?' said Thanet.

Mallard puffed out his lips, expelled air softly and shook his head. 'You don't give up, do you, Luke? You know as well as I do that it's impossible to be accurate.'

Thanet grinned. They went through this charade every time. 'Oh come on, Doc, just give us some idea.'

Mallard considered, head on one side, and then said reluctantly, 'Some time in the last three hours? And earlier in that period, rather than later.'

Thanet glanced at his watch. Ten-thirty. Between 7.30 and 9.30. then, probably. 'Thanks. You've finished here, now?'

Mallard snapped his bag shut. 'I have. It's off to my nice warm bed for me.'

'Don't rub it in. I'll walk you to your car.'

'Don't bother.'

'It'll be good to get some fresh air.'

Outside, Thanet gratefully inhaled the clean, moist air, anxious to rid his nostrils of the smell of death, the taint of murder. As they emerged from the passageway he saw that the ambulance had arrived at last and some more cars were pulling in.

'Draco won't be here, I suppose,' said Mallard. 'Didn't Angharad have another test this week?'

'Yes. On Wednesday. They went up today for the result.'

In the early years of Superintendent Draco's reign in Sturrenden he had galvanised the place into becoming the most efficient Division in the South-East. He was ubiquitous and his men never knew when he would suddenly materialise, breathing down their necks. But a couple of years ago his beautiful and much-loved wife Angharad had had leukaemia diagnosed and overnight Draco had become a changed man. Gone were the light of enthusiasm in his eyes, the hectoring tone in his voice, the infuriating bounce from his step. Although his men had all complained bitterly at the way the Super had harried and chivvied them, they had grown to admire, respect and even to like him, and there was not one of them who would not have suffered the worst of harassments to see Draco back on his original form. There were signs that Angharad's condition was improving, but she was still trailing up to London regularly for bone-marrow tests and Draco's staff always knew when another test was coming up: for days beforehand he would become increasingly abstracted and morose. He always accompanied his wife both for the test and for the results two days later and for the last six months or so had got into the habit of taking her away to a hotel for a day or two afterwards.

Mallard sighed. 'Living through all that is not an experience I'd wish on my worst enemy.'

Thanet glanced at the little doctor, aware that Mallard was remembering his own bitter years. The Thanets and the Mallards were good friends, Thanet having known the older man since childhood. He and Joan were very fond of Helen, Mallard's second wife, and grateful to her for rescuing the little doctor from the years of depression which had followed the lingering death of his first wife from cancer. Thanet was saved from a reply – for what could usefully be said? – by the approach of the two ambulancemen, carrying a stretcher. He knew them both by sight.

'Sorry we took so long, Inspector. Been a spate of accidents this evening.'

Thanet shook his head. 'There's no hurry with this one. Anyway, it's all clear now. Just check that the SOCOs have finished and you can take him away.'

Hard on their heels came more of his men. He sent them to find Lineham. 'I'll be with you in a few moments.'

At the car Mallard turned. 'How's Bridget these days? Helen was saying the other day we hadn't seen her for ages. I know she misses their cookery sessions.'

Helen Mallard, a well-known cookery writer, had encouraged Bridget in her choice of career and at one time the two of them regularly used to spend afternoons together concocting new dishes for Helen's latest project.

'She's down for a long weekend, as a matter of fact. I picked her up at the station earlier this evening.'

Something in Thanet's tone must have alerted Mallard to his concern.

'Nothing wrong, is there?'

'We don't know for certain, yet. But she seems pretty down in the mouth.'

'Alexander?'

'More than likely, I should think.'

'Who'd be young again?' said Mallard, unlocking his

car. He patted the old Rover affectionately. 'There's a lot to be said for growing old together. So much more comfortable.'

Thanet laughed. 'So far as I can recall, at the age of twenty it wasn't comfort I was looking for!' He watched Mallard drive off and then set purposefully off back to the laboratory. Action was now called for: get the men organised; then interview the chap who had discovered the body, Vintage.

He was eager to get on with it.

TWO

The yew hedge was tall, dense, thick, planted no doubt as an evergreen screen to preserve the Randishes' privacy in winter and summer alike. Living over the shop, so to speak, must have certain disadvantages, thought Thanet as he followed Lineham through the tall arched wrought-iron gate which fitted snugly into a clipped opening in the hedge.

Though this house would compensate for most.

It was Tudor, black and white, the marriage of beams and plasterwork a delight to the eye. The curtains were drawn in the room to the left of the front door but lights still blazed from most of the windows, illuminating the neat front cottage garden. This was past its best now but still sported clumps of flowers here and there, their colours indistinguishable in the dim light. The path of ancient paving stones was bordered by a dwarf lavender hedge which in summer must release its sweet scent as visitors brushed by.

Thanet waited for the inevitable remark from Lineham. Anything larger than the sergeant's own modest dwelling invariably provoked a comment.

Lineham did not disappoint him.

'Not exactly on the breadline, are they?' said the

sergeant as they approached the massive front door with its shallow medieval arch. 'Where's the doorbell?'

'Is this it?' Thanet grasped the curlicue on the end of a piece of stout wire dangling to the right of the door, and tugged. In the distance a bell tinkled.

'Sounds like it,' said Lineham. 'This place really is the genuine article, isn't it? Be interesting to see what it's like inside.'

'We're not house-hunting, Mike.' But Thanet's tone was mild. He, too, would be interested to see the interior. People's houses were very revealing, he found.

Footsteps approached, unseen hands fumbled with a latch, and the door opened. The man was broad-shouldered, with a thatch of thick, white hair.

'Detective Inspector Thanet and Detective Sergeant Lineham, Sturrenden CID,' said Thanet.

'Owen Landers.' The man stood back. 'Come in.' He closed the door behind them. 'Randish is – was – my son-in-law.'

They were in a narrow hall, the patina on its panelled walls a mute testimony to centuries of polishing. The floor was of flagstones, partly concealed by the rich sub-dued colours of a red and blue Persian rug.

Thanet offered his condolences and then said, 'We understand that it was a Mr Vintage who found the body and we were told he was here.'

Landers would be in his late fifties, Thanet thought, and a farmer, at a guess. That ruddy, weatherbeaten complexion could only be the result of years of exposure to the caprices of the British climate, and his clothes were what Thanet thought of as top quality country gear – cord trousers, cable-stitch sweater and brogues.

'Yes.' Landers gestured to a half-open door. 'Come in.'

A wave of heat greeted them as they stepped inside. It

was the kind of room often seen in the pages of glossy magazines: beamed, low-ceilinged, with casement windows on three sides and a huge inglenook fireplace. There were more Persian rugs on the floor of polished brick, linen curtains and upholstery in glowing colours and several pieces of fine antique furniture, all displayed to advantage by the light of strategically placed table lamps. The three people in it looked up apprehensively – a middle-aged woman, a woman in her thirties and a slightly younger man.

'My wife, my daughter and Vintage,' said Landers. He introduced Thanet and Lineham and then added, 'They want a word with you, Oliver.'

Vintage was standing in front of the fireplace, his back to the wood-burning stove. 'Yes, of course.' He was young, twenty-seven or twenty-eight at a guess, and whipcord thin with a shock of straight black hair which flopped across a high, bony forehead. He looked, Thanet thought, like a man on the verge of collapse. His shoulders drooped, his hands hung limply by his sides, his eyes were dull in their deep-hollowed eye-sockets, his skin tallow-white. His clothes were as creased and stained as if he had worked and slept in them for weeks. Indifference, overuse or simple neglect? Thanet wondered. In any case, it was clear that, the murder aside, Vintage was a man who had been under stress for some considerable time.

And a man under stress can snap.

'You can use the dining room,' said Landers.

After the first apprehensive glance Mrs Randish had ignored them. Hunched on the edge of her chair, hands outstretched to the stove, she seemed oblivious of their presence, sunk in private misery. Her tear-stained face and swollen eyes told their own story. The older woman's attention was focused on her daughter. Perched on the arm of the chair beside her she watched her steadily with a fierce, protective gaze.

Thanet was glad to get out of the room. Dressed in his outdoor clothes he felt he couldn't have stood the heat in there much longer. He was relieved to find the dining room cooler, but he and Lineham still took off their raincoats before sitting down at the round oak gate-legged table.

Vintage remained standing.

'Do sit down, Mr Vintage.'

'If I do I shall never get up again.' Nevertheless, apparently unable to resist the temptation, he sat, slumping in the chair as if his muscles no longer had the strength to hold him upright. After a moment he straightened his shoulders and sat up a little, presumably to brace himself for the interview.

'It must all have been a terrible shock,' said Thanet.

'Yes it was, of course. But it's not just that. I've been working flat out for weeks now. It's the busiest time of the year. It's OK while you keep going, but when you stop it hits you, you know?'

Thanet nodded sympathetically. 'Pretty long hours, I imagine.'

'I don't usually get to bed till two or three and then I'm up again to get here and start work at 7.30.'

'You actually make the wine?'

'With some supervision from Zak – that's Mr Randish, yes.'

Zak, thought Thanet. What an outlandish name. Short for Zachariah, perhaps?

'He's the winemaker, I'm his assistant,' Vintage was explaining. 'He's been training me for the last four years so in practice most of the time he leaves me to get on with it.'

'Just the two of you make the wine?'

'Yes. But he's also the winemaker for another vineyard, at Chasing Manor, and he divides his time between the two. So a lot of the time I'm here by myself. It's pretty hectic because we not only press the grapes from this vineyard but from a lot of smaller vineyards in the area. Most don't have their own presses, you see.'

'So you were here by yourself today?'

'Zak was here for a couple of hours this morning, as usual, before going to Chasing.' Vintage's tone was guarded.

'Anything unusual happen?'

'No.'

But he was lying, Thanet was sure of it. 'What did you do?'

'Discussed yesterday's work, today's arrangements. Made one batch of wine.'

What could the man be hiding? 'Together?'

'Yes.'

'Was that usual?'

'Not unusual.'

It all seemed innocuous, but Thanet was still convinced there was more to it than this. It would keep, however. He pressed on.

'And how long does a batch take?'

'Two and a half hours.'

'So Mr Randish left at – what? Ten?'

'Nearer half past, I should think.'

'And what time did he get back?'

The routine during harvest was that Randish usually got back from Chasing Manor vineyard at about six, had a bite to eat and then came up to the press where Vintage was working. They would sort out any problems that had cropped up during the day and then work through the evening, sometimes together, but more often than not individually. Randish would divide his time between laboratory and office.

'There's a lot of paperwork, then?' said Thanet.

Vintage passed a hand wearily over his forehead. 'Oh God, yes, you wouldn't believe it. Everything, but everything, has to be catalogued for the Customs and Excise. If you sneeze, they want to know it.'

'What sort of information do they require?'

'They have to know exactly what happened, what date, what went where, how many ounces of sugar you used with each batch, how much yeast went in. They want to know every movement from tank to tank, every single fluid ounce you've got in there, how much you lost after fermentation when you rack a tank off, all your losses through the process.' Vintage put his head in his hands. 'How I'm going to manage to do all that as well as the winemaking, I just don't know.'

It certainly sounded a mammoth task for one man. 'Perhaps you'll be able to get someone in to give you a hand.'

'Where from? Anyone who'd be of any use is working flat out at the moment, like me.' He shook his head in despair. 'Sorry, Inspector, not your problem, is it?'

'You say Mr Randish usually divided his time between the office and the laboratory. What would he be doing in the laboratory?'

'Checking sulphur levels, sugar levels, fermentation, Ph, acidity and so on and then noting it all down, putting it on computer.'

'And would you see him during the evening? Would you have to go over to the laboratory or the office for anything?'

A shrug. 'Sometimes. Depends.'

'And tonight?'

'No. I had a lot of other things to do.'

Vintage was holding back again. What had been going on? No doubt they'd find out, sooner or later.

'So exactly what did happen this evening?'

According to Vintage he and Randish had followed their usual routine. They had worked together from 6.30 to 7, doing the turnaround between batches, which involved a lot of manual work that always went more quickly if there were two of you. Randish then went across to the office and that was the last Vintage saw of him until 9.30, when the next batch finished. That was when he went to the laboratory and found him dead.

'Did you go in?'

'Just a couple of steps inside the door.' Vintage grimaced. 'I didn't need to go any further.'

He had gone straight to the phone in the office next door, rung the police and Mr Landers, then hurried down to the house to warn Mrs Randish of their arrival, and the reason for it. She had insisted on coming to see her husband's body for herself.

'I tried to stop her, but she wouldn't listen. Short of physically restraining her, there was nothing I could do to stop her.'

No wonder she was so upset, thought Thanet. The shock of a husband's sudden death is enough, but to see him in that condition ... 'Did she go into the room, touch anything?'

'Just a couple of steps, like me. Then she came to a dead halt, stood staring for a minute, then went outside and was sick. I'm not surprised.'

They had then returned to the house, by which time Mrs Randish's parents had arrived. They lived less than a mile away.

'So that would have been, let me see, at about ten to ten?'

Vintage thought. 'Something like that, yes. And the police arrived about five minutes later.'

'Did Mr Landers go up to the laboratory?'

'Yes. He wanted to see for himself, as well. I don't think any of them could believe it, really.' This time Vintage anticipated Thanet's question. 'But he only went just inside the door, too.'

'So no one actually touched the body?'

Vintage shook his head.

Thanet considered. 'Was there anyone else working here this evening?'

'No.' Vintage pulled a face. 'Drops me in it, doesn't it?'

'Should it?'

'What do you mean?'

'Did you have any reason to kill Mr Randish?'

'No!'

But again, it didn't ring quite true.

'Do you realise you haven't shown the slightest sign of regret over his death?'

'Haven't I?' Vintage rubbed his hands nervously together. 'I don't suppose it's sunk in yet. But believe me, I'd rather have him alive than dead.'

'Why?'

'Purely selfish reasons. Because it really does leave me in a hell of a mess here. And also, in the long term, because I still had a lot to learn from him. He was a bloody good winemaker.'

'I notice you don't say anything about liking him or missing him as a friend.'

'You don't have to like someone to work with him.'

No, but it helps, thought Thanet, glancing at Lineham who was to him almost indispensible. The sergeant was

23

listening intently, making the occasional note. There was one other question that had to be put. Let Lineham ask it. 'Do you have any further questions to put, Sergeant?'

Lineham glanced down at his notebook, as if consulting it. 'You say you were working here alone all evening, Mr Vintage. Did you see anyone else around, at any time?'

'No! Oh, hang on . . . Yes . . .' Vintage stopped.

It was obvious that he'd suddenly remembered, had said so without thinking and then had second thoughts. Why?

'Yes, or no?' said Lineham.

'Yes,' said Vintage reluctantly, aware no doubt that retracting now could lead to all sorts of complications. 'I'd forgotten because it was early on, soon after Zak went across to the office.'

Lineham waited expectantly.

'Reg Mason came up. He'd been to see Mrs Randish, he said.'

'Who's he?'

'A local builder. He's been converting a complex of farm buildings on their land into holiday cottages.'

'What did he want to see her about?'

'He didn't say. Why should he? It's none of my business.'

Thanet sighed inwardly. Vintage was not a good liar.

Lineham wasn't prepared to let the matter go. 'So why did he come up to see you?'

'Search me. Just to say hullo. Perhaps he just felt like a natter.'

'So did he stay talking long?'

'No, just a few minutes. He could see I was busy.'

'Did you see him leave?'

'Yes.'

'You're sure he didn't go into the bottling plant?'

'No, he didn't!'

'The press is that stainless-steel machine underneath the open-sided shed at the far side of the yard?'

'Yes.'

'Then you'd have had a clear view of the big doors into the bottling plant all evening. No one would have been able to go in or out without your seeing them.'

Vintage laughed. 'You must be joking! If I'd stood there beside it like a dummy all the time then yes, that would be true, I grant you. But I was all over the place, shifting things about, swilling out, hosing down, moving supplies of sugar, batches of waiting grapes, cleaning out some of the fermentation vessels in an adjoining shed . . . Shall I go on?'

'I think you've made your point. So it would have been easy for someone to slip into the laboratory without your seeing them.'

'Right!'

'Did you hear anything, then? Cars arriving or leaving?'

'If you'd heard the noise the press makes when the compressor comes on you wouldn't be asking me that, either.'

Thanet couldn't make up his mind if Vintage was deliberately being unhelpful, or whether he was just trying to make it clear that although he had been alone here there had been ample opportunity for anyone else to get in if they had watched for the opportunity.

Lineham glanced at Thanet. *I don't think we're going to get any further.*

Thanet nodded. 'Well, I think that's all for the moment, Mr Vintage. We'll need to talk to you again tomorrow, and you can make a formal statement then. But you can go home now, try and get a decent night's sleep for once.'

'Will I be able to go on pressing tomorrow?'

Thanet shook his head. 'I'm sorry, that's out of the question.'

'But I have to! We've got four batches booked in, from small vineyards, and more the next day. And the day after that! We can't just not deal with them. This is these people's livelihood, Inspector, they work all year for this. We've just got to go on.'

'I'm sorry,' Thanet repeated, 'but I can't have people tramping around all over the place tomorrow. The vineyard will have to be closed. But I do understand what you're saying and I'll do my level best to make sure you're able to go on the following day.'

Vintage compressed his lips but could see that it was pointless to argue. With an ill grace, he left.

THREE

Lineham tossed his notebook on to the table. 'He knows more than he's telling, doesn't he?'

'Yes. But is it relevant? That's the point.' People were, Thanet knew, prepared to go to astonishing lengths to preserve their privacy and even in a murder investigation would tell the police only what they felt they ought to know. Understandable but infuriating. All the same, he was intrigued by Oliver Vintage. 'I wouldn't mind betting there's more to his condition than just plain tiredness.'

'He's ill, you mean?'

'Not ill, but ... Well, I'd say he's a man with a problem, a problem that's really getting him down. And he's having an especially hard time coping with it at the moment, because of the demands his work is making on him.'

'You think Randish was the problem?'

'Could be. If so, no doubt we'll find out sooner or later.'

It was, he thought, an extraordinary way to earn a living. Here he sat, in a dead man's chair at a dead man's table, trying to feel his way into a dead man's life. If anyone had asked him why he did it he supposed he'd say, well, someone has to. And if asked to elaborate, even knowing that he risked sounding grandiose, he'd say that some of us have to try to balance the scales of justice, or evil would flourish unchecked and the world would descend into anarchy. His own contribution towards the struggle might be small, but it was what gave meaning and purpose to his life.

'Pity they all went tramping into the laboratory,' Lineham said.

'I know. No doubt they'll all have glass embedded in their shoes, so we won't be able to eliminate any of them that way.'

'Except Mrs Landers.'

'True.'

'So, what now, sir?'

'We'd better have a word with Mrs Randish, if she's up to it. Let's go and see.'

As soon as they entered the sitting room Thanet could sense the tension in the air. It showed in Landers' aggressive pose in front of the hearth, chin thrust forward, legs apart and hands clasped behind his back; showed too in Mrs Landers' worried expression and in the rigidity of Alice Randish's back. Alice was still huddled on the edge of her seat as close to the woodstove as she could get, stretching out her hands to its warmth and rubbing them together from time to time. With her long fair hair falling forward to hide her face and her slight, almost girlish figure, she could easily have been taken for a teenager, Thanet thought. Her mother was still perched on the arm of the chair beside her.

What had they been arguing about? Thanet wondered. 'Mrs Randish,' he said, 'I really am very sorry to have to trouble you at a time like this. I mean that. But it would help us enormously if you could answer just a few questions.'

'Can't it wait till morning?' snapped Landers. 'I've sent

for the doctor. Alice will need something to help her sleep tonight. I thought we'd take her home with us. The children too, of course. It'll mean waking them up, but that can't be helped.'

'Daddy, do stop fussing,' Alice said wearily, without looking up. 'I told you, I'll be perfectly all right.'

Was this the cause of the disagreement? Thanet doubted it. Whether Alice should go or stay was surely not a sufficiently emotive issue. He said nothing, simply stood, waiting, and in a moment Alice did glance up.

'Do sit down, Inspector.'

'Alice . . .'

'Daddy, please!'

Thanet took a seat on the opposite side of the hearth, wishing that it weren't so hot in here. Already he could feel sweat pricking at his back.

'How old are the children?' he said, hoping to break the ice.

Landers answered for her. 'Eight and six.' He was still standing in front of the hearth, a physical barrier between Thanet and Alice.

Thanet had had enough of this. 'Would you mind taking a seat, sir? And if you'd like to stay –'

'Of course I'm staying!'

'Then I'd be grateful if you would refrain from interrupting. Otherwise I'm afraid I shall have to insist on seeing Mrs Randish alone.'

Landers didn't like it but with an ill grace retreated to a sofa at the far side of the room.

Thanet guessed that Alice was an only child and had probably been both over-protected and over-indulged. He wondered how Landers would have felt if he knew that Randish had been knocking his beloved daughter about. That was a thought. Perhaps he had known. Somehow

Thanet had to find out if there was any foundation for Louise's suspicions and if there were, whether Landers had been aware of the situation.

But not yet. Such delicate matters could not be rushed.

He turned back to Alice. 'Now, Mrs Randish, I understand that your husband was away for most of the day.'

For the first time she lifted her head and looked at Thanet properly.

Her eyes were astonishing, he thought, a deep cornflower blue, fringed with long lashes. Her features were regular, the bone structure delicate, its underlying beauty unmarred by the superficial marks of grief. She was aptly named, he thought, remembering Tenniel's famous illustrations for Alice in Wonderland.

'Yes, that's right,' she said. Her tone was heavy with despair and he felt a surge of pity for her.

Be careful, said a small voice in his head. She could have done it herself. He had a lightning vision of the slender figure before him galvanised with fury, the flower-like face contorted with rage, that ladylike voice hurling imprecations at Randish. It would have taken no strength at all to sweep bottles, test tubes, flasks off the benches, to seize and hurl some of them at her husband.

Thanet shook his head to clear it. He needed all his wits about him to tread the tightrope he always had to walk when interviewing a bereaved husband or wife. Statistics make it more than likely that you are talking to the murderer, but this can never be taken for granted. And you are in any case addressing a person whose private world has been destroyed for ever.

Noticing that her lower lip had begun to tremble and her eyes to fill with tears he tried to make his tone as matter-of-fact as possible. 'What time did he leave this morning?' *I hate this.*

'I don't know. I was out on Rosie. My horse.'

'And what time did he come back?'

'Just before six, as usual.'

Her voice was steadying, Thanet noticed with relief.

'We always eat early during harvest, so that he can work right through the evening without stopping.'

'So you had supper, and then?'

'He left to go up to the winery, about 6.30.'

'Did you see him again during the evening?'

She bit her lip and shook her head, the long hair swaying from side to side.

'What did you do after he left?'

'Put the children to bed, read them a story. Watched television.'

'So you were alone for the rest of the evening?'

Suddenly tension was back in the air. She glanced at her father, hesitated. 'No.'

Her mother also looked at Landers, somewhat apprehensively, Thanet thought.

What was going on?

'I was here for a while, Inspector,' said Landers.

Thanet was intrigued. So a father had called to see his daughter. Why this reaction? There could be only one reason. The visit must have a possible connection with the murder, in their opinion at least.

'Why was that?' Thanet asked Alice, but she was avoiding his eye, it seemed, staring fixedly at the woodstove and twisting a lock of hair round and round a forefinger.

Mrs Landers had suddenly become engrossed in scraping at an invisible spot on her skirt with her thumbnail.

'Mrs Randish?' Thanet persisted. 'What was the reason for your father's visit?'

'Oh, for God's sake!' Landers exploded. He jumped up and strode across the room towards them. 'Do I have to

31

have a reason to call on my own daughter? You don't think I have to ring up and make an appointment, do you?'

What was it that Landers was trying to prevent her saying? The answer to what had originally been a casual enquiry had become important. Thanet noticed with amusement that Lineham had stopped writing and was staring fixedly at Landers as if trying to read his mind, his nose pointing like a gundog on the trail.

This, clearly, was what the argument had been about. Landers had wanted to hold something back from the police, his daughter had disagreed with him.

'Mrs Randish?' Thanet said again.

Alice looked at her father. 'Oh, what's the point, Daddy? Can't you see you're just making matters worse? I told you they'd be bound to find out sooner or later.'

Very neat. Landers was no match for his daughter, thought Thanet. Alice was obviously skilled at getting her own way. She hadn't openly gone against his wishes but had yet managed to manoeuvre him into the position where it had become obvious that he had something to hide.

Landers was understandably looking baffled and exasperated.

Thanet glanced from one to the other. 'Know what?' He guessed who would be the one to reply.

'Oh, very well!' said Landers. He took up his original position in front of the hearth, unconsciously betraying his agitation by shoving his hand in his pocket and jingling some coins. 'It's just that it's a private matter and rather complicated and as it had been resolved anyway it seemed pointless to mention it, especially as it has no bearing whatsoever on what happened here tonight.'

Thanet said nothing; waited.

Landers shifted from one foot to the other. 'My daughter and her husband have been having some work done by a local builder.'

'Reg Mason,' said Thanet, remembering Vintage's evasiveness on the subject. Perhaps he was now going to find out what all that was about.

They all looked startled.

'Yes. How did you . . .?'

'Mr Vintage told me he'd called to see Mrs Randish this evening.'

Alice shot a triumphant glance at her father. *You see?*

'Go on, Mr Landers.'

It was the sort of sad little tale which had become all too familiar during the recession years. Landers was patently reluctant to tell it and Thanet had to prompt and probe in order to get the details.

Reg Mason's firm was small and he tended to take on only one big project at a time. In the boom years of the late eighties when there had been so much work about that builders could pick and choose and virtually name their own price, he had, like many people, overstretched his resources by buying a much bigger house, with a correspondingly huge mortgage padded out by a bank loan. At that time the future seemed golden, the supply of work endless and confidence was high. Then in '90 and '91 everything went wrong. The bottom fell out of the property market, building work virtually ground to a halt, interest rates shot up. The mortgage became crippling and there was no money coming in. Reg had realised he must retrench. He had put his house on the market but no one could afford to buy it at the price he had to ask. He had reduced it, repeatedly, to no avail. He had had to lay off some of the small team of workmen he had employed for years.

Then Randish's project came along, the conversion of a group of farm buildings into holiday cottages, and Mason had jumped at the chance to tender for it. Randish's credit was good and Mason saw it as a safe enterprise which would keep his firm ticking over until the economic situation improved. Work had started about eighteen months ago and to begin with there had been no problems, Randish paying up reasonably promptly once a month, as agreed. Mason could not afford to pay his suppliers without a regular income from his client.

As always with such work the most expensive months were the last, when floors were tiled, central heating put in, kitchens and bathrooms installed, and it was when these larger bills started to come in that the trouble began. Randish disputed them, claiming that they were far beyond the original estimate. Mason said that this was because Randish had altered the initial specifications, choosing more expensive finishes and introducing additional features. The dispute had been put into the hands of solicitors and had been running for over six months.

Until the matter of the disputed bills, which over three months amounted to a sum of some sixty thousand pounds, Mason had managed to limp along. But after that the situation had become increasingly desperate. His building merchants, unpaid, refused to provide further supplies, thus preventing him from taking on other work until the matter was settled. Both bank and building society pressed progressively harder as unpaid mortgage and interest payments mounted up. A month ago they had lost patience and today he had received a letter from the building society's solicitors saying that they were seeking a court hearing with a view to repossession. The situation was exacerbated by the fact that Mason's wife had a heart condition which was being adversely affected by the strain and anxiety.

Mason had come tonight to make one more attempt to persuade Randish to pay at least a part of the sum owing, much of which was well within the original agreed estimate. Alice had advised him against attempting to talk to her husband that evening. Zak was tired and overworked and would not be in a receptive mood. But she felt sorry for Reg, whom she had known since she was a child, and she promised to do her best to try to persuade her husband to change his mind. Knowing, however, that this was most unlikely, when Reg left she had decided to ask her father's advice. She had rung Landers and asked him to come over.

Thanet could understand why Landers hadn't wanted all this to come out. Mason was obviously a desperate man. His anger and resentment must have been building up for months, justifiably so far as Thanet could see. Even if his bills had been extortionate, most of the money had apparently legitimately been owed to him. In view of Mason's dire financial position Randish could, in all decency, at least have paid him that sum and taken legal action only over the excess amount. The letter informing Mason that repossession was imminent must have been the last straw. That scene of destruction in the laboratory spoke eloquently of an explosion of anger. Mason now seemed a prime candidate and Landers must know it. But it was obvious from the way that Landers had spoken of Mason and presented his story that he was very much on the builder's side. They had probably been boys together and old loyalties die hard. It was equally obvious that Landers had not been fond of his son-in-law and wasn't sorry to see the last of him.

'So,' Thanet said to Alice, 'you had the impression that Mr Mason was going to do as you suggested and not attempt to see your husband tonight?'

'Yes.' She frowned. 'But if Oliver saw him he must have gone up to the winery.'

'Yes, he did. But he didn't see Mr Randish. Mr Vintage says he only stayed a few minutes, then left.'

Landers looked relieved.

'However,' Thanet added, 'Mr Vintage has also made it clear that although he was working at the winery all evening he was moving about a lot and anyone could have got into the bottling plant without being seen.'

'You're not suggesting Reg came back, are you?' said Landers sharply.

'It's possible.'

'No!'

Without warning the door swung open and they all turned towards it, startled.

On the threshold stood a miniature version of Alice Randish, bare-footed and wearing a Snoopy nightshirt. Bridget used to have one exactly like it, Thanet remembered. The little girl blinked at the unexpected sight of a roomful of people.

Her appearance galvanised Alice Randish into action. 'Fiona!' She was across the room in a flash, stooping to put her arms around her daughter. 'Darling, what's the matter?'

'I was thirsty, Mummy. I called, but you didn't come.' Her eyes travelled from face to face. 'Where's Daddy?'

There was a brief, pregnant silence. What would Alice Randish do? Thanet wondered. Break the news of Randish's death to her daughter now, when she herself was at her most vulnerable and least fit to cope with Fiona's reaction? Or wait until morning?

The decision was taken out of her hands. Landers stepped in. He crossed to his granddaughter and swung her up into his arms. 'Grandad will get you a drink, sweetheart. And then we thought it might be fun for you all to come and stay with us for a few days. Would you like that?' Without waiting for an answer he bore Fiona away.

Having told her father she would prefer to stay at home, Alice was understandably looking irritated at his high-handedness. Her lips tightened and she glanced at her mother, who shook her head resignedly. *What did you expect?*

So far, Thanet realised, Mrs Landers hadn't said a single word. He wondered if her relationship with her husband was always so overshadowed by that between him and Alice.

She spoke now. 'Actually, your father's right, dear. Apart from anything else it will be very disturbing for the children to be here over the next few days. There's bound to be a lot of activity, isn't that so, Inspector?'

'Inevitably, I'm afraid.'

'And it really would be better for you, too, to be away from all this. Do reconsider.'

Alice was silent for a few moments, then she sighed. 'I suppose you're right.' She pulled a face. 'I'm just being feeble, I suppose. The thought of organising the packing ...' She ran a hand through her hair and gave a defeated shrug. 'I just can't seem to think straight.'

Her mother put an arm around her shoulders. 'That's not surprising. Don't worry, I'll see to all that. We won't need to take much tonight, anyway. We can come back tomorrow.'

In the hall a bell tinkled.

'That'll be the doctor,' said Mrs Landers.

There was a sudden flurry of activity: the doctor was admitted; Thanet and Lineham retired once more to the dining room. As they were crossing the hall Landers returned with Fiona and handed her over to her grandmother, who bore her off upstairs. Thanet asked Landers to accompany them. Clearly reluctant, he complied.

'You seem very certain that Mason couldn't have come back,' said Thanet, as if their conversation had not been interrupted.

The phone rang in the hall.

Thanet cursed as Landers jumped up with alacrity. 'I'd better answer that.'

He closed the door behind him and Thanet heard him murmuring responses. A moment or two later he returned, looking stunned. He slumped down into his seat. 'My God,' he said. 'I just don't believe it.'

FOUR

'Bad news, sir?' said Thanet.

'I don't believe it,' Landers repeated. 'They say lightning never strikes twice in the same place. That was my daughter's sister-in-law – Zak's sister. They were very close. She's a widow, and older than him and ... Well, anyway, she's got two children, twins, a boy and a girl. She was ringing to say the girl, Zak's niece, died this evening. She was only twenty. She's been in hospital for some time, but even so ...'

The same age as Bridget, thought Thanet, with a pang of sympathy for this unknown woman.

Landers jumped up and began pacing about. The shock seemed to have loosened his tongue. 'I don't know how Alice will take this, especially after what's happened here tonight. She was very fond of her niece. They've always been close, ever since Karen and Jonathan came to stay here for a few days when their mother was in hospital. That was years ago, just before Fiona was born. In fact, Karen seemed to get on better with Alice than with her uncle. So how Alice is going to react ...' He stopped pacing and turned to face Thanet. 'Oh, you may have thought Alice was calm enough just now, but I know her and believe me, she's just hanging on by the skin of her teeth. She was besotted with that husband of hers. I expect you thought I was coming on a bit strong with her, didn't you? Playing the heavy father? Well that was because I knew it was the only way to stop her falling apart over these first few hours. Give her something to kick against and she'd be OK until the doctor could knock her out. If I'd gone all mushy on her she'd never have been able to cope.'

It all sounded very logical but Thanet wasn't so sure. It wouldn't surprise him to discover that Landers was really talking about himself, that it was he who wouldn't have been able to cope if Alice had 'fallen apart', as he put it. Especially, perhaps, if he had committed the murder himself and was the cause of the disintegration.

'Did you tell Mr Randish's sister about his death?'

'No. Fortunately she wasn't expecting him to come over tonight. She knows he works all hours during harvest, and she asked me to tell him not to. Said she'd just got back from the hospital, she was exhausted and was going to bed. She'd see him tomorrow, she said. I suppose I'll have to go round and break the news of Zak's death to her myself. There's no one else to do it. God knows how she's going to take it.' Landers was obviously dreading the prospect, and Thanet couldn't blame him. Breaking the news of the death of a close relative was high on the list of jobs all policemen hated most.

'We could do it if you like, sir.'

'Oh.' Landers looked taken aback. 'That's very decent of you, Thanet. But no, I think Alice would want me to. Thanks all the same.'

They heard the door across the passageway open and Landers hurried into the hall. There was a brief consultation with the doctor, who had prescribed Alice a sedative, Thanet gathered, and was advising that Mr and Mrs

Landers now took her home and got her to bed. Consulted, Thanet said that there were a few more questions he had to ask Landers before he left. At this point Mrs Landers came back downstairs with Fiona, carrying a younger child, the little boy, swathed in a duvet. It was decided that Mrs Landers, Alice and the children should go on ahead, Mrs Landers driving Alice's car, and that Landers would follow shortly.

When, finally, they had gone, Thanet and Lineham returned to the sitting room with Landers and Thanet put his question for the third time. Perhaps this time he would get an answer.

'You seemed very emphatic, Mr Landers, that Mr Mason couldn't have come back later, after Mr Vintage had seen him leave.'

'That was because Reg and I were together.'

'Really? Where?'

'In the pub, in the village.'

'What time was this?'

Landers ran his fingers through his thick white hair. 'Straight after I left here.'

Patiently, Thanet worked out the timings.

Alice had rung Landers to ask him to come over at around 7.45. Landers and his wife were just finishing their evening meal and he left about twenty minutes later, reaching the vineyard five minutes after that. He knew Mason's van and noticed it in the car park of the village pub as he drove past.

Alice was watching a favourite sitcom when he arrived and they had seen the end of it together before discussing Mason's predicament.

Landers had come up with a possible solution.

'There's an empty cottage on my farm, quite a decent one, detached and with a small garden. I told Alice I'd decided to offer it to Reg, at a nominal rent, until he could get his business back on its feet again.'

'That was very generous of you, Mr Landers.'

Landers looked embarrassed. 'Yes, well, Reg and I go back a long way.'

'You're good friends?'

'I wouldn't say that. But we've known each other since we were boys and we've always been on good terms. He's worked hard all his life and I don't want to see him go under.'

'So you decided to tell him about the cottage?'

'Well, Alice said she'd have one more go at trying to persuade Zak to change his mind about paying Reg at least a proportion of the money owing to him. But yes, we decided that in any case I'd have a word with Reg to reassure him that whatever happened, he'd still have a roof over his head. So that's what I did.'

Landers had left Alice at around 8.45 and seeing Mason's van still in the car park at the pub had called in to have a drink with him and give him the good news. He and Mason had left the pub together at around 9.15 and he, Landers, had arrived home shortly afterwards. Mason had said he was going straight home to tell his wife about Landers' offer.

'That's why I'm so certain Reg didn't come back here later. He was itching to get home and tell Kath, his wife, about the cottage. And in any case, the offer had taken the pressure off him, don't you see?'

They let Landers go. The Mercedes in the vineyard car park was his. They watched its tail-lights disappear down the drive and then Lineham said, 'Mason certainly isn't off the hook, as far as I can see. According to Vintage, Mason left about ten to eight but Vintage didn't actually see him leave the premises. He could easily have sneaked back into the bottling plant without Vintage seeing him. I know Landers says he saw Mason's van parked at the pub when he went by at ten past eight but that was twenty minutes later. And Mason had another opportunity to come back later on, after leaving Landers outside the pub. It's all very well saying the offer of the house had taken the pressure off him, but that doesn't mean he'd stop feeling angry with Randish, who had got him into the mess in the first place.'

'Quite.'

'So do we go and see him, sir?'

'I suppose so.' Thanet peered at his watch. It was just after midnight. He didn't like disturbing people at this hour, but murder was murder. If he left it until morning vital evidence could disappear and Mason would have time to compose himself and get his story straight. No, it would have to be tonight.

The village of Charthurst was only half a mile from the vineyard, just a few minutes away by car, and at this time of night was silent and deserted. Most of the houses were in darkness but lights illuminated the well-kept forecourt of the Harrow, the pub where Landers and Mason had met. Lineham was right, Thanet thought. Twenty minutes would have been ample for Mason to have slipped back into the laboratory, committed the murder and got down here by the time Landers drove past. When Mason first went up to the winery that night, had he told Vintage he wanted to talk to Randish, and why? And had Vintage advised him against it? If so, why hadn't Vintage said so? If this was what Vintage had been hiding, why should he be so concerned to protect Mason? Because he was sorry for him? Felt he'd been ill-treated?

In any case, perhaps Mason had pretended to leave because he would have been embarrassed to be seen going into the bottling plant against the advice of both Alice Randish and Vintage. But if he had waited until Vintage's back was turned, or if he had slipped back later, and if Randish had been particularly tactless or dismissive in his refusal to listen to his plea, then Mason might well have finally snapped, lost control. And there was no doubt about it, whoever killed Randish had been completely out of control. Yes, Mason might well be their man.

Landers had told them where Mason lived and from his description they found the house without difficulty. Even without the 'FOR SALE' sign outside they could scarcely have missed it. The last street lamp in the village illuminated a high brick wall and tall wrought-iron gates flanked by pillars from which two lions gazed haughtily down on passers-by. Someone obviously had delusions of grandeur. Mason, or a previous owner? Thanet wondered.

The house itself was set well back from the road behind large areas of lawn and as they drove up the curving drive a row of security lights spaced out along its façade clicked on. It had been built some time in the last ten years, Thanet guessed, and it was big, a good sixty to eighty feet long, with a four-car garage. Although it was not to his taste Thanet could see why, in the heady years of the housing boom, Mason had been tempted into overstretching himself to buy it. It shouted 'SUCCESS' from every picture window.

Lineham gave a low whistle. 'No wonder he can't sell it. I wonder how much he's asking for it.'

Houses like this, in the higher price brackets, were the last to move in the still sluggish housing market. 'Thinking of putting in a bid, Mike?'

'Ha, ha, very funny. That'd be the day.'

The doorbell sounded unnaturally loud in the darkness and silence.

44

'I hate hauling people out of bed at this hour,' muttered Thanet. 'Makes me feel like the secret police.'

'Got to be done, sir.'

'Maybe. That doesn't make me feel any better about it, though.'

Above, there was the sound of a window opening and a man's voice called out, 'Who is it?'

Thanet and Lineham stepped back, peered up. 'Sorry to disturb you, sir. It's the police.'

'I'll come down.'

The silhouetted head disappeared and a moment later a light clicked on in the hall. Someone approached the front door inside and there was a brief pause. Thanet guessed that Mason was inspecting them through the spyhole. Finally the door opened on a chain and a hand emerged through the crack. 'Your identification, please.'

Thanet handed over his warrant card and eventually the door swung wide.

'Sorry about that,' said Mason. 'But you can't be too careful these days.'

He was short and stocky, with a squarish head, cropped brown hair and wary brown eyes. He was wearing an old-fashioned woollen dressing gown in a brown and fawn check pattern and striped flannel pyjamas. He led them into a big sitting room where dralon-upholstered chairs and settees were dotted uneasily about on a sea of heavily patterned carpet. There were a couple of occasional tables and an elaborate arrangement of artificial flowers. No books, no newspapers, no magazines, not even a television set, Thanet noted. The effect was as bleak and impersonal as a dentist's waiting room and Mason looked completely out of place in it. It was cold, too, with a damp, penetrating chill. Thanet guessed that the Masons had been forced to economise on their central heating and that this room was no longer in use.

Mason shivered and pulled his dressing gown more closely about him. 'I'll light the fire.'

It was a gas fire of imitation logs and when he had lit it he stood with his back to it, rubbing his arms. 'What's all this about?'

'I understand you went up to the vineyard to see Mr Randish this evening, sir?'

'Yes. Why?'

'He was found dead tonight. In his laboratory.'

Mason stopped rubbing his arms and became quite still. 'Dead?' He looked astounded.

Genuine astonishment or not? Thanet had no idea.

'But how? I mean, he was perfectly all right when I last saw him.'

'When was that, Mr Mason?'

'Yesterday afternoon.'

'You didn't see him tonight?'

'No. I wanted to, yes, but . . . Look, why all the questions?'

'Mr Randish was murdered, sir.'

If Mason was acting he was making a good job of it. His jaw dropped open and he groped blindly for the arm of the nearest chair, sank down into it. 'Murdered? I don't . . .'

The door swung open and a girl of about eighteen came into the room. 'What's going on, Dad?'

She too was short and stockily built, with long dark curly hair, blunt nose and square, determined jaw. Her quilted dressing gown was tightly belted beneath her ample breasts, her solid legs terminating in large feet incongruously thrust into high-heeled mules trimmed with swansdown.

'It's the police, love. Mr Randish . . .' Mason looked helplessly at Thanet. *How can I tell her?*

Her eyes narrowed and she glanced from her father to the two policemen. 'What about him?'

She'd have to know sooner or later, and in any case Thanet suspected she was a lot tougher than her father's attitude would suggest. 'Mr Randish was found dead tonight, Miss Mason. He'd been murdered.'

Her eyebrows shot up. 'Murdered!' She glanced at her father and Thanet had the impression that she was thinking fast, working out the implications. 'Well, well, well!' she said at last, and sauntered towards them, wobbling slightly on the impossibly high heels. 'Good riddance to bad rubbish, I say.'

'Sharon!'

'Don't "Sharon" me, Dad. You know what I thought of that creep! What's the point in being hypocritical about it?' She turned to Thanet. 'All the same, I don't see what you're doing here. What d'you want with us?'

'We understand your father went to see Mr Randish tonight, Miss Mason.'

'So what? Oh I see . . . So that's it! Someone told you about Dad's little problem and bingo, you added two and two together to make five. Typical!'

'Sharon, no one's said anything about –'

'No, they don't need to, do they? Come on, Dad, who d'you think you're kidding? Why else d'you think they've got you out of bed at this hour? Better go and get your clothes on, pack your suitcase or they're going to be dragging you off to the police station in your pyjamas.'

'You're jumping the gun somewhat, Miss Mason. At this stage we simply want to ask your father some questions.'

'Oh, I see, the arrest is the next stage, is it? Well I can

tell you straight off you're barking up the wrong tree. Dad wouldn't hurt a fly. And he didn't even see Mr Skinflint Randish this evening. Did you tell them that, Dad?'

Thanet was getting a little tired of this. 'Your father hasn't had a chance to tell us anything yet,' he snapped. 'All we know so far is what we have heard from other people. That's why we've come to see him.'

'Well go on then, Dad. Tell them.'

And Sharon planted herself in front of the fire, arms folded belligerently across her substantial bosom.

They all looked at Mason.

He shrugged. 'There's not much to tell. I did go up to the vineyard, yes, but I didn't see Mr Randish.'

'Why not?' said Thanet. 'No, begin at the beginning. What time was this?'

Mason's story tallied with what Alice and Vintage had told them. He had arrived at the vineyard at about 7.30 and had spent ten minutes or so talking to Alice Randish, a further ten talking to Vintage. Then he had left.

'Mrs Randish tells us that she advised you not to see Mr Randish this evening, that she thought it would be better for her to speak to him first. So why did you go up to the winery?'

'I thought if Mr Randish knew how serious my position was, he might –'

'And pigs might fly!' said Sharon. 'I told you there was no point in going, didn't I? If you'd listened to me you wouldn't be in this mess now, would you?'

Thanet ignored the interruption. 'So why didn't you speak to him?'

'Because Oliver also advised me not to.'

So Mason *had* told Vintage that he intended to speak to Randish.

'Oh, did he? Why was that?'

'He didn't think it was a good moment to approach him.'

'Any particular reason?'

'Mr Randish wasn't in a very good mood, he said.'

'Did he say why?'

Mason hesitated and before he could reply the door opened again. An older woman this time, Mason's wife, presumably. She stood supporting herself with one hand against the door post. 'Reg? What's happening?'

Mason jumped up and both he and his daughter hurried to assist her.

'Kath, you shouldn't be here . . .'

'Mum, what are you doing up?'

Mrs Mason peered past them at Thanet and Lineham. 'Who's this? What are they doing here? It's nearly one in the morning.'

'And you should be in bed,' said Mason gently, attempting to steer his wife back out of the door again.

She detached her elbow from his grasp. 'Reg, please . . . I want to know what's going on.'

'There's been an accident in the village, Mum,' said Sharon. 'It's the police. They're making some inquiries.'

'What accident? Why is it so urgent? Why can't it wait till morning?'

She was clearly determined not to be fobbed off and they seemed equally determined not to tell her. Thanet now remembered Landers telling him that Mrs Mason had a heart condition. Perhaps he should, after all, have waited until morning to question the builder, when he could have got him on his own.

She was becoming exasperated. 'Reg, for goodness' sake stop treating me like a child and tell me straight what's happened.'

'All right, love. But come and sit down first.'

He glanced at Sharon and some unspoken communication passed between them. Sharon left the room.

Mason led his wife to a settee and sat down beside her, taking her hand. Gently, he broke the news to her.

She drew in her breath sharply and he watched her anxiously.

Sharon came quietly back into the room. She was holding something in her hand. Thanet couldn't see what it was.

Mrs Mason looked up at Thanet. 'I still don't understand what you're doing here. What's it got to do with –' She broke off and turned back to her husband. 'Reg, you went up there tonight. Is that . . .' Her hand flew to her chest as realisation hit her and Sharon hurried forward, stumbling in her haste as one of her heels caught on the edge of the hearthrug. If the look she directed at Thanet and Lineham could have killed, they would have fallen dead on the spot. She dropped to her knees in front of her mother, shaking some tiny tablets out of the pill bottle she was holding.

This was what she had gone to fetch, Thanet realised. She and her father had been afraid this might happen.

She handed a tablet to her mother, who put it under her tongue.

They all watched Mrs Mason anxiously. In a minute or two she began to breathe more evenly and the hand she was pressing against her chest relaxed.

Thanet became aware that he had been holding his breath. He and Lineham exchanged relieved glances.

'It's all right,' she said feebly. 'I'm fine now.' She patted her daughter's hand. 'Thanks, love.'

Sharon stood up, coming to her feet like a released spring. 'I think you'd better go,' she said to Thanet and

Lineham in tones of barely suppressed fury. 'You've done enough damage for one night.'

Thanet was inclined to agree with her. He could finish questioning Mason tomorrow. It was obvious that the builder wasn't going anywhere.

It was not until he was almost home that he realised there was something he had forgotten to do. One of the reasons why he had not wanted to leave the interview with Mason until the next day was that he had intended to take away the shoes Mason had been wearing that night, in case there were fragments of glass embedded in their soles. His concern for Mrs Mason and his relief that she seemed to have recovered had driven this completely out of his mind.

He hoped that at this very moment vital evidence was not being destroyed.

FIVE

Joan was fast asleep when Thanet got home and he was careful not to wake her. Next morning she brought him a cup of tea in bed. Usually it was the other way around.

He blinked himself awake, peered at the clock, sank back with a sigh of relief. Seven o'clock. He hadn't overslept, then. 'What are you doing up at this hour, love? Got to go in to work today?'

Joan was a probation officer and usually had Saturdays off. Occasionally, though, there was some special task to perform.

She drew the curtains back and a grey, mournful light crept into the room. 'No. I just woke up early, that's all. What a miserable day.'

'Is it raining?'

'No.' She peered up at the sky. 'I wouldn't be surprised if it did later, though.'

She sounded uncharacteristically gloomy and looked tired, Thanet thought. 'Do I gather you've found out what's wrong with Bridget?'

'Yes. We had a talk last night, after you'd gone.' She came back, sat down on the bed, a dispirited slump to her shoulders. 'It's as we thought. Alexander has broken it off.'

'Just like that.'

'Just like that?'

'No warning, no hint of what was coming?'

'Apparently not. Oh, I suppose there must have been signs, but if there were, Bridget didn't see them. Or didn't want to see them, perhaps.'

'Did he give any particular reason?'

'Only that he doesn't feel ready for a long-term commitment yet.'

Thanet experienced a spurt of anger. How dare this handsome, privileged, debonair young man float into Bridget's life and then toss her aside, careless of any damage he might have inflicted? 'How's she taking it?'

'Well, you saw for yourself.'

'Quite. Well, I don't suppose there's much we can do for her at the moment, except give her moral support. Anyway, let's try to look on the bright side. She's still young, she'll get over it eventually, I suppose.' He hoped.

'Maybe. But I'm afraid she's going to have a bad time for a while. She really was very fond of him. And inevitably she's asking herself where she went wrong.'

'If we could help her to see that it was Alexander's problem, not hers . . .'

'I know. Oh Luke, it's such a shame. He was such a nice young man.'

'Maybe. But I never did think he was right for her, as you know.'

'I never really understood why.'

Thanet leaned forward and kissed her. 'Darling, much as I'd love to have a deep and earnest conversation on the merits or otherwise of Alexander as a suitor for our daughter, if I don't get up soon I shan't want to get up at all.'

She laughed and stood up. 'I'll go and get you some breakfast.'

'No need. I can do it myself.'

'I know that. But I thought I'd cook something for a change.'

Thanet wasn't going to argue with that. Cooked break-fasts were a rare treat nowadays, indulged in only occasionally at weekends.

Neither Bridget nor Ben put in an appearance and they had a leisurely breakfast à deux. Fortified by bacon, egg, toast and marmalade, several cups of freshly brewed coffee and a pipe, Thanet arrived at the office feeling ready to tackle anything. As usual, Lineham was already at work. Thanet could never be sure whether the sergeant invariably arrived early because he loved his job and couldn't wait to get to his desk each morning, or whether he found the early-morning chaos of life with a young family so trying that it was a relief to escape from it. In any case, he suspected that by now it was a matter of pride to Lineham to arrive before his boss.

'Morning, Mike. Anything new?'

'The *Kent Messenger*'s been on the phone, sir. And TVS.'

Thanet groaned. He hated the public relations side of his job, but forced himself to take it in his stride. Occasionally the police really needed the cooperation of the media and he was careful not to antagonise them. After all, like him they were only doing their job. 'Tell them I'll give them a statement this evening but that there'll be nothing until then. Perhaps that'll keep them from being underfoot all day.'

'In time for the six o'clock news, sir?'

'I suppose so. Anything else?'

'PM's arranged for later on today.'

'Good.' Thanet glanced at his watch. Time for the morning meeting, a ritual instituted by Draco when he first arrived, and which they had kept up whether he was there to take it or not. 'Look, while I'm at the meeting get a message out to the vineyard. The regular staff will no doubt be turning up for work as usual. Make sure they're not allowed home until they've all been questioned. Get Carson and Bentley out there to do it. And give Reg Mason a ring. I want to talk to him again, but not at home. I don't want a repeat performance of last night with Mrs Mason. Ask him to come in to Headquarters, as soon after nine as possible.'

At the meeting Chief Inspector Tody, who acted as Draco's deputy in his absence, confirmed that Draco had intended taking his wife away for the weekend after getting the results of her latest test the previous day.

'Let's hope the news is good,' he said.

On the way back upstairs Thanet ran into DC Wakeham, hovering outside his door. This was a recent recruit to Thanet's team, keen as mustard but still unsure of himself. Thanet always kept a close eye on new arrivals. It was very interesting to see how they settled in – important, too. Nothing was as disruptive to teamwork as disharmony between its members. Wakeham would do, he thought. The DC was feeling his way carefully, trying to learn and to pull his weight without treading on anyone's toes.

'You've got something for me, Chris?'

Wakeham wore a worried frown. 'I'm not sure, sir. I don't even know if I ought to mention it, when . . .'

'Come on in. Let's hear it all the same.'

Inside, Wakeham looked if anything even more worried. 'I hope I'm not jumping the gun, sir. I mean, I don't even know if there's any point in mentioning it at the moment . . .'

'Chris,' said Thanet patiently, 'you've said that once,

already. But you're here now, so just get on with it, will you?' Then, as Wakeham still hesitated, 'Well come on, man, spit it out. It's obvious you'll go on worrying about it until you do.'

'It's just that I've been looking at the photographs. Of the murder victim, sir. And I'm sure I've seen him before.'

'Where? And when?'

Wakeham looked downcast. 'Well, that's why I wondered if I ought to mention it at the moment, sir. I can't remember.'

Thanet laughed. 'I know the feeling, Chris, I know the feeling. We all do, for that matter. But don't worry, it'll come to you. And when it does, let me know. Meanwhile my advice is try to forget about it. Let your subconscious do the work for you. Sooner or later it'll come up with the answer.'

'Right, sir. Thank you.'

Wakeham was almost at the door when Thanet called him back. 'There's a little job I'd like you to do. One of the suspects in the Randish case is a chap called Reg Mason. He's coming in for questioning this morning and when he leaves I'd like you to go home with him and pick up the clothes he was wearing on his visit to the vineyard last night. Especially the shoes. Get all the stuff sent off to the lab, asking them particularly to look out for fragments of glass embedded in the soles of the shoes. And then I want you to do a little digging about those shoes, just to make sure he's given you the right ones. Talk to Vintage, the assistant winemaker at the vineyard, see if he can remember what shoes Mason was wearing last night. Also, have a word with Randish's father-in-law and the landlord at the pub. Anyone, in fact, who might have noticed. Use your initiative.'

Wakeham went off looking like a Labrador who had just spotted an especially juicy bone.

'That should distract him all right,' said Thanet with a grin.

'He's a good lad,' said Lineham. 'A bit too much of a worrier at the moment, but only because he's so anxious to do the right thing. He'll get over that.'

'I agree. Now, what did you fix up with Mason?'

'I missed him, sir. He'd already left.' Watching Thanet's face, Lineham grinned. 'But before you explode, let me say it's only because he was already on his way here, of his own accord. In fact, he should be arriving any minute now.'

'Check, will you?'

Mason was already waiting downstairs and it was arranged that Lineham would question him today.

Slumped at the table in an interview room in a brown leather jacket which had seen better days, Mason looked tired and depressed. Thanet guessed that he hadn't slept much the previous night. His eyes were weary, the skin beneath them slack and puffy.

'How's Mrs Mason?' Thanet asked.

'All right. But I didn't want her upset again, so in case there was anything else you wanted to ask me I thought I'd come in, so you didn't have to come to the house.'

'A good idea,' said Lineham. 'There were one or two points . . .'

'Fire away, then.' Mason leaned back in his chair, shoving his hands into his pockets. He looked resigned, as if unpleasant experiences had become the norm for him of late.

'You realise that you're in a very difficult position, Mr Mason.'

The builder gave a short, unamused bark of laughter.

'You can say that again! In fact, you might say things couldn't be much worse.'

'We understand that because of the dispute with Mr Randish, there's a question of your house being repossessed.'

'That's what I meant.'

Lineham frowned. 'Don't play games, Mr Mason. It wasn't what I meant, as I'm sure you're aware. But I'll spell it out. I'm referring to Mr Randish's murder. You obviously had a grudge against him and you were there, at the vineyard, at the time when the crime was committed. What's more, when you went up there last night you must have been feeling pretty desperate.'

'OK, OK.' Mason waved a weary hand. 'So I was feeling pretty desperate. That doesn't mean I knocked him off, does it? If we all went around bumping off everyone we felt angry with, pretty soon there'd be no one left, would there?'

'All the same, you must have been very determined to see him, make one last appeal to his better nature, shall we say.'

That short bark of laughter again. 'You must be joking. Better nature! What better nature?'

'You didn't like him, did you? In fact you hated his guts.'

Suddenly, Mason leaned forward. 'Wouldn't you?' he spat. 'If someone wouldn't pay you what he rightfully owed you and as a result *your* family was going to be out on the street, wouldn't you hate his guts?' He subsided, indignation already fading. 'No, I don't deny it, I did hate him for what he's done to me, to us. But that still doesn't mean I'd commit murder just to get my own back.'

'Maybe you didn't go up there intending to. Maybe you just wanted to have a reasonable, rational discussion

58

with him, man to man. But what if he wouldn't play ball? What if he just told you to get lost, or worse, just laughed at you? What then? Wouldn't all your good intentions fly out the window? Come on, Mr Mason, why not admit it? It's so easy to snap, isn't it, when you've been under a strain for a long time, as you have, so easy to lose your temper, pick up a bottle and throw it at him in sheer frustration. Then another and another, and before you know where you are, it's too late, he's dead . . .'

Mason's jaw had dropped. 'You must be out of your tiny mind! Look, ask anyone, anyone who knows me, anyone who's ever known me. OK, I might get a bit irritable from time to time, but I bet you won't find a single person who's seen me lose my temper, not ever.'

'They say that every man has his breaking point, Mr Mason. Perhaps you'd reached yours.'

'No! I never even saw him, I told you!'

Lineham leaned forward. 'We find it very difficult to believe that. Try to look at it from our point of view. You're frantic about losing your home. You go up there to make one last appeal. You see Mrs Randish. She says she'll speak to her husband on your behalf and suggests you don't approach him again until after she's done so. So what do you do? Go home? No. You came intending to see Mr Randish and see him you will. So you go up to the winery and ask Mr Vintage where Randish is. And then, surprise, surprise, where Mrs Randish has failed to convince you, Mr Vintage succeeds. You take his advice and off you go, like a little lamb. So what we want to know is why? Why listen to him and not to Randish's wife, who presumably knows her husband best?'

'I told you last night! Because Mr Randish was in a bad mood, Oliver said, and he thought it would do my case more harm than good to tackle him last night.'

Thanet wasn't surprised to learn that, as he had suspected when he last spoke to Mason, Vintage had indeed known why Mason wanted to see Randish and had been reluctant to say so to the police because he was in sympathy with the builder's cause. No doubt the dispute was common knowledge in the village, as such things are in a small community. But it still didn't explain why Mason had taken his advice.

'Yes, I know you told us that,' said Lineham. 'But he must have put forward some very convincing argument, to get you to listen to him. What was it?'

Once again Mason hesitated, as he had last night.

Mason shrugged. 'It was enough, to know he was in a bad mood. I mean, what was the point of putting his back up?' But his tone lacked conviction.

He was definitely holding something back, thought Thanet. And he was beginning to waver. *Go on Mike, press home your advantage.*

Lineham was shaking his head, 'Not good enough, Mr Mason. Look, I don't think you realise the seriousness of your position. You were there, on the spot, when a man you hated was murdered. If you refuse to be frank with us and fail to give us a convincing reason why you gave up and went away without seeing him, you can't blame us for drawing our own conclusions.'

'But I didn't go near him, I swear it!'

Lineham said nothing, just gazed steadily at Mason, whose eyes eventually fell away. 'It was because they'd had a row,' he muttered.

Lineham must have been pleased at Mason's capitulation, but he didn't show it. 'Who had a row? Mr Randish and Mr Vintage?'

Mason nodded.

'Then why on earth didn't you say so before?'

Thanet could guess why. Mason had hesitated to point the finger of suspicion at Vintage for the same reason that Vintage had been reluctant to talk about Mason's visit: they had evidently both been ill-treated in some way by Zak Randish and had not wanted to implicate a fellow-sufferer. What had the row between Vintage and Randish been about? he wondered.

Mason had not replied, just shook his head, and Lineham sounded exasperated as he said, 'Well, what was the row about?'

'None of my business, I'm afraid. I didn't ask.'

That didn't mean that Vintage hadn't told him, though, thought Thanet. But by the stubborn line to Mason's lips he guessed that Lineham wasn't going to succeed in getting him to say any more on this subject. He was right. The sergeant tried various tacks and then, recognising that it was a hopeless task, went on to question Mason about the rest of the evening. Mason's account tallied with what Landers had told them.

'And when you left the pub at 9.15 with Mr Landers?'

'I went straight home to tell my wife about Mr Landers' offer. I knew she'd be relieved to know we had somewhere to go.'

And Lineham could not shake him.

They watched him depart with DC Wakeham and then Lineham said, 'So, the plot thickens. Mr Vintage was keeping very quiet about that row, wasn't he?'

'Wouldn't you, if you'd had a row with someone and a couple of hours later he was found murdered?'

Lineham laughed. 'Put like that, yes, I suppose I would. Anyway, d'you think Mason was telling the truth?'

Thanet pursed his lips. 'Some of it, yes. All of it? I'm not sure. In any case, Vintage certainly has some explaining to do. Let's go.'

SIX

The first drops of the rain which Joan had forecast spotted the windscreen as Lineham turned into the entrance to the vineyard.

Alice Randish and Fiona were just getting into a Range Rover. They were both wearing corduroy trousers, rollneck sweaters and Puffa waistcoats, Fiona's outfit a scaled-down version of her mother's. Alice, Thanet remembered, owned a horse and Fiona probably had a pony. Livestock had to be attended to whatever crisis its owners were going through. Thanet raised a hand in greeting and Alice acknowledged it with a tight nod as she drove away. Her face was set, as if she were hanging on to her self-control by the most slender of threads. Thanet wondered if she had been told about her niece's death yet.

The rain was coming down more steadily now and with increasing force. Lights were on in the shop and two women inside turned curious faces as Thanet and Lineham hurried past to the bottling plant.

Inside the big double doors they took off their raincoats and shook them before the water could soak into the fabric. Carson had come to meet them and he now led them into the office, where he gave them an update on the various searches and inquiries that were going on. Most of the staff had been interviewed and allowed to go home, but two of the women had been held back. One of the girls who served in the shop had told him that Oliver Vintage had been 'in a mood' the previous day, though she didn't know why. She usually worked in the shop only on Saturdays, but had come in to help out yesterday because the regular girl was ill, so she knew nothing of what had been going on at the vineyard during the days leading up to the murder. The manageress was a different matter. Both Carson and Bentley were sure that she knew more than she was telling, but had failed to get her to open up.

'Has Vintage shown up yet?' said Thanet. 'I told him I'd want to see him again this morning.'

'Yes, some time ago. He went off into the vineyard to look at some grapes,' said Carson. He glanced at the rain, which was now beating relentlessly against the windows. 'I shouldn't think he'll stay out long, in this.'

The manageress's name was Mrs Prote and she was waiting in the shop.

'Prote. What sort of name is that?' said Lineham.

While they waited for Carson to fetch her Lineham prowled around the office, coming to a halt in front of the computer. The sergeant had been hooked on computers ever since he'd done a course a few years back. 'Nice computer system, sir.'

Thanet wasn't interested. 'Really?'

'Yes. Expensive. New, by the look of it. And a laser printer. I'm surprised he didn't get something cheaper, for a business of this size.'

Carson was back. 'Mrs Prote, sir.'

The manageress was in her late thirties, tall and dark, with horn-rimmed spectacles and hair swept back into a neat French roll. The pleats in her navy blue skirt were crisp, her shoes highly polished. She looked as if she were used to having everything under control and her expression was apprehensive and somewhat bewildered – hurt, even, as if life had unexpectedly let her down. As she came in she cast a proprietorial glance around the office as if to check that these interlopers had not been tampering with her arrangements. She sat down primly, knees together, feet neatly aligned.

She had worked at the vineyard for four years, Thanet learned, and was in charge of the hiring of staff and of the administration of both vineyard and tea shop, leaving Randish free for his work as winemaker and consultant.

'What sort of consultant?' said Lineham.

'He advises people who are setting up their own vineyards on the types of grapes to plant, explains to them the various advantages and disadvantages of the two main systems of growing, and also acts as agent for winemaking equipment. Anything, really, to do with the growing of grapes and the making of wine. He's – he was, very much respected as a winemaker.'

'How did you get on with him, Mrs Prote?' said Thanet.

Interesting, he thought. A toe on her right foot had twitched. Feet were often a giveaway. People could school themselves to control their facial muscles, but their extremities seemed to have a life of their own. She had obviously had reservations about her employer.

'All right.'

'You don't sound too enthusiastic.'

'We got along perfectly well as employer and employee. I know my job, I'm reasonably good at it, I think, and he was satisfied with my work. Otherwise I wouldn't have stayed as long as I have.'

'What about Mr Vintage?'

Extraordinary things, eyes, thought Thanet. Fascinating, how they reflect one's inner feelings and attitudes. Mrs Prote did not blink, nor did her expression alter even slightly, except for her eyes. There, it was just as if a shutter had closed. And her right toe twitched again.

'What about him?'

'How do you get on with him?'

'Fine. Though we don't actually have a lot to do with each other. He works outside and I work inside and our responsibilities don't often overlap.'

'What do you think of his work?'

'He's hardworking and conscientious, anxious to learn. I know Mr Randish thought he was becoming a very good winemaker.'

She had relaxed a little, pleased to present Vintage in a good light. Time to try to get under her guard.

'What was the row about, between Vintage and Mr Randish?'

She blinked and this time she twisted her right foot around her left ankle. 'What row?'

Thanet sighed. 'Look, Mrs Prote, I'm not going to insult your intelligence by playing games. I'll be frank with you. One of your members of staff has told us that Oliver Vintage was "in a mood" all day yesterday, and we know from another source that Vintage and your employer had a row last night . . .'

'Last night?' At once, she looked as though she wished she hadn't spoken.

'You're surprised. Interestingly enough, not by the fact that they had a row at all, but by the fact that it was last night. Why is that?'

She shook her head to convey – what? Confusion? Reluctance?

'What can I say to convince you that you have to be frank with us? This is, I must stress, a murder inquiry. If you know anything, anything at all, which could help us, it really is your duty to say so.'

But duties could conflict, as Thanet knew only too well, and people frequently chose to give their loyalty to people rather than to the abstract cause of justice.

'There's really not much point in hiding anything, you know,' Thanet added softly. 'We always find out, sooner or later, I assure you. I can see we are talking about someone you obviously like and respect and I can understand your reluctance to tell us anything you feel might incriminate him. But surely it's better that we learn anything there is to be learnt from someone who is on his side.'

'I doubt that you'd find anyone who isn't. Not that he is in need of such support, of course.'

'Nevertheless . . .'

Thanet let the silence stretch out, aware of its power to exert pressure where words have failed.

Mrs Prote had turned her head and was gazing out of the window as if seeking the answer to her dilemma in the familiar view outside.

She had come to a decision. Her lips tightened.

She's not going to tell me, thought Thanet.

She shook her head. 'I'm sorry, Inspector, I can't help you. But I will say this. I've worked with Oliver Vintage for four years now and I honestly do not believe he could have anything to do with what happened here last night.'

Thanet could see that there was no point in pursuing the matter. Her mind was made up and that was that. He sent Lineham to find Vintage.

While he waited he stared out of the window at the view which had greeted Randish every day of his working life. What had the man been like? So far he hadn't even begun to understand what made him tick. They seemed to have been plunged at once into suspects and motives. But it was Randish who was the key to the mystery, Randish whose behaviour had for some reason hurled someone into a fit of ungovernable rage. Thanet realised he should have discussed him at greater length with Mrs Prote, but he had been so intent upon trying to get her to talk about the row with Vintage that he had let the chance slip. He could always see her again, of course, but meanwhile he wasn't going to make the same mistake with Vintage.

The heavy shower had eased off and the sky was lightening. Perhaps it would clear up later after all. Vintage, however, had obviously caught the worst of it. His old waxed jacket streamed with water and his hair was plastered to his scalp, accentuating the skull-like effect imparted by the deep eye-sockets and the hollows beneath the cheekbones. The early night didn't seem to have done him much good. He still looked bone-weary.

He took off his coat, dropped it on the floor and perched on the edge of a desk, taking out a green-spotted handkerchief to mop his face. 'Bloody rain. We could do without this, on top of everything else.'

Thanet leaned back in a relaxed manner and said, 'Tell us about Mr Randish. What was he like?'

'Like?' Vintage frowned. 'In what way?'

Thanet waved a hand. 'Any way.'

'Well, he was ambitious. Always looking for ways to expand his business, to make more money. But hard-working, mind.'

'Ruthless, perhaps?'

'A bit, yes, I suppose. All successful businessmen are, aren't they?'

'Go on.'

Vintage frowned. 'It's difficult, when you work with someone every day. You don't stand back and look at them, you tend to take them for granted.'

'Try.'

'Well, he had a very good opinion of himself.'

'Egotists are by definition very self-centred.'

No response.

'They tend to be somewhat dismissive of other people's feelings.' And that shot had gone home, Thanet thought. Vintage's eyes had dropped and he had compressed his lips.

Vintage shifted uncomfortably. 'I don't really like talking about him like this.'

'Speaking ill of the dead, you mean?'

'Yes.'

'Understandable, but really rather pointless, don't you think? I'm not asking you to spread malicious gossip, just to give me your own frank, personal opinion of him. Nothing you can say will harm him now and it might help us to understand what happened last night.'

'I don't see how.'

'Just take my word for it, Mr Vintage.'

Vintage slid off the desk and walked to the window, stood looking out, with his back to them. 'I still can't quite take it in, that he's dead. He was so very much alive, if you see what I mean. Always full of energy, always looking for new avenues to explore.'

Vintage was prevaricating, Thanet realised, while he tried to make up his mind how much to tell them. Thanet was happy to go along with this if it would encourage Vintage to open up. 'Yes, I understand he had a number of strings to his bow. He must have had a lot of contacts. I believe his sister lives locally, so I imagine he grew up in the area.'

'Yes he did, I think.'

'How did he get into vine-growing, do you know?'

Vintage returned to his perch, settled down again. 'I think he was always interested in farming, used to work on farms in the school holidays and joined the Young Farmers' Club. That was where he met Mark Benton, I believe – Mark's father, James Benton, owns the other vineyard where Zak is – was – winemaker, at Chasing Manor. That was where Zak really became interested in vines, through going out to the vineyard with Mark. He started working there during the holidays after that, instead of on a farm. Mr Benton was winemaker there at the time, of course, but by the time he retired Zak had had quite a lot of experience and I suppose it was natural for him to take over. Mr Benton still owns the vineyard, though.'

'Mark Benton didn't take over when his father retired?'

'No. He went into something completely different. He's an accountant.'

'His father must have been disappointed.'

'Zak told me Mark was never interested in the vineyard. You can't force these things.'

'No. Presumably Mr Randish went to college to study – what do you call it, the study of vine-growing? Viticulture?'

'That's right, viticulture. No, he couldn't. At that time there was no such course at any college in the country. Now, there is a course in vine-growing and winemaking, at Plumpton. It started a few years ago. Oddly enough, it was to Plumpton Agricultural College that Zak went. No, like me, Zak went to some workshop courses at Alfriston, run by the Agricultural Training Board. It was the only way to learn viticulture at the time. But I was lucky. My old man could afford to pay for me to go to

Australia. The vineyards out there are amazing and I got in a couple of years' very useful experience, learnt a hell of a lot.'

'You're saying that Mr Randish's family couldn't have afforded to send him to do something like that?'

'Well I could be wrong but that's certainly the impression I've got.'

'So how did he acquire this place?' Though Thanet suspected he could guess.

'I really don't know.'

'How did he meet his wife, do you know?'

'In the Young Farmers', I believe.'

Yes, a good place for an impecunious and ambitious lad interested in farming to meet a prospective bride, thought Thanet. Or was he being unfair to Randish? 'How did they get on?'

'Oh, for God's sake! If you want to discuss his marriage, you'll have to ask his wife.'

Thanet didn't know what made him then ask, 'Are you married, Mr Vintage?' He watched a bleakness seep into Vintage's expression. What was wrong there?

'Yes. But what's that got to do with it?'

'Just wondered. Been married long?'

'Two years.'

Thanet filed away a question mark over Vintage's marriage, for further investigation later if necessary. 'How did Mr Randish get on with his father-in-law, Mr Landers?'

Another hit, it seemed. Once again there was an evasive look in Vintage's eyes. 'None of my business.'

'But you must have had an opinion.'

'I thought you weren't asking for gossip. My personal opinion of Zak's character, you said you wanted.'

Vintage was getting annoyed. Good. Thanet hadn't

deliberately set out to needle him, but anger frequently
led to loss of control and hence indiscretion. Time to
edge towards the main point of the interview.

'Why didn't you tell us about Reg Mason's dispute
with Mr Randish?'

Vintage blinked at the sudden change of tack. 'That
was none of my business, either.'

'I'm getting a little tired of people trying to protect
other people. It's understandable, but misguided and completely pointless. As I was saying to Mrs Prote a moment
ago, we always find out sooner or later. She, of course,
was trying to protect you.'

Vintage's eyebrows went up, but Thanet could tell that
his surprise was not genuine and there was even a touch
of resignation in his voice as he said, 'Me?'

'Yes, you, Mr Vintage.'

Suddenly, Thanet was fed up. Interviewing was the
part of his work that he enjoyed most. He enjoyed plan-
ning tactics, drawing on his accumulated experience in
order to coax information out of reluctant witnesses. But
just occasionally he became tired of all the manoeuvring.
He sighed. 'How on earth can I get it into your head that
there really is no point in trying to hide things from us?'
He leaned forward, allowing his frustration to show. 'I
honestly don't think you realise the seriousness of your
position. Your employer was killed here yesterday. This
is a murder investigation, and in a murder investigation
everyone, but everyone connected with the victim comes
under a searchlight and especially those who are known to
have quarrelled with him. You all seem to think you live
in little worlds of your own, but those worlds overlap, all
the time. People see things, they hear things, and even if
they don't want to tell us about them through misguided
but perhaps understandable loyalty, sooner or later the

truth will come out. As it has in your case. We *know* you had a row with Mr Randish yesterday and we want to know what it was about. So I suggest you stop pretending you don't know what I'm talking about, and tell us.'

Had he got through? Thanet wondered. If not, which tack should he try next? He was aware of Lineham's waiting stillness, of the almost palpable tension in the room.

Vintage's face was expressionless but Thanet guessed he was thinking furiously. His eyes were narrowed as he stared at Thanet and bunched cheek muscles betrayed clenched teeth.

At last he took a deep breath, blew the air out softly between pursed lips. 'I suppose you're right. You're bound to find out sooner or later, so you might as well hear it from me.'

SEVEN

Vintage slid off the desk again and went to look out of the window. 'It takes years to build up a place like this,' he said. 'I wonder what'll happen to it now.' He glanced at Thanet. 'How much do you know about English wines?'

'Virtually nothing.'

Vintage turned to face them, resting his buttocks on the windowsill. 'Well, before I explain about yesterday, just let me give you a little bit of background. It'll help you to understand what happened.

'If you want to produce a good wine, having the technical knowledge is important, of course. You've got to understand soil structure and soil management, know about the correct use of fertilisers and disease and pest control. But say you have that knowledge, say you've made a major investment, bought the land, planted your wines, tended them for years, picked your first harvest and got a pretty good wine from it, what then? The trouble is, English wine is not cheap and represents only about a third of a per cent of all the wine that's drunk in England. We don't get any of the grants the French and Germans get. So this is where you come up against your main problem: selling. With all other agricultural crops you have a ready-made market, but with wine you have to go out and sell your product and the competition is incredibly stiff. So, even assuming you employ all the right marketing techniques, if you really want to take off you still need something to make your wine stand out from all the rest. A major award, for example.'

Here, Thanet realised, was a true enthusiast. Vintage's eyes were glowing, the words flowed off his tongue as fluently as if he were giving a lecture he had delivered many times. This was a subject which he had pondered, discussed and studied from every angle.

'Of course, it's perfectly possible to make a moderate commercial success of a small vineyard and it has become an increasingly popular thing to do. You need so little land, you see. The reality is that if you have ten acres, once you're up and running, most years you will get thirty to forty thousand bottles of wine. But as I say, the problem is you have to shift it or you're going to end up with barns full of wine and no money to live on. Somehow you have to build up a demand for your product. You also have to decide whether you're going for quality or for a cheaper, more commercial proposition. A good wine-maker like Zak, of course, only ever goes for quality, and his reputation matters. He can do a lot to influence the way the wine turns out; he really holds the strings.

'I'm telling you all this because although I work a lot of the time here at Sturrenden, I've also been getting my own vineyard going. I told you how generous my father was, in sending me to Australia for a couple of years. Well, when I got back and he saw how keen I still was, he bought me a cottage with thirty acres to set myself up. I'm an only child, my mother died years ago, and he said I might as well have the money now, when I needed it, than wait until after he was dead to inherit it. Right at the outset I decided I was going for quality. If I could only win a couple of awards I'd be on my way.

'Well, I've done fairly well in a modest sort of way. I picked my first grapes two years ago and I've managed to shift quite a bit of my stock. But this year I knew I was going to get my big chance. This year, for the first time ever, I had perfectly ripe Pinot noir grapes, as perfect as they get them in Burgundy. The weather conditions were excellent and as the summer went on I was getting more and more excited about them. Believe me, the amount of care I put into looking after those grapes ... Anyway, I was going around telling everyone how great this wine was going to be, and finally, just over a week ago, we picked them and brought them over here for pressing. We put them into plastic picking bins and stacked them. You then leave them for a week and the natural yeast in the grapes starts to ferment. You don't actually add anything. You can only do this if you have a good summer, with really ripe grapes – it's how they make wine in Burgundy.

'So, we covered the bins with sheets and left them to stand, stirring every day by hand. In the beginning the juice was very light in colour but as the days went on it got darker and richer and I got more and more excited. Every night I said to Zak, let's press it, let's press it, but no, every night he kept saying, we'll leave it one more night, one more night. I could have done it myself but I didn't want to. I wanted those grapes to get every ounce of Zak's expertise. Finally he decided we would press it on Thursday night but we got a bit late with the previous load so he promised he'd stay on here late next morning – yesterday – and we'd do it together.'

'Which you did,' said Thanet. 'I remember you telling me you'd pressed a load together.' He also remembered being certain at the time that Vintage was not telling the whole story. Though he didn't see where all this was leading.

'Which we did.' Vintage was nodding, but his expression was sour. 'The problem was, when I got in yesterday I discovered that one of the bins had split.'

'Ah . . . You lost all the juice from it?'

'Yes. There it was, all over the floor. My special, potentially award-winning wine! If Zak hadn't kept on putting it off and putting it off . . . I've told you all this because it was no secret, everybody knew about it and I'd rather you heard the story from me than from anybody else.'

No wonder Vintage had been 'in a mood' all day yesterday. 'So you had a row with Randish.'

'I wouldn't put it quite like that. I couldn't afford to really let fly. I was still dependent on Zak's skill to see me through making the rest of the batch, wasn't I?'

'You mean you were afraid that if you had a real bust-up with him, he might deliberately spoil it?'

Vintage shook his head vigorously. 'Oh no. His professional pride wouldn't allow him to do that. But he might have, well, taken a little less care over it, shall we say. Not even deliberately, perhaps. But your concentration is never very good after a row, is it? Apart from which, I didn't want to lose my job here. Zak was my employer, after all, and I still had a lot to learn from him. No, I couldn't take the risk. Anyway, Zak apologised, handsomely. So that was that.'

'I see.' Thanet did. Unable to give full vent to his anger, Vintage had bottled it up all day. The perfect recipe for the kind of explosive situation in which Randish had met his death. It also explained why Mrs Prote had been surprised to hear that Vintage and Randish had had a row in the evening – if, indeed, they had. No doubt she would have known about yesterday morning's disaster and assumed, by the fact that the two men had proceeded to press the batch together, that the matter had been settled between them.

'But the impression we got from Mr Mason was that you had a row with Mr Randish last night.'

Vintage was shaking his head. 'To be honest, I deliberately misled him. I told him I didn't think it would be a good idea to have another go at Zak last night because I'd had a row with him myself earlier and he wasn't in a very good mood. Which was true. I didn't say when, deliberately. I thought Reg would do his cause more harm than good if he tackled Zak when he was tired and on edge.'

And Vintage stuck to his story: he had been fully occupied with the load he was pressing. He had not seen Randish between 7 and 9.30, when he had gone across to the laboratory to tell him the load was finished, and had found him dead, nor had he seen anyone else enter or leave the bottling plant.

'You realise you're in a very difficult position,' said Thanet, 'entirely alone here all evening, apart from the brief conversation with Mr Mason.'

'No need to rub it in,' said Vintage wearily. 'I'm not an idiot. But I repeat, I didn't do it, so you'll never be able to prove otherwise.'

And there, Thanet agreed, was the rub. Lack of proof. And if Vintage were guilty, he didn't see how they would ever get it. The man must have been in the lab thousands of times, so scientific evidence of his presence there wouldn't help. They'd check his clothes, of course, for bloodstains, but Thanet didn't think the murderer would have been standing close enough to have been splashed with blood. Randish's throat had been cut by broken glass as he lost his balance and fell backwards through the window. Still, you never knew. Past experience had shown that it was surprising what might turn up.

Vintage was anxious to see if he could recruit someone who could at least help him out with the manual work involved in pressing when the vineyard resumed working next day, and Thanet let him go.

'God knows how we're ever going to catch up,' said Vintage gloomily as he went off.

Thanet and Lineham watched him walk to the car park and get into a mud-spattered Land-Rover.

'What d'you think, Mike?' said Thanet.

Lineham closed his notebook with a snap. 'I really don't know. I mean, it's all very well for him to say "that was that" after Randish apologised, but how could he have just put it out of his mind? Working alone all day like that he'd have had plenty of time to brood, plenty of time for his sense of grievance to grow ... Maybe he had intended to let the matter rest, but suppose that during the evening he had to go across to the lab for some reason and Randish said or did something to trigger him off? It wouldn't have taken much, I shouldn't think. And the rest of his wine was safely pressed by then, remember, so he wouldn't have had that to make him hold back as he did in the morning.'

'Quite.'

'So what now, sir?'

'Keep digging, I suppose. While we're here we might as well take a look at Randish's papers, in case there are any more skeletons in his closet.'

They spoke to Mrs Prote again first, but learnt nothing of interest. She refused to be drawn into giving a personal opinion of Randish's character and was adamant that to her knowledge, apart from the long-running dispute with Mason, there had been no disagreement or conflict in his business life which could possibly have led to last night's tragedy. 'If there had been, I'd have known about it.'

A quick skim through the files of correspondence in the office seemed to bear this out, and Thanet and Lineham next went down to the house, to see if they could turn up anything more interesting there.

Randish's study overlooked an uninspired back garden, an oblong patch of lawn surrounded by bedraggled flower-beds. The room was small and square and most of the space was taken up by a wing chair and an oversized pedestal desk, but attempts had been made to give it a masculine air: the wing chair was covered in dark green leather and there were hunting prints on the walls.

They worked their way quickly down through the desk drawers, Thanet on one side, Lineham on the other, find-ing only the usual odds and ends which seem to accumu-late in any desk, together with stationery, bank statements (healthy without being remarkable), old cheque-book stubs and household bills and receipts. Lineham reached the bottom drawer first, Thanet having been held up by a perusal of the bank statements.

'Hullo, this one's locked,' said the sergeant on an opti-mistic note. 'Lucky we kept those keys.' He fished out of his pocket the keyring which had been found in Randish's pocket last night and which they had held back for just this type of eventuality.

There were a number of keys on the ring but only three small enough to be possible. The second one Line-ham tried turned smoothly in the lock. He slid the drawer right out and put it down on top of the desk. 'Letters,' he said. He opened a cardboard box in one corner. 'And photographs.'

The photographs were all of girls, mostly taken alone, sometimes with a younger, slimmer Randish, and in all sorts of situations: sitting on bicycles, perched on gates, seated on walls, sprawled on grass, leaning against trees.

'Wild oats,' said Lineham. 'Quite a Don Juan, wasn't he?'

Thanet was shuffling through the photographs again. There was something . . . some message which his brain was trying to pick up, here. He shook his head. It was no good, he couldn't think what it was.

They picked up the bundles of letters and began glancing at them.

'These are all from girls, too,' said Lineham. 'You can see why he wouldn't want his wife to read them.'

'Ancient history, though,' said Thanet. 'They seem to date mostly – exclusively, in fact – from the time when he was away at college.'

'Even so . . . And look at this lot.' Lineham had picked up the fattest bundle. 'I've glanced at one or two. They're written over a period of three years, mostly headed Trews Farm, Charthurst and signed Alice. From his wife, no doubt, before they were married.' He handed them to Thanet.

'So he was going out with her then.'

'All the time he was away, by the look of it.'

Thanet flicked through the bundle. Some of the envelopes were addressed to Randish at Plumpton Agricultural College, some to c/o Mr K Darks, Wentley Farm, Nr Hassocks, Sussex, the rest to c/o Mrs Wood, Jasmine Cottage, Plumpton, Nr Lewes, Sussex. This latter batch had foreign stamps, Thanet noticed. He peered at them. Switzerland. 'Looks as though Mrs Randish was away at finishing school during his last year at college.'

'And he was two-timing her, that's the point, for the whole three years. Or should I say three-timing her, or even four, five or six. No wonder he kept this drawer locked.' Lineham was picking envelopes up at random, peering at postmarks. 'These others are from all over the place, Bradford, Plymouth, Norwich, from heaven knows where, as well as from Plumpton. And all sent to an address in Sturrenden.'

Thanet was trying to decipher the dates on postmarks. 'Written to Randish during college holidays, by the look of it.' He wondered how Alice Randish was going to feel when she came across these, as she must, eventually. Would it make it easier or harder for her to come to terms with his death?

'If he was two-timing her then,' said Lineham, 'then I bet he was two-timing her now.'

'The thought had crossed my mind. But if so, with whom?'

They stared at each other, thinking.

'Did you notice,' said Thanet slowly, 'that Vintage seemed a bit cagey, when I asked him how long he'd been married?'

'Yes, I did. I definitely had the impression there was something wrong. You're suggesting his wife . . . and Randish?'

'Could be. Perhaps we'll pay her a little call later on this morning.'

'In any case, it does open up interesting possibilities, doesn't it, if he was a ladies' man? A leopard doesn't change his spots, as they say.'

'Very profound, Mike. But I agree. If it's not Mrs Vintage, it could be someone else.'

'I wonder how Mrs Randish's father would have taken that, sir. I mean, if Randish was in the habit of playing around. And especially if what Louise suspected was true, and Randish got a bit rough with his wife from time to time. Landers certainly wouldn't have liked that.'

'Quite. We certainly can't count him out, I agree. Which is one of the reasons why I want to see him next. I'd like another word with Mrs Randish too. With any luck we'll catch her there.' He glanced at his watch. 'We'd better get a move on.' He began to stack the letters back in the drawer and Lineham joined in. 'Make sure you lock these up again. And then we'll be on our way.'

EIGHT

Landers and his wife lived on the far side of Charthurst. Most of the village lay just off the main road and although Thanet had passed through it on a couple of occasions he had never looked at it properly before. Last night, of course, it had been dark, but even by daylight it was unremarkable, typical of the hundreds of villages scattered all over Kent, with a nucleus of older houses, mostly brick and tile-hung, weather-boarded or Tudor black and white, a sprinkle of Victorian cottages, a rash of new houses squeezed in wherever possible and the ubiquitous council estate. There was a church, a dilapidated village hall, a pub, a post office-cum-stores and a village school, which like so many had unfortunately long since been converted into a house. That, no doubt, mused Thanet as they drove past it, was where the bonds of rural loyalty between Landers and Mason had been forged. Landers had probably been sent away to school later on, but to begin with he and Mason would have shared a classroom, perhaps even a desk. The amalgamation of so many small schools like this one was, he believed, one of the many factors responsible for the decline in rural life. Ferried by school bus or by accommodating parents, children were taught from infancy to look away from their communities for their activities, hobbies and satisfactions. It was scarcely surprising that when they grew up they either moved to the towns or regarded the villages as little more than dormitories.

By daylight Mason's house still looked as if it were trying to proclaim the prosperity of its owner, an impression marred by the fact that the sole vehicle parked in the drive was an old pick-up truck which looked as though it were on its last legs – the only transport Mason was now able to afford, Thanet presumed.

Trews Farm was about a mile beyond the village and looked prosperous – probably was, thought Thanet, remembering the Mercedes. The house itself was about four hundred yards from the road and the surface of the long drive was smoothly tarmacked, the verges mown, the hedges well trimmed. On one side were orderly rows of raspberry canes trained on wires, on the other an orchard which had recently been picked; the branches were bare of fruit and the windfalls had been raked into little piles at the end of each line of trees. If first impressions were anything to go by, Landers was to be congratulated. Farmers, Thanet knew, had been having a very bad time. Over the last few years there had been more bankruptcies and more suicides in the farming industry than there had ever been before and Kent had been badly hit. But it looked as though Landers was efficient enough – or perhaps lucky enough – to have escaped the worst of the recession. Perhaps he had weathered the storm by having long-standing contracts to supply some of the larger supermarket chains.

In any case, Thanet guessed that the packing sheds, cold store and other, larger agricultural buildings associated with the work of the farm were elsewhere; the cluster of buildings at the end of the track was too picturesque to be businesslike on the scale which successful modern fruit farming demanded. It was characteristically Kentish: a brick and tile-hung farmhouse, an oast house with conical roof and white-painted cowl, a wooden barn and a range of open-fronted cart-sheds in which were parked the Range Rover Alice Randish had been driving earlier and a trim little silver-blue Rover Metro.

'Glad it's stopped raining,' said Lineham as they got out of the car.

'Mmm.' Thanet was watching Mrs Landers, who was crossing the yard with the little boy they had last seen bundled up in a duvet. He was riding a bright red tricycle which reminded Thanet of one Ben had had when he was that age. They were accompanied by a golden Labrador which now came bounding across to investigate the newcomers, sending up sprays of water as it splashed through the puddles.

'Good boy,' said Lineham placatingly, putting out a slightly nervous hand to pat the dog's handsome head as it skidded to a halt. He flinched and shuffled backwards as it sat down and lifted a friendly but very wet and muddy paw to greet him.

'Timon, here!' called Mrs Landers, and the dog trotted obediently back to its mistress.

'He's well trained,' said Thanet with some relief as he and Lineham approached her. He liked dogs as long as they were kept under control. Like postmen, policemen all too frequently have to suffer from the unwelcome attentions of badly behaved pets watched admiringly by their doting owners.

Last night Mrs Landers had taken so little part in the conversation that he had not paid her much attention. Now he looked at her properly. She was, he guessed, used to being overshadowed by her husband, and her

unremarkable physical appearance matched the unobtru-
sive role she habitually played: neatly styled greying hair,
clothes chosen for comfort and serviceability rather than
elegance or style. Her eyes were a faded version of her
daughter's. But Thanet remembered the fierce, protective
stare with which she had watched Alice last night and
reminded himself not to underestimate her; there was
steel beneath that misleadingly innocuous exterior.

'I don't like badly behaved dogs,' said Mrs Landers,
her expression softening as she glanced at the Labrador.
'Especially big ones. If you don't train them properly
your friends soon stop calling.'

'And what's your name?' said Lineham, smiling down
at the child.

'Malcolm,' said the boy shyly. He had his father's
sturdy frame, thick dark curly hair and regular features.

'I've got a little boy like you,' said Lineham, squatting.
'Well, a bit older, I suppose. He's called Richard.'

'Has he got a tricycle?'

'He used to. But he's got a bicycle now.'

'When I'm a bit bigger Daddy's going to teach me to
ride a bicycle.'

A shadow fell over the conversation.

Thanet and Lineham glanced at Mrs Landers, who
shook her head. 'We've told them, but he hasn't taken it in.'

'He'll need time,' said Thanet.

They all turned as a car approached at speed up the
drive: Landers' white Mercedes. It slowed as it entered
the yard and rolled neatly into one of the sections of the
cart-shed. Landers got out, looking grim.

Of course, Thanet remembered, this morning Landers
had had the unenviable task of breaking the news of her
brother's death to Randish's sister, whose daughter had
also died last night.

The dog had gone bounding to meet him, followed by Malcolm on his tricycle, and Landers stooped to pat one and smile at the other before coming on. He nodded a greeting at Thanet and Lineham and said, 'Excuse me for a moment, will you?' He took both his wife's hands and drew her aside. 'You won't believe this, Dulce . . .' The dog was nuzzling at his hand and he said, 'Stop it, Timon. Lie down.'

The dog subsided obediently on to the ground.

'What?' said Mrs Landers, watching her husband's face. 'Not more bad news, surely? There just can't be.'

'When I got to Rachael's house there was no reply. So I went next door. The neighbour told me Rachael was still at the hospital. Because' – and Landers gave his wife's hands a little shake, as if warning her to brace herself for what was coming – 'because *Jonathan* had an accident last night.'

'Oh, no . . . I don't believe it. Poor Rachael!'

'Apparently the police came around last night shortly after she got back from the hospital – it must have been just after she rang Alice's house and spoke to me – to tell her. She went straight back and she's been there all night.'

'So how is he? You went to the hospital?'

'Yes.' Landers shook his head. 'It's not good, Dulce. He's still unconscious.' Landers released his wife's hands. 'Jonathan is Zak's nephew,' he said to Thanet, 'the twin brother of the girl who died last night. He and his sister have always been very close.' He turned back to his wife. 'Apparently Jonathan was with Karen when she died. Rachael says she can only assume that he was so upset he was driving carelessly. And of course, on a motorcycle you're so vulnerable.'

'So how badly hurt is he?'

87

Landers shrugged. 'No bones broken, but he's seriously concussed. As I say, he hasn't regained consciousness yet. He's just . . . lying there.'

Poor woman, thought Thanet. He'd occasionally come across this type of situation before, when someone seemed to suffer a positive avalanche of disaster. The resilience of the human spirit never failed to amaze him. He'd often wondered how people could bear it when they lost their entire family at one fell swoop, in a fire, perhaps, or a car crash. How did they cope, when suddenly there was not a single member of their family left to turn to for consolation? This lad was not dead yet, of course, and with any luck would survive, but even so, Randish's sister must meanwhile be in a pretty parlous state.

'So how is Rachael taking it?' said Mrs Landers. 'Did you tell her about Zak?'

'Yes. I didn't want to, mind, but I thought, if I don't she'll only read about it in the papers or hear it from a neighbour or on television and I didn't want to risk that. But I think she's in such a daze about Karen and Jonathan she didn't really take it in. She just stared at me, didn't say a word.'

'I'll have to go to her.'

'We'd better tell Alice about Jonathan, first.'

'Do we have to, for the moment? She's still reeling from hearing about Karen, after last night.'

'I suppose we could leave it until tomorrow, when there might be better news. Where is she?'

'Lying down. Ever since she and Fiona got back from seeing to the horses.'

Landers turned to Thanet again. 'Sorry about all this, Inspector.'

'No need to apologise! I'm only sorry to hear that you've had yet more bad news.'

'It's not as though we're especially close to Zak's sister, but she is all alone and you can't help feeling sorry for her. And we're naturally concerned as to how our daughter will take it . . . Are you just leaving, or arriving?'

'Arriving, I'm afraid. There are some more questions I really must ask you.'

'We'd better go in.'

'Did you want me for anything, Inspector?' said Mrs Randish. 'Because if not, I'd really like to go down to the hospital.'

Thanet shook his head. 'Go, by all means.'

'Thank you. Fiona's in the playroom, Owen. I'll take Malcolm along to join her. If you could just look in on them from time to time, while Alice is lying down . . .'

She went off upstairs with her grandson.

'I could do with a cup of coffee,' said Landers. 'Would you like one?'

They accepted the offer and followed him to a door at the end of the wide corridor which served as a hall, the Labrador padding along behind.

The kitchen was big, with a huge pine table in the centre and a dresser at one end, and had a pleasantly lived-in air. Thanet guessed that it had been modernised recently, but the alterations had been cleverly done: the pine units looked mellowed by time, as though they had always been there. Landers filled a kettle and put it on the Aga. In what seemed a matter of seconds it had boiled, the coffee was made and they were seated at the table, the dog sitting down beside Landers and watching its master expectantly.

He caressed its broad head absent-mindedly and took a long swallow of coffee. 'So,' he said. 'Go ahead.'

Landers seemed in a much more cooperative mood this morning, thought Thanet. Good. Perhaps it was because he was no longer trying to protect Reg Mason, or perhaps because he was pleased that his daughter was back under his roof. And possibly, from what they were learning about Zak Randish, because he was relieved that his son-in-law was permanently out of the picture. That, Thanet reminded himself, was what they were here to find out: what had been Landers' attitude towards Zak Randish? 'I was hoping you'd be able to fill me in a little on Mr Randish's background, sir.'

'In what way?'

'Anything you care to tell me. I gather he's known your daughter a long time.'

Landers' lips tightened. 'Since she was sixteen.'

'How did they meet?'

'Look, what possible relevance can this have? It's ancient history now.'

'Believe me, Mr Landers, anything I can learn about Mr Randish will help, anything at all. Bear with me, will you?'

Landers was reluctant to talk but little by little an amplified version of what Vintage had told them emerged. Alice and Randish had in fact met when Randish was fruit-picking on Landers' farm during the school holidays.

'It doesn't sound as though you were too keen on the relationship,' said Thanet.

'Alice was too young to have a steady boyfriend – any steady boyfriend.'

It took all Thanet's skill to extract any further information, but he gathered that for Landers' precious only daughter the fruit farmer had wanted an altogether more advantageous match. Randish's background was undesirable – his father had been a mere labourer on the roads and the family had lived in a council house.

'Any father wants the best for his children,' said Landers defensively.

And he was right, of course. Any father did. Thanet did. But people's ideas as to what 'the best' was varied enormously. Landers had disapproved of Randish because of his humble background, Thanet had disapproved of Alexander because of his privileged one. Which of them was right? Neither, thought Thanet. We're both judging by the wrong criteria. He tucked the thought away for future examination. 'Of course,' he said.

'And Zak never was "the best" as far as you were concerned, was he, Dad?' Alice was standing in the doorway and her tone was bitter.

Thanet wondered how long she had been listening.

She walked across to stand with her back to the Aga, holding out her hands to the warmth as she had to the woodstove last night. A sleepless night had bruised the delicate skin beneath her eyes and the long fair hair hung lank and lustreless on her shoulders. 'Why don't you tell the Inspector some of the good things about him? Yes, his background was poor, his father a drunken lout and his mother pathetic, downtrodden, but it was the fact that he was able to rise above all that and put it behind him that made him so special. And you certainly couldn't complain that he was lazy. He worked like a slave to get the vineyard where it is today and you know it.'

'Alice . . .' Her father got up, followed by the dog, and went to put an arm around her shoulders. 'I know all that. It's just that . . .'

She shook his arm off and put her hand up to run her fingers through her hair. The loose sleeve of her blouse fell back and all three men saw it, a large discoloured patch on the tender flesh of the inside upper arm.

Thanet and Lineham exchanged glances. There was

only one way that such a bruise could have been inflicted in that particular position. Louise had been right.

And Landers had seen them noticing. Not realising that he was offering the policeman a weapon to use against him, he was unable to resist casting a triumphant glance at Thanet. *You see what I mean?*

Intent on her grievance Alice was unaware of what she had unintentionally revealed. '"It's just that" what?' she said. 'It's just that it really doesn't matter any more if you come out into the open and say what you really think of him? It's just that he's been such a thorn in your flesh for so long you're merely relieved he's gone? You never did like him, did you, Dad, and I bet you're delighted you'll never have to set eyes on him again!'

The Labrador was standing watching them, tail drooping, clearly unhappy about this argument between two of its people.

'Alice ...' Landers attempted to put his arm around her shoulders again but once more she shook him off.

'Don't "Alice" me!' she cried. And rushed out.

Landers' glance at Thanet and Lineham somehow contrived to be apologetic, humorous, indulgent and rueful, all at once. He returned to his seat. 'She's upset,' he said, the understatement intended as a joke.

The dog pushed its nose into his hand, seeking reassurance that all was now well and again he patted it automatically.

'She's very loyal,' said Thanet, unsmiling.

'She's always been the same, as far as Zak was concerned.'

Time to stop pussy-footing around, thought Thanet. 'How long have you known that he was ill-treating her? And don't pretend you don't know what I mean. We all saw that bruise and it was obvious you realised its significance.'

'I've known for years,' said Landers bitterly. 'Have you got any children, Inspector?'

Thanet nodded. 'Two.'

'Either of them married?'

'No.'

'Just wait,' said Landers grimly. 'I hope, for your sake, that you like the partners they choose. Because believe me, there's nothing you can do about it. If you disapprove and say so, you risk losing them altogether. You just have to stand by and watch it happen, hope it'll all work out for the best in the end.'

'Which is what you did with your daughter.'

'Didn't have much choice, did I? I've only got one child, more's the pity. And I had to stand by and see her throw herself away on that . . . on Randish. I did my best to smooth the way for her, of course, but when it comes down to it there's nothing you can do about their day-to-day relationship. You just have to let them get on with it.'

'And did it get to the stage where you'd had enough of letting them get on with it?'

'Did I go up there last night and shove him through that window, you mean? No, I didn't. She had me over a barrel, you see.'

'What do you mean?'

'Alice thought the sun shone out of him,' said Landers. He looked bewildered and his tone was almost plaintive as he went on. 'I could never understand why. But from the moment she first set eyes on Randish she was besotted. I thought, when it first dawned on me that he was knocking her about, that she'd come to her senses. I waited and waited, but no, he could always get her eating out of his hand. And if you love someone, really love someone, you want what's best for them, however you feel about it.

You see my dilemma? If I got rid of Randish – and I'll admit there have been many occasions when I could cheerfully have thrown him through a window – I'd be depriving her of her greatest happiness, incomprehensible though that was to me. So my hands were tied. No, you'll have to look elsewhere for your murderer, Inspector. Sorry.'

'D'you know if Mr Randish was playing around?'

'Was he having an affair, you mean? Not so far as I know.'

But Landers was lying, Thanet was certain of it. The fruit farmer might have been caught out once, but he wasn't going to hand Thanet another motive on a plate, even if it might point the finger of suspicion in another direction.

'Do you know of anyone apart from Mr Mason who might have had a grudge against Mr Randish?'

The mention of Reg Mason's name made Landers scowl. 'I told you, you can leave Reg out of it. He just isn't the type to lose his temper and whoever caused that mess up there last night was beside himself with rage, as I'm sure you'll agree. But no, Zak might have trodden on a few toes, but I can't think of anyone who'd hate him to that degree.'

'Mr Vintage told us that your son-in-law also made the wine for another vineyard, at Chasing Manor. How did he get on with the people there?'

'The Bentons? Fine, to my knowledge. They've known him since he was a teenager and I hardly think James Benton would have let Zak take over the winemaking there if there'd been any problems between them.'

'They could have arisen recently.'

'I doubt it. Anyway, you'll have to ask him.'

'Don't worry, we intend to.'

As they walked to the car, Lineham asked, 'Are we going to Chasing Manor next?'

'Let's have a look at the map.'

They held it out between them.

'As I thought,' said Thanet. 'Vintage's house is on the way. Let's pay a call on Mrs Vintage first, see what's going on there. If she was Randish's current girlfriend I'd like to know.'

NINE

The hollow sensation in Thanet's stomach reminded him that it was a long time since breakfast, so they pulled in at the pub in the village.

'We can check Mason's alibi, such as it is, at the same time.'

Although it hadn't started raining again the sky was still overcast and the air was damp and raw. Thanet shivered as they crossed the car park and decided he would eschew his usual sandwich and have something hot.

'Shepherd's pie, I think,' he said with satisfaction, scanning the bar menu. One of his favourites.

'Me, too,' said Lineham.

While they were waiting for the food they questioned the landlord. He had been on duty the night before and although he couldn't be certain of the precise time at which Mason arrived, he confirmed that Landers had later joined him and that the two men had left together about half an hour after that. He also said that although Mason had seemed depressed before Landers arrived, by the time they left he had looked considerably more cheerful.

'Because Landers had offered him the house, presumably,' said Thanet as they carried their drinks to a table in the corner. 'All of which confirms what they've both told us.'

'Still doesn't alter the fact that Mason had the opportunity both before and after he was in here.'

'True.'

When it arrived the pie was excellent, generous helpings with plenty of meat and real, not substitute, potato on top.

'We'll have to come here again,' said Thanet.

While they were eating they discussed the morning's interviews.

'Don't seem to have made much progress, do we?' Lineham was uncharacteristically gloomy.

'Oh, I don't know. I think we're getting there, slowly.' A picture of Randish was, Thanet felt, gradually beginning to emerge: a man whose driving ambition had been forged by his deprived childhood, who saw even his wife, perhaps, as a means to an end; a man powerless to prevent himself repeating in his own marriage the pattern of violence which Thanet suspected Randish's 'drunken lout' of a father had inflicted upon his 'pathetic, downtrodden' mother; a man, Thanet was beginning to believe, for whom other people's feelings did not exist. Well, it looked as though he had trampled on someone else's sensibilities once too often.

Enough of the case, for now. Thanet laid down his fork and patted his pockets, feeling for pipe, pouch, matches. Out of consideration for Lineham he waited until the sergeant had finished eating before lighting up. Then he sat back, puffing contentedly. 'How's Louise getting on?'

Lineham's wife was a trained nurse and until the children came along had been a staff nurse at Sturrenden

General. She had then devoted herself to full-time motherhood and had found it a great strain. Eventually she had taken a part-time job, looking forward to the day when Richard started school and she would be free to resume her career. But like so many women, when that day finally arrived she found that she had lost her confidence. Eventually she had been persuaded to take a retraining course for working mothers and she was now halfway through it.

'Fine,' said Lineham. 'Progressively better and better, as a matter of fact, as she gets her confidence back. The course is very well designed, she has one day in the classroom and one in the wards, and she's expected to do half a day's studying as well. And the hours are so convenient, especially tailored to the needs of mothers with children at school. If only we could get Richard sorted out everything in the garden would be lovely.'

'But I thought he'd seen the – what did you call her? The dyslexic support teacher? – and had an assessment and a special programme worked out for him.'

The previous year Lineham's son Richard, now aged eight, had been diagnosed dyslexic. Lineham and Louise had been worried about him for some time, realising that something was wrong but unable to put their finger on the problem. The diagnosis had been a shock but there had also been a measure of relief: at least now, they thought, something constructive could be done, at once.

They were wrong.

Help was theoretically available, but in practice, they discovered, it took a long time to arrive. Kent County Council was getting itself increasingly organised to provide specialised tuition for children like Richard, but resources were as yet inadequate to provide the degree of help each child needed. Richard had had to take his place in the queue and for three months nothing had happened while his application was being 'processed'. There was only one dyslexic support teacher for the entire area and she was grossly overworked. At last, however, she had seen him for his assessment and Lineham and Louise had had high hopes of the results.

'Yes, she did see him, and he is working on the programme she set up for him.'

'So why the gloom?'

'Guess how much special tuition he's getting.'

'I've no idea. A couple of hours a week?'

'Try again,' said Lineham grimly.

'One hour, then.'

'And again.'

'Not less than an hour, surely.'

'He gets, believe it or not, twenty minutes a week.'

'Twenty minutes a *week*! But that's hopeless!'

'Quite. The trouble is, there just aren't enough special support teachers around. There are thirty-two between eighty-five schools. And Richard's dyslexia is apparently not as severe as some, so he doesn't qualify for as much help. Another problem is that because the dyslexia provision has only been set up relatively recently there's still a backlog of children who were late being diagnosed and are desperately behind, so they naturally come first.'

'So there's nothing you can do?'

'We've tried everything, believe me. But it's like banging your head against a brick wall. The school takes the attitude that it's doing its best, but that if the help simply isn't available, there's nothing to be done about it.'

'Have you taken it up with the Education Authority?'

'Yes. But it's the same old story. It takes for ever to get any kind of response, and when we do they simply say that everything that can be done is being done, but that they simply haven't the funding to provide adequately for every single child with special needs. There is a very good special unit, at the Malling School near Maidstone, but children can't go there until they're eleven, even if they're lucky enough to get in. It's so frustrating!'

'How's Richard reacting to all this?'

'I think he's coming to believe more and more that he's just plain stupid. And how can we convince him otherwise, when as far as he's concerned all the apparent evidence is to the contrary? To make matters worse, he's just gone up a form and from what he tells me I suspect his new teacher is one of the old school, who privately thinks dyslexia is just a fancy label to hang around the neck of a pupil who is really either stupid, lazy or just plain difficult.'

'I thought that attitude had gone out with the Ark.'

'Unfortunately, no, it seems. Old habits die hard, I'm afraid.'

'It must be very depressing for you, not finding any way of doing something constructive to help him.'

'You can say that again! And we're not alone, believe me. You wouldn't credit the number of times we've heard this story over and over again from other parents of dyslexic children. Still, we haven't given up yet. At the moment we're enquiring about private tuition. The trouble is, there are so few people qualified to give it.'

Outside it had started raining again and they had to make a dash for the car. As he drove Lineham was unwontedly quiet – brooding, Thanet suspected, on Richard's predicament. Thanet had always been grateful that Bridget and Ben had been normal healthy children, and the courage and devotion of those parents who were not so fortunate never failed to arouse his heartfelt admiration. Would he have been able to find such reserves of strength in himself, had he been called upon to do so? He doubted it. But then, perhaps one never knew, unless one was actually put to the test. Richard, of course, appeared in every way a perfectly bright healthy child, but in one respect this made things even more difficult: people were less inclined to make allowances for him.

Usually Thanet enjoyed a drive through the countryside but this afternoon there was little pleasure in it. The foliage was beginning to turn colour and on a sunny day the woods and hedgerows would have been splashed with gold, streaked with scarlet, but the blanket of lowering cloud and flurries of driving rain cast a pall over everything. There were puddles in the furrows of newly ploughed fields and tree branches drooped, heavy with the weight of water in their sodden leaves.

It took about fifteen minutes to get to Vintage's house. This was a much more modest set-up. There was a simple signboard announcing 'AMBERLY VINEYARD, WINES FOR SALE', and a short drive up to a pretty weatherboarded house. Looking about him, though, Thanet could see the potential of the place: ample space for a big car park and two substantial barns for storage. The neat rows of vines had a well-tended air.

'I think I'm in the wrong job,' said Lineham. 'How big did he say this place is?'

'Thirty acres.'

'And how much wine a year did he say could be produced off ten? Thirty to forty thousand bottles, wasn't it?' Lineham screwed up his face, calculating. 'So on thirty acres that's – no, wait a minute, I'm getting lost in all the noughts . . .'

'Mike! We're not here to do mental arithmetic. You can amuse yourself with that when you're off duty. Anyway, don't forget what he said. The main problem is selling it.'

Thanet was pleased to see that there was a car parked in front of one of the barns, an old green Morris Traveller. Mrs Vintage was probably in, then. The house, however, had a neglected air. The windows were dirty, streaked with grime from the morning's rain, and some of the curtains were drawn, some not. There was an accumulation of leaves around the front door as though it hadn't been used for some time. Perhaps it hadn't, thought Thanet as they knocked. Farming people often habitually use the back door because of all the mud that is carried in. Someone was in, anyway: inside a radio or television set was blaring out, almost but not quite drowning another sound, that of a baby crying.

No reply.

They knocked again, harder; still no response. Thanet was becoming uneasy. There was something wrong here, he could sense it.

Lineham evidently felt the same. 'Don't like the look of this, sir.'

'Perhaps she hasn't heard because of the noise.'

'Do we go around the back?'

Thanet nodded.

On the way past the window to the right of the door he stooped to peer in between the half-drawn curtains. This was the room with the television set. It stood in the corner beside the fireplace and opposite, at right angles to the window, slumped on a settee, was a woman, her profile masked by her hair. Thanet tapped at the window, but she gave no indication of having heard. He knocked harder and called Lineham back, knocked again, still with no response.

At last, as they peered in together, to Thanet's intense relief, the woman stirred. Slowly she turned her head to look at them. Her eyes were blank, incurious, and although she couldn't have been more than a few feet away, the sight of two strange men peering in at her initially produced no reaction whatsoever.

'Mrs Vintage?' Thanet called. 'Police.' He fished out his warrant card and held it up to the glass.

She continued to stare at him as if he were speaking in a foreign tongue and then slowly, very slowly, as if she were walking through water, she rose and approached the window. She was wearing a dressing gown, Thanet realised, and slippers. She'd been ill, perhaps, or still was. She was very pale, with dark circles beneath her eyes, and her long brown hair hung lank and greasy as if it were long overdue for a wash.

She was now close enough for them to speak to her. They had arranged that this time Lineham should take the interview and he also pressed his warrant card against the windowpane. 'Could we have a word, Mrs Vintage?'

Thanet half expected her to say no or at least to indicate that she would dress, first. It seemed to take a few moments for Lineham's request to penetrate but then, without a word, still with that curious trancelike motion, she turned and left the room through a door at the far side.

Thanet and Lineham looked at each other, eyebrows raised, mouths tugged down at the corners.

'Drugs?' said Lineham.

They returned to the front door but when there was no sound from inside hurried around to the back. She was waiting for them, leaning against the edge of the half-open door, a tabby cat weaving around her bare legs.

'What is it?' she said. Her voice was hoarse, as if she had a cold, and she cleared her throat.

'We're inquiring into the death of Mr Randish,' said Lineham. 'And we wondered if we could have a few words with you.'

She frowned, and again it seemed to take several moments before the meaning of what he had said penetrated.

Definitely drugged, Thanet decided. Tranquillisers, he suspected.

'Mr Randish? Dead?' The news seemed to have shaken her into a greater awareness and she stood back, held the door wider. 'Come in.'

But why the surprise? Thanet wondered. Why hadn't her husband told her the news before he left for the vineyard this morning?

Inside she glanced about her as if becoming aware of her surroundings for the first time. 'It's a bit of a mess,' she said vaguely, but without real concern.

And that was an understatement if ever he'd heard one, thought Thanet. Every square inch of surface was piled high with opened tins, dirty dishes encrusted with food and used saucepans. The floor hadn't been swept or washed for some time and there was a row of empty saucers beside which the cat had stationed itself, watching its mistress with an optimistic stare. Someone, however, had been at work recently: a huge pile of washing up had been left to drain beside the sink, and on the filthy cooker, standing in a pan of water, stood a baby's bottle full of milk. Two more bottles were lined up nearby. The child must be due for a feed, thought Thanet. Inside the house the noise of its crying was much louder and it sounded frantic. Mrs Vintage, however, made no move to turn on the heat under the saucepan.

'We'll go in the other room.' She led the way. The baby was upstairs and in the hall the noise it was making intensified. How could any mother ignore such a desperate appeal for attention? Thanet wondered. Lineham, he could tell, was thinking the same.

In the sitting room she made no move to turn down the volume on the set, simply returned to her seat and sat down, tugging the edges of her dressing gown together across her bare legs. The shoulders, Thanet noticed, were encrusted here and there with little patches of dried vomit, where the baby had brought up wind.

'Do you mind if we have the TV off, ma'am?' said Lineham.

She shook her head.

The sound of the baby's cries seemed magnified in the ensuing silence.

'We don't mind waiting, if you want to attend to the baby,' said the sergeant.

'He'll be all right for a few minutes.'

Then, shockingly, she got up and shut the door, reducing the sound to a distant wail. She returned to her seat.

Thanet and Lineham exchanged glances. What could they do? You couldn't force a mother to look after her baby.

'Didn't your husband tell you about Mr Randish?'

She shook her head. 'I was asleep when he got home last night. And when he left this morning.'

Her voice had lost its hoarseness and Thanet suddenly realised why. It had been the roughness not of illness but of disuse. With a sudden flash of comprehension he glimpsed what this woman's life was like. By the sound of its cry the baby was very young and therefore very demanding. The first weeks of a child's life were always exhausting for the mother, a time when she herself was not fully restored to health and needed help to cope with the extra demands upon her time and energy. Vintage had told them that the harvest was the busiest time of year, that for weeks now he had been rising very early and not getting to bed until two or three in the morning.

During that period he had probably hardly even spoken to his wife. Mrs Vintage had had to cope alone and clearly the task had been too much for her. Thanet guessed too that there was more to it than that. She was, he was willing to bet, suffering from post-natal depression and had been given tranquillisers to help her cope. Vintage must know that something was wrong, but fully stretched as he was he had probably shut his eyes to the extent of the problem. It was he, probably, who had prepared those bottles for the baby and done that washing-up before leaving this morning.

This, Thanet was sure, was the reason for Vintage's unease when speaking about his marriage. They would have to look elsewhere for Randish's mistress, if he'd had one. Meanwhile, what was to be done about this situation? Theoretically, nothing. It certainly wasn't his responsibility to sort out suspects' domestic problems. On the other hand, there was the child to consider.

Lineham was giving Mrs Vintage a brief account of Randish's death. Outside a car drew up, a door slammed. Thanet rose to look out of the window: Vintage. Here, perhaps, was his opportunity. Unobtrusively, he withdrew to the kitchen. Vintage was just coming in through the back door. He was scowling.

'What are you doing here?' But there was no real aggression in his tone, just a weary acceptance.

No wonder the man looked so exhausted, Thanet thought. He must feel as though his life was completely out of control. 'I'm afraid we turn up everywhere in this sort of inquiry.'

Vintage had registered the baby's frantic crying. He glanced at the cooker, took in the three untouched bottles of baby feed, moved at once to turn on the heat beneath the one in the saucepan of water.

'Where's my wife?'

'In the sitting room, with Sergeant Lineham.'

'Excuse me.'

Before Thanet could say anything Vintage left the room and Thanet heard him trudge upstairs. Briefly, the crying stopped, then started again. He was, Thanet guessed, changing the child's nappy. A few minutes later he returned to the kitchen cradling the baby. It was indeed very young, less than eight weeks old, Thanet guessed. It was scarlet with frustration, its scrap of hair wet with perspiration, its face screwed up in agonised appeal as it continued to wail with every ounce of energy it still possessed. Not for the first time Thanet marvelled that something so small could make so much noise and cause so much disruption.

With his free hand Vintage snatched the bottle out of the saucepan, sprinkled a few drops of milk on the back of his other hand to test the temperature and shoved the teat into the baby's gaping mouth. Its lips clamped around the rubber and it began to suck with desperate urgency. Vintage hooked his foot around one of the chairs, dragged it away from the cluttered table and sat down.

There was a blissful silence.

Both men watched the child without speaking for a few moments. Then Thanet also pulled out a chair and sat down. There would never be a better time to say this, he thought.

'You realise your wife is ill, Mr Vintage.'

Vintage glanced up, briefly. 'It's none of your business.'

'Maybe not. But a child at risk is.'

'She's seen a doctor.'

'Where? Here?' Thanet's glance underlined the chaos in the room. 'Or at the surgery?' He did not add, *where she and the baby would have been dressed and tidied up for public inspection.* The implication was obvious.

'Yes,' admitted Vintage reluctantly.

'Then it's up to you to spell out to him just how bad things are, so that he can keep a close eye on her. Oh, I do realise how difficult it must have been for you, over the last few weeks. But all the same, it can't go on, you must see that.'

Vintage put the bottle down and laid the baby gently against his shoulder, patted its back to bring up the wind. He sighed, a long slow sigh of capitulation. 'I know. You're right. I suppose I didn't want to admit how serious the problem was. I kept saying to myself, if she can just hang on until harvest is finished . . . As it is, I just don't see how I can cope. And this business with Zak has just made things ten times worse, if that's possible.'

'Is there no one who could come and stay, to help look after the baby?' Vintage's mother, Thanet remembered, was dead. 'Your wife's mother, perhaps?'

'She couldn't even begin to manage. She's just out of hospital after a hysterectomy.'

'Brothers, sisters?'

'I haven't got any.' The baby burped obligingly and Vintage set the teat to its mouth again. 'Beth has a sister, but she lives up north and has four children of her own. I don't see how she could possibly leave them for any period of time.'

'There must be someone.'

'That's the trouble,' said Vintage. 'There isn't. Only me.' This time the look he directed at Thanet was one of despair. 'What am I going to do?'

Thanet thought. 'Is there any chance of hiring a nanny for a while, until your wife is on her feet again?'

'We can't afford it. The doctor said it could take months.'

'I appreciate that, but can you afford not to? I'm not sure if you realise just how serious this is. If it were my wife I'd be prepared if not to steal at least to beg or borrow, to help her through it. You may not like the idea, but desperate situations demand desperate remedies. Perhaps you could arrange a loan from the bank. Or would your father lend you the money?'

'He might. But I'd hate to ask. He was so generous in setting us up here that I've spent the last four years trying to prove how independent I can be.'

'Have you actually discussed the situation with him?'

Vintage shook his head. 'No. Anyway, he's been away on business for the last fortnight, in Thailand, and it's only during that period that things have got so bad.'

'When's he due back?'

'Monday.'

'Well, I suggest you swallow your pride and see what he can do. I would have thought that if he appreciates it's a question of his grandchild's welfare, he'd be more than willing to lend a hand.'

Vintage sighed again. 'You're right.'

The teat had slipped out of the baby's mouth and it slept, exhausted and replete. Vintage pushed aside a plate on the table to make room for the bottle and looked down at the child. 'We'll manage something, won't we?' he murmured.

Thanet stood up. 'Good.'

On cue, he heard the sitting-room door open and Lineham appeared.

'All finished?' he asked the sergeant.

Lineham nodded.

Vintage watched them go. 'Thanks, Inspector.'

Thanet grinned. 'All in a day's work!' he said.

TEN

'Did Vintage tell you what the doctor's diagnosis was?' said Lineham.

On their way to Chasing Manor vineyard they had been discussing what they had learnt at Vintage's house. Not a lot, they had decided, and had been silent for a while mulling things over.

'Not in so many words, no. But it's obvious, isn't it?'

'Post-natal depression. Yes. But what I'm wondering is if it's *too* obvious.'

'What do you mean, Mike?'

'Well, you take one look at Mrs Vintage and the set-up there and immediately that's the conclusion you jump to.'

'I still don't see what you're getting at.'

'What if her illness has a completely different cause? What if the reason she's depressed is because she was having an affair with Randish and when she discovered she was pregnant he threw her over? What if the baby is Randish's? Just think what a motive that would give her husband!'

Thanet remembered Vintage's concern for the child, the tenderness with which he had handled it. 'I can't believe that.' He didn't want to believe it, he realised. He was sorry for Vintage and sympathetic to the difficult situation in which he found himself. He would have to be careful. He mustn't allow bias to warp his judgement. 'If you'd seen him with the baby . . .'

'All right. Perhaps I'm wrong about the baby. Or perhaps I'm right and he just doesn't realise it isn't his. But in any case I could still be right about the affair – I say "I", but it was you who suggested it in the first place!'

'I know that. But having seen Mrs Randish I'm not so sure.'

'That's because you're thinking of her as she is now. At her worst. But while I was talking to her I was trying to visualise what she'd look like in good health, with make-up on and so on, and I bet she'd turn heads any day of the week.'

'Maybe. All right. Let's say she and Randish were having an affair. What, exactly, are you suggesting, Mike? That Vintage has known about it all along? In which case, why do nothing until last night? Or are you suggesting he's only just found out?'

'That he's only just found out.'

'How?'

'No idea. Perhaps someone told him. Perhaps something was said which made him put two and two together.'

'And come up with five, most likely! No, sorry, Mike, I'm still sceptical. In any case, there's one big objection to the idea that his wife might have been Randish's mistress.'

'What's that?'

'When we told her Randish was dead, don't you think we would have got more of a reaction?'

'But she was doped up to the eyeballs, we could both see that! All her reactions were about as low-key as they could get! And if Vintage did somehow find out last night, he would fit the bill perfectly. For one thing, he was there alone most of the evening, and for another, whoever killed Randish just exploded with rage, didn't he? Just think about it! Vintage was very tired, exhausted in fact, which means his self-control would be at its lowest. Also, because of Randish he'd just lost a substantial portion of the very special wine he was hoping would launch him on the road to success. Then he learns his wife had been having an affair with the man! It's enough to make anyone snap!'

'Mike, this is pure speculation and you know it.' Thanet's tone was indulgent. Lineham's enthusiasm was one of his more endearing qualities and Thanet was used to the fact that the sergeant sometimes got carried away.

'That doesn't mean it can't be true.'

'No, just that we have to wait until we have some hard evidence to support the idea before we can take it any further. So let's drop it for the moment, shall we? Anyway, isn't this the vineyard coming up?'

Lineham slowed down. 'Looks like it.'

The signboard for Chasing Manor vineyard had been designed to look like a wine label, the label which no doubt was put on their bottles. In the centre was a cameo of the vineyard, a sketch of a classic Georgian house set in well-ordered rows of vines.

'I'm beginning to feel as though we're on a tour of the vineyards of Kent,' said Thanet. 'I never knew there were so many.'

'Oh yes, there are dozens of them. There's one at Tenterden, one at Biddenden, one at Frittenden, one at Leeds, one at Bearsted . . .'

'All right, Mike. I didn't ask for a catalogue. Anyway, how do you know so much about it?'

'I've got a neighbour who's a wine buff. His favourite

pastime at weekends is touring vineyards. This one doesn't look as though it's doing too badly.'

Thanet looked around. Over to his right, set well back behind a brick wall and a generous front garden, was the house on the signboard, translated into bricks and mortar. It was a classic example of Georgian architecture: front door in the centre, two sash windows to right and left, five above. For once the architect had got the proportions exactly right and not even the grey light of a damp October afternoon could dim the beauty which had mellowed through the centuries. Sitting serenely in its setting of well-kept lawns and flowerbeds it seemed to encapsulate so much of what people envisage when they think of the beauty of rural England. What must it be like to live in a house like that? Thanet wondered.

'A real hive of activity, in fact,' said Lineham.

Thanet tore his eyes away from the house. The sergeant was right. There was a coach in the car park and a number of cars. Machinery hummed and there were people moving about. As they walked towards the buildings ahead the noise got louder and they met a group of people leaving the shop, carrying bottles and packs of wine. The coach party, probably, thought Thanet, and by the laughter and chatter he guessed that they had probably attended a wine-tasting session before making their purchases.

The noise intensified. It sounded like the spin on a giant washing machine. It was emanating, they discovered, from a cylindrical stainless-steel wine press identical to the one at Sturrenden.

Lineham raised his voice to make himself heard. 'That must be what Vintage meant, when he talked about the noise the press makes when the compressor comes on.'

Thanet nodded. 'Probably.'

There were in fact two presses, one on each side of a wide covered area, but only one was working at the moment. Preparations were in progress for starting off another batch in the other press: a man on a tractor was backing a trailer-load of grapes up to a smaller bin-shaped trailer of sturdy green plastic which had been connected to the press by a thick corrugated hose about 5 inches in diameter. Another man was standing by, watching, and a third man was hosing out a huge black plastic barrel. As they approached he picked up a broom and began to sweep the water towards a runnel leading to a drain.

Although Benton had retired Thanet guessed that in the circumstances the former winemaker would have stepped in to do Randish's job. He picked out the man watching as the most likely candidate. He had an air of authority about him. Thanet raised his voice to make himself heard. 'Mr Benton?'

The man turned. 'Yes?'

Warm brown eyes regarded him with affable curiosity. If Benton was in his early sixties he was very well preserved, with thick brown curly hair untouched by grey and a luxuriant beard.

'Mr James Benton?'

'That's right.'

Thanet introduced himself and Lineham, watching the bleakness creep into Benton's eyes.

Benton half turned, spoke to the man on the tractor. 'Can you manage for a while, Mark?'

'Is that your son, sir?'

Benton nodded. 'Yes, why?'

Randish's childhood friend, now an accountant, according to Vintage. What a bit of luck, thought Thanet. He certainly hadn't expected to find him here today. Presumably the younger Benton had also stepped in to help out in the emergency. With two presses in operation this vineyard must have double the workload of Sturrenden to cope with. 'I'd like him to join us, please.'

Benton frowned. 'We're rather behind here. Would you mind waiting a few minutes while we start this batch off? Then we'll be free for a while.'

'Fine.'

Thanet and Lineham watched with interest. The trailer connected to the press, they discovered, had a huge stainless-steel screw running across the bottom inside, from front to back. When it started to revolve it would feed the grapes into the hose leading to the press. They watched while the grapes were emptied in and the process started, then Benton led the way across the yard and up an outside staircase to an office on the upper floor of one of the barns. He sat down behind the desk and offered Thanet the only other chair. Mark Benton perched on the desk edge and Lineham went to lean against the window-sill.

'We still can't believe it,' said Benton. 'Murder is something you read about in the newspapers or hear about on the radio or television. You just don't think it could ever happen to someone you know.'

Thanet nodded sympathetically. He'd heard this said so many times before, and he could believe it.

'I mean, here we are, perfectly ordinary people leading perfectly ordinary lives and then wham ... I suppose until now we've been lucky.' He glanced at his son. 'It's just that we've known Zak since he was in his teens.'

'You were fond of him?' Thanet was intrigued. Apart from Alice Randish this was the first time he'd heard anyone speak of the dead man with anything approaching affection.

Benton hesitated. 'I wouldn't say "fond" was the right

word. He'd been around so long he was practically one of the family, wasn't he, Mark? And I suppose my attitude to him was pretty much what it would be to one of my own children. I took his faults for granted.'

Mark Benton grinned. 'Thanks, Dad!'

Mark Benton must take after his mother, Thanet thought. He was shorter than his father and much less robust in appearance, with straight floppy brown hair and gold-rimmed spectacles which gave him a studious look.

Benton waved a hand. 'You know perfectly well what I mean.'

'So what were his faults, would you say?' said Thanet.

Benton frowned, ran his hand through his thick hair, then leaned forward to ease his waxed jacket off. He tossed it on to the floor beside him. 'That's tricky. You never sit down and actually list people's characteristics in your mind, do you? I mean, what usually occurs is that something happens and you think, God, he's an impatient beggar, or he's a heartless blighter, or he'd trample over anyone who got in his way, and so on. D'you see what I mean?'

'Yes. Were you thinking of Mr Randish just then, when you were speaking? Was he in fact impatient, heartless, ruthless?'

Benton shifted uncomfortably in his chair and glanced at his son. 'I suppose I was, to a certain extent. Sorry, Mark, but there's no point in trying to make out that Zak was some sort of saint, because he wasn't.'

'I've never suggested otherwise.'

'And in any case, we would be doing him a disservice if we tried to pull the wool over the inspector's eyes.'

'Don't treat me like an idiot, Dad, I realise that! I don't know what you're going on like this for in any case. You know Zak and I hardly ever saw each other any more.'

'Oh? Why was that, sir?' Thanet was interested.

Mark shrugged. 'We just drifted apart. Our paths divided, I suppose, and we went different ways. I don't actually work on the vineyard, I reneged and became a white-collar worker.'

'An accountant, I believe.'

Mark looked surprised and a little wary. 'That's right. You're very well informed, Inspector.'

'But you had known Mr Randish a long time.'

'As my father said, since we were in our teens, yes.'

'And – correct me if I'm wrong – but I had the impression, just now, that it wasn't just because your ways divided that you didn't see much of each other any more, but also perhaps because you didn't like him as much as you once did.'

'Yes, that's true. But – look, I hope you're not about to suggest that I went over to Sturrenden last night and bumped him off, are you?'

Mark Benton's tone was jocular, but his father jumped in before Thanet could respond. 'Don't be ridiculous, Mark! The inspector's suggesting no such thing.'

'Quite right, I'm not suggesting anything of the sort. It's just that I'm trying to find out as much as I can about Mr Randish, and the only way I can do that is to ask questions of the people who knew him. And you, Mr Benton, are in a position where you could be especially useful to us. You've known him a long time but you're not so close to him now that you can't stand back a little and give us a more impartial view than people he was involved with on a day-to-day basis.'

'I was, as I'm sure you realised, Inspector, joking. Anything I can do to help . . . Ask away.'

Much of what Mark Benton told them simply confirmed what they had already heard. Randish had met

Alice when he was fruit-picking on her father's farm during the school holidays and it was she who introduced him to the Young Farmers' Club, which was where he met Mark.

'She was absolutely crazy about him. All the while they were together, even in a crowd, she'd hardly take her eyes off him. It was as if the rest of us simply didn't exist.'

'Did he feel the same about her?'

'He was keen, certainly, but not to that degree. I think he just went along with it, to begin with, at least.'

'And then?'

Mark Benton looked uncomfortable. 'Well, to be honest, I think it dawned on him that he might be on to a good thing.'

'Because she was an only child, you mean, and her father had a large farm.'

Mark nodded reluctantly. 'Yes.'

Benton intervened. 'I don't know if what Mark is saying is true, Inspector, it well might be. In fact, it wouldn't surprise me in the least. All the same, I do feel that we might be giving you the wrong impression. Zak had many good qualities, or I wouldn't have employed him to take over here when I retired. He was reliable, very hard-working and as far as I was concerned absolutely trust-worthy.'

'Oh come on, Dad, don't be a humbug! Who was apologising to me a few minutes ago for being too frank about Zak? I don't like saying these things about him any more than you do, especially when he can't defend him-self, but let's face it, people don't get themselves killed because they're reliable, hardworking and trustworthy. They get themselves killed, presumably, because they've treated someone badly – very badly.'

'All the same, I think it has to be said. Zak worked

incredibly hard to get where he did, and when you consider his background . . . His father was a drunken brute, Inspector, who used to beat his wife and children without any excuse at all. There was some very nasty publicity once, when a neighbour reported him to the NSPCC. I imagine the whole family heaved a sigh of relief when he got drunk one night and landed up in the river. Fortunately he couldn't swim. There was no foul play, there were plenty of witnesses around. Zak was around fourteen then, I believe.'

'I had the impression that Mr Landers wasn't too keen on Mr Randish's association with his daughter,' said Thanet.

'Can you blame him, with a background like that?' said Benton senior. 'If Mark had had a sister I wouldn't have been too keen on Zak as a prospective suitor for her, I can tell you. And not because I'm a snob, either. The poverty of his background wouldn't have worried me if his parents were good people. But bad blood is a different matter.'

And so was an undesirable example. Had the Bentons known or suspected that Randish was beating his wife, as his father had beaten his mother?

'And would your anxiety have been justified, sir?'

'What do you mean?'

Benton was looking puzzled, but Mark had understood, Thanet could see it in his face. 'Are you married, sir?' he asked the younger man, on a sudden inspiration.

'Yes. Why?'

'Just wondered.'

'It was through Alice that Mark met Zoë – his wife – as a matter of fact,' said Benton. 'She and Alice were at the same finishing school in Switzerland, and Alice invited her to stay when they left.'

That explained a lot, thought Thanet. If the two girls were friends and the two young men had known each other for a long time, no doubt they had seen quite a lot of each other in the early years of their marriages. And if Randish had started knocking Alice about, Zoë – like Lineham's wife, Louise – might well have noticed, or guessed. In which case, even if the two young women had kept up their friendship, Mark Benton might well out of distaste have allowed his friendship with Zak to lapse. 'It was during Mr Randish's final year at college that Mrs Randish – Miss Landers as she was then – was away in Switzerland, wasn't it?'

'Yes. I think Landers sent her away in the hope that separation might break the relationship up. A vain hope, I'm afraid. The experiment was a dismal failure. The minute Alice got back she and Zak were inseparable again. Not long afterwards they announced their engagement.'

'Mr Landers gave his consent to the marriage?'

'Well, Alice was nineteen by then. Strictly speaking she didn't need it.'

But that wouldn't have suited Randish's plans at all, thought Thanet. He needed Landers' blessing.

'What happened,' said Mark, 'was that Mr Landers agreed, provided they waited two years before getting married. If they still wanted to go ahead at the end of that time, he would not oppose it.'

'I suppose he thought that if they were still determined then, he might as well give in gracefully,' said Benton. 'Which, of course, is what happened.'

'I assume he set them up in the house and vineyard?'

'It was his wedding present,' said Benton.

So Randish's patience had been amply rewarded.

Lineham shifted from one foot to the other and Thanet

could hear his unspoken comment. *Some wedding present!*

'And meanwhile Mr Randish was working here?'

'Yes. I told you, I couldn't fault him in that respect. He learned fast as he had a real flair for winemaking. Some have got it and some haven't. He did.'

'You were saying,' said Thanet to Mark Benton, 'that Mr Randish was never as keen on his wife as she was on him.' He paused, choosing his next words carefully. 'Do you know if he had other girlfriends at the same time, while he was away at college, for instance?'

'Good God, yes!' said Mark Benton. 'His attitude was that he should make hay while the sun was shining.'

'Didn't Miss Landers suspect?'

'I can't think how he got away with it, but he seemed to. It must have been some juggling act, during his second year at least, because her father gave her a car for her seventeenth birthday and once she passed her test there was no holding her, she was off to Plumpton every week-end.'

'Hence the finishing school during Zak's final year there, I imagine,' said Benton.

'He had a particularly torrid affair while she was away, I remember,' said Mark. 'With his landlady's daughter, I believe. I met her once. Interestingly enough, she looked a bit like Alice, except that she was dark instead of fair. She was the same type, I suppose – small, slight, rather fragile-looking.'

Of course! thought Thanet. That was what had been eluding him when he was looking at those photographs. All Zak's girlfriends had been the same physical type. 'And did his attitude change after he was married?' he said, arriving at last at the point up to which he had been leading.

'Ah,' said Benton. 'Now there, I certainly can't help you.' There was a brief silence. He glanced at Mark.

'So that's what you've been getting at,' said Mark. 'You're thinking in terms of a jealous husband, or lover.'

'It's a possible explanation.'

'Well, all I can say is that I do know for a fact that Zak wasn't exactly the most faithful husband in the world. But whether or not he had a current girlfriend, mistress, whatever, I'm afraid I have no idea. And that's the truth.'

'So,' said Lineham as they walked back to the car. 'Surprise, surprise, we're back to "*cherchez la femme*".'

'You've been working on your French accent, Mike.'

'Shouldn't be too much of a problem, sir, should it, to round up all the small, slight, fragile-looking girls in the area and find out which of them was Randish's mistress?'

'Ha ha. Very funny.'

Lineham cocked his head. 'Isn't that the car radio?' He hurried off.

Thanet's shoelace was undone and he stopped to fix it. The call was brief and by the time he arrived at the car Lineham was replacing the handset.

The sergeant leaned across to unlock the passenger door. He was grinning from ear to ear.

'What's up?' said Thanet.

'You won't believe this!' said Lineham.

ELEVEN

Thanet got into the car. 'Believe what? Well, come on, Mike, stop grinning like a Cheshire cat and spit it out.'

'It looks as though we've found the *femme*!'

'Oh?' Thanet was wary. He wanted to hear more before he started rejoicing.

'That was a message from DC Wakeham. You remember he was saying this morning that he was sure he'd seen Randish before? Well, he remembered where. It was at a restaurant in Lenham. Randish was with a girl and they were very engrossed in each other. Wakeham especially noticed them because he fancied the girl. Anyway, and this is the point, the friend Wakeham was with knew who she was. He works in computers and so does she. You remember the new system I commented on, at the vineyard? I bet that was how Randish met her.'

'Could be. When was this, that Wakeham saw them?'

'Couple of weeks ago, sir.'

'But he didn't know the name of the girl? Or the firm she works for?'

'No. But he's trying to get hold of his friend, to find out.'

'Good. Well, let's hope you're right.' It all sounded feasible and if so it was a lucky break. It wasn't often that an answer fell into their laps almost before they'd asked the question.

'Where now, sir? Back to Headquarters? You promised that statement to the press.'

Thanet groaned. 'I suppose so.'

It was nearly 9.30 before he at last reached home. Joan and Bridget were watching a film on television.

'Your supper's in the oven,' Joan said. 'Side salad in the fridge.'

'Thanks, love.' In the kitchen the table was laid for one. Thanet turned off the oven, took an oven-cloth and removed the dish inside. A mouth-watering aroma rose to greet him. As he expected it was one of Bridget's specialities, salmon and prawn lasagne. Bridget was a Cordon Bleu cook, a freelance professional who cooked for directors' dining rooms in the City. The effortless ease with which she produced delicious meals never failed to arouse her mother's envy and admiration and invariably, when she was home, despite Joan's protests that it was no break for her, she cooked for the family. Thanet inhaled appreciatively, suddenly realising how hungry he was. He was glad to see that they'd left him a generous helping.

As usual, at the end of a long day, his back was aching and he adjusted himself into the most comfortable position before beginning to eat. Gradually, as he enjoyed his meal, the strains and tensions began to seep away and by the time he'd finished, cleared away and lit his pipe he was feeling a new man. He put his head around the sitting-room door. 'Tea, coffee, Horlicks, cocoa, chocolate?'

Briefly they turned smiling faces towards him. They both wanted tea.

He returned to the kitchen, made tea for three. The front door slammed and Ben wandered into the kitchen.

'Hi.'

'You're early for a Saturday night.'

'Yeah. Got a training session in the morning. Have to get up early, groan, groan.'

'Want some tea? I've just made some.'

'Think I'll really live it up, have some chocolate instead. Don't worry, I'll make it myself. Saw you on the box tonight, by the way. Great performance, Dad. We'll make a star of you yet.'

'No comment,' said Thanet, departing with the tray of tea.

The play was just finishing.

'Well timed, darling,' said Joan.

'How are things?' said Thanet.

Bridget pulled a face. 'Not exactly great.'

'Oh?' Thanet was surprised. Surely Bridget wasn't going to talk about Alexander here, now, with Ben about to come in?

Joan had guessed what he was thinking. 'It's Karen, Luke. You remember Bridget's friend Karen, the one with anorexia?'

Thanet was nodding.

'Well, she died last night.'

Thanet stared at her as wheels clicked in his brain. Karen. He heard Landers' voice. *Zak's niece died this evening. She was only twenty. She's been in hospital for some time.*

Joan glanced uneasily at Bridget, who was staring down at her hands, her expression grim. 'And that wasn't all.'

Thanet knew what was coming next. Landers' voice again: *Jonathan had an accident last night ... the twin brother of the girl who died ... he and his sister have always been very close ...*

'Bridget went around to Karen's house,' Joan was

saying, 'and there was no one in. But the next-door neighbour heard her knocking and came out. She told her about Karen, then said that Karen's mother was still at the hospital because Karen's brother Jonathan had had an accident . . .' Joan stopped. 'You're not looking surprised,' she said.

'I'd already heard. I'm sorry about your friend, Sprig,' he said to Bridget. He rarely used her childhood nickname these days but this time it just slipped out.

Bridget looked close to tears. 'It was such a shock,' she said. 'I knew she wasn't getting on very well. Last time I was home she'd gone down to five stone again. But I didn't think . . . And then, Jonathan, too. I rang the hospital and he's still unconscious.'

'Who's still unconscious?' Ben came in carrying a mug and a triple-decker sandwich.

No one commented on the latter. They were used, by now, to Ben's late-night snacks.

'Jonathan Redman,' said Joan. Quickly, she filled Ben in on what they had been saying.

'A motorbike accident!' said Ben, glancing at his father.

Thanet nodded. With what he considered superhuman restraint he refrained from saying anything. The question of a motorbike was a bone of contention between them and he hoped that Ben would have enough sense to draw his own conclusions. He remembered thinking the same thing last night when he'd passed the scene of that accident. It struck him now that it might well have been Jonathan Redman on the stretcher.

'But how did you know about all this, Luke?' said Joan.

'This murder I'm working on. The victim was Karen's uncle, Mrs Redman's brother.'

All three stared at him, taken aback. Joan was the first to speak. 'Oh no!' she said. 'Poor woman! She must be absolutely devastated by all this.'

'I know,' said Thanet. 'I was thinking earlier on that I can't imagine how anyone in her situation even begins to cope.'

'I'll go and see her tomorrow,' said Bridget suddenly. 'In case I can do anything to help.'

'Her brother's mother-in-law, Mrs Landers, was going around to keep her company today,' said Thanet. 'But of course, in the circumstances, she can't stay with her all the time. Mrs Landers' daughter is naturally very upset over her husband's death, and there are the grandchildren to think of.'

'Quite,' said Bridget. 'But Mrs Redman will be feeling so alone. She hasn't got anybody else, to my knowledge. She's incredibly shy and awkward in company and it puts people off. I don't think she has any close friends.'

'I'm not surprised,' said Ben. 'She and Mr Redman were a pair of oddballs, in my opinion. I went there once with you, do you remember, when he was still alive? Mrs Redman wouldn't say "boo" to a goose and Mr Redman gave me the creeps.' He took a huge bite out of his sandwich.

'In what way?' said Joan.

Somehow Ben managed simultaneously to screw up his face in distaste at the memory and masticate energetically. He swallowed. 'Dunno. This was yonks ago. I couldn't have been more than, what, eleven? at the time, so I don't suppose I stopped to analyse what I didn't like about him. All I knew was that I wasn't too anxious to go back there.' He returned to his sandwich.

'I don't blame you,' said Bridget. 'It wasn't much fun going to the Redmans', especially if Mr Redman was there. He was a bit of a religious maniac. Very strict. Like something out of the dark ages, really. He wouldn't allow a television set in the house, or a radio. I'm sure he didn't approve of me. He had very rigid rules about the way they were all supposed to behave, even about how they should dress – Karen wasn't allowed to wear bright colours, short skirts, jeans or T-shirts, and as for make-up, that was absolutely *verboten*.' Like Ben she pulled a face. 'He gave me the creeps too.'

Thanet had a feeling that she could have said more, that there was in fact something specific that she was holding back. He had had a case once in which a similar family was involved, he remembered. And there, too, the extremity of the father's views had led to tragedy. The roots of Karen's anorexia had no doubt lain in the warped relationships within her family.

He said as much to Joan as they were getting ready for bed. 'And I have a feeling that Bridget knows more than she's telling.' He swung his legs into bed and lay down, feeling the tense muscles of his aching back relax into the blissful support of the orthopaedic mattress in which they had invested some years ago.

Joan was patting moisture cream into her face. 'You could be right. She and Karen were very close at one time.' She finished creaming her face and got into bed. She sighed. 'It's such a waste, isn't it, a young girl like that, dying unnecessarily. Anorexia is a dreadful thing and I'm only thankful Bridget never succumbed.'

'As far as she's concerned, the one positive aspect of all this is that it has given her something other than Alexander to think about.'

'Quite.'

'How's she been today?'

'Well, there's no doubt about it, it's been an awful

blow to her self-confidence. She'll bounce back eventually, I imagine, she's pretty resilient, but it's bound to take time. And, of course, hearing about Karen has rather overshadowed everything else. But as you heard downstairs, she is trying to be positive. She's arranged to go and have coffee with Helen tomorrow morning.'

'Helen will be pleased. Doc M. told me only last night that Helen was saying recently that she hadn't seen Bridget for ages. She misses their cookery sessions, he says.'

'And we're going to Mother's for tea.'

Thanet grinned. 'It all sounds rather dull for a twenty-year-old, but highly therapeutic.'

To spend time with people who loved and valued her was just what Bridget needed, he thought next morning, looking at his daughter's drawn face as she came into the kitchen. It wrenched at his heart to see her like this and to feel so powerless to help her. He was standing waiting for the kettle to boil and went to put his arm around her shoulders, give her a hug. 'What are you doing up at this unearthly hour on a Sunday morning?' Almost before the words were out, he knew he shouldn't have asked.

'I didn't sleep very well.'

The opening was there, he had to take it. In any case they couldn't go on avoiding the subject as they had been. 'I was sorry to hear about Alexander,' he said.

She twisted to look up at him; disengaged herself. 'Were you, Dad?' she said bitterly. 'I'd have thought you might be relieved. You never did like him, did you?'

She was hurt and angry, he saw, angry with Alexander, with herself, with life. Now, briefly, her anger had found a focus in him. Well, there was no point in being anything but honest. But how to do it, without inflicting more pain? 'I did like him.' But his reservations showed in his tone of voice, he realised. 'I just wasn't sure he was right for you.'

'Why not?' said Bridget passionately. And then, 'Oh, what's the point in going over and over it? It's finished now, anyway.' And, putting up a hand to dash away the tears which had sprung into her eyes, she rushed from the room.

Thanet was reminded of the scene between Alice Randish and her father yesterday, which had been over much the same issue – parental disapproval of choice of partner – and had ended in much the same way, and he felt a pang of sympathy for Landers. Despite his rationalisation of a moment ago, he was upset. How not to administer comfort, in one easy lesson, he thought wryly.

He made the tea and, before sitting down to breakfast, carried a cup upstairs. Joan, he knew, would still be asleep, she usually had a lie-in on a Sunday morning before going to church. He tapped softly on Bridget's door. 'Cup of tea,' he murmured.

No response.

With a sigh he deposited it on the floor and went back downstairs. She would come around, he knew. Meanwhile the memory of the brief and uncomfortable little scene lodged like a splinter in his consciousness. It would, he knew, lie there festering all day. It was rare indeed for him to be on bad terms with Bridget, however briefly.

He had little appetite for breakfast but knowing how uncertain meal times were when he was working on a case made himself eat some cereal. Outside, however, the sun was trying to break through, his pipe consoled him a little and by the time he arrived in the office he was feeling marginally more cheerful. It was depressing therefore to find that the usually ebullient Lineham, there before him as usual, was looking gloomy.

Reluctantly, Thanet removed his pipe out of consideration for the sergeant and tapped it out in the stout ashtray which stood on his desk for that purpose. 'It can't be as bad as that, surely, Mike.'

Lineham tossed the report he had been reading on to his desk. 'Nothing!' he said. 'Nothing of any use, anyway. And if there's nothing coming in at this stage, what's it going to be like later?'

'Oh come on, stop being so pessimistic. You know perfectly well one can simply never tell what's going to turn up next. You've said yourself that's one of the things you like about this job.'

'True.'

'So? There must be something to report, surely, even if it's all negative.'

'The PM report is in, but it doesn't tell us anything we didn't already know.' Lineham passed it over and Thanet glanced through it. Randish had apparently been in very good shape and in layman's terms had, as they surmised, quite simply bled to death as a result of the gash in his throat.

'What about the girl DC Wakeham saw?' said Thanet. 'Has he tracked down the friend who knows her, yet?'

Lineham shook his head. 'Couldn't get hold of him last night, sir. Not surprising, as it was Saturday night. Wakeham's gone off to have another go. If he fails, we could always make inquiries at the vineyard. If Randish did meet her through the firm who sold him his new computer system Mrs Prote would know who they are. If she's not at work today – and it is Sunday, after all – we've got her address. She might even know who the girl is. As I said, it's an expensive system and the firm might well have sent this girl to work at the vineyard for a couple of days to make sure their clients knew how to handle it. They often do. In which case, come to think of it, Vintage probably met her too.'

'You're assuming a lot, Mike. It might be pure coincidence that she works in computers. Randish could have met her in a dozen different ways. Still, I agree, it would be worth a try. Has Wakeham sent Mason's shoes off to forensic?'

'Yes. But they say they're snowed under and can't promise to come back to us for several days, at least.'

'Surprise, surprise.'

The morning meeting was brief again, Thanet's report once more being the longest. There was still no news of the results of Angharad's latest test. They all hoped that in this case no news did indeed mean good news. They should know tomorrow morning, when Draco returned.

Back in the office Thanet found Mallard waiting for him, alone. Lineham had evidently gone off on some errand.

'Morning, Luke. Don't suppose you've got any queries about the PM, it was all pretty straightforward, but I thought I'd pop in just in case.'

Thanet shook his head. 'Don't think so, thanks. It's all crystal clear.'

'He would have been good for another forty or fifty years, you know, barring accidents.'

'So I gathered.'

'How's it going?'

'We're feeling our way, as usual, not getting very far at the moment.'

'Actually, I really called to ask how Bridget is. I don't know if she told you, but she's coming around for coffee with Helen this morning. Is Alexander the problem?'

'I'm afraid so.' Briefly, Thanet gave Mallard a summary of the situation. 'We're hoping Helen will cheer her up.'

'She's very good at cheering people up,' said Mallard. 'Look what a good job she did on me!'

'True,' said Thanet smiling.

Thoughts of his own past must have reminded Mallard of Draco's present. 'Any news of Angharad?' he asked.

Thanet shook his head. 'We're keeping our fingers crossed.'

'So am I,' said Mallard grimly. 'This is a really important test, you know.'

'More so than the last? Why?'

'How much do you know about leukaemia?'

'Only snippets I've gathered here and there. I used to think it was invariably fatal, but we've all been astounded to see how Angharad has picked up over the last year.'

After the diagnosis they had all watched fearfully as Angharad had become a shadow of her former self. She had lost all her wonderful red hair and scorning a wig had taken to wearing exotic turbans. The ghost of her former, exceptional beauty had lingered only in the bone structure of her face. And then, miraculously, she had begun to improve. Little by little she had put on weight: had even, eventually, discarded the turbans and emerged like a freshly hatched chick with a fine frizz of hair the colour of a new-minted penny. Colour had begun to return to her cheeks and vitality to her movements.

'As you know,' said Mallard, 'Angharad has acute myeloid leukaemia. It was diagnosed two years ago. So you'll understand just how astounding that improvement is if I tell you that the average outlook is two years of life from diagnosis, with one or more remissions, each shorter than the last because of the disease becoming resistant to treatment. The first remission is on average one year, the second six months, the third – and you might not get one – four weeks. If someone recovers, it is always during first remission. If you have a second remission you will die unless you have a transplant, and that's a very risky business.'

'You're saying that Angharad is still in her first remission?'

'Yes. So far she's been one of the lucky ones.'

'I'd no idea. To begin with I think we were all afraid to talk to the Super about it, for fear of making him more depressed. No, to tell you the truth, I think we were just too cowardly, in case the news was bad and we wouldn't know what to say.'

'Understandable,' said Mallard.

'And then of course, when she seemed to start getting better I think we felt that to comment on the improvement would somehow be tempting fate. So we just stood by and kept our fingers crossed that it would continue.'

'Yes. Well, I'm afraid we're not out of the wood yet. Patients can do extraordinarily well and survive several years without relapses, but only about ten per cent of the total are cured and never relapse. After five years without a relapse you can be pretty sure. This particular test is important because for the first two years you have tests every two months and this is the last of the series. If she's clear it'll be a major landmark in her recovery.'

'But even if she is, they'll still have three more years to go before they can really begin to feel safe.'

'Yes. But if it is clear this time, she'll at least be in with a chance. From now on, all being well, it'll be every three to four months between tests, for a further two years. Then every six months for a couple of years. Then every year.'

Thanet had always shied away from imagining too vividly what it must be like for a relatively young woman of thirty-seven like Angharad to live with the shadow of death always hovering over her, to have to summon up over and over again sufficient courage to live through yet another course of debilitating chemotherapy. He fervently hoped that for the Dracos the worst of the nightmare would now be over.

Lineham hurried into the room. The spring was back in his step, his eyes alight with enthusiasm. 'We've got it, sir! Oh, sorry, Doc, morning.'

Mallard acknowledged the sergeant's greeting with a nod, an indulgent twinkle in his eye.

'Got what, Mike?' said Thanet.

'The girl's name. DC Wakeham just rang in. It's Elaine Wood. Wakeham's friend wasn't sure which firm she works for, though. He met her at some conference.'

'This is Randish's latest girlfriend, apparently,' Thanet explained to Mallard. 'Or could be.'

'Well, don't mind me. I'm just off anyway.'

'Right. We'll go out to the vineyard, then, Mike, test this theory of yours and see if they can tell us where to find her.'

'Want a bet on it, sir?'

'A pint, at lunchtime?'

'Done!'

'Tut, tut,' said Mallard. He clicked his tongue in mock disapproval. 'Gambling in the ranks. What would Super-intendent Draco say?'

TWELVE

With the resumption of work Sturrenden vineyard had come to life. The car park was surprisingly full for this hour on a Sunday morning and there were a number of customers in the shop.

'Murder is always good for business,' muttered Lineham cynically as they got out of the car.

Thanet grunted. The prurient attitude of the public towards anything to do with murder never failed to disgust him. Heads turned and necks craned as they went past.

Lights were on in the office but it was empty. Perhaps Mrs Prote wasn't in and they'd have to talk to Vintage instead.

In the covered yard the press was in operation and hoses of different thicknesses and colours snaked off in all directions. Vintage had evidently found someone to help him out: a young man Thanet had never seen before was hosing down the pressing area. He was wearing a long black rubber apron and wellington boots. As they picked their way towards him he dropped the hose, picked up a bass broom and began to sweep the water vigorously towards a central drain. Reflections of the neon lights above fragmented and reformed as the water rolled across them. A strong fruity smell hung in the air.

'Sturrenden CID,' said Lineham. 'Is Mrs Prote in today?'

The young man stopped sweeping. He was about twenty, with cropped black hair and an incipient beard. There was a sheen of perspiration on his forehead. 'Who?'

'Mrs Prote. The manageress.'

'I've just come in for the day, to help out, so I don't know people here. What does she look like?'

'Tall, dark, horn-rimmed glasses.'

'Yes, she's about somewhere.'

'There she is, Mike,' said Thanet.

Mrs Prote was descending the outside staircase from the Tea Room, which was in the upper floor of the barn housing the shop. As they crossed the yard Thanet said, 'Let's hope she's less prickly than she was yesterday, or you'll have your work cut out.'

Lineham, they had agreed, was to take this interview.

They waited for her at the bottom of the staircase. Once again she was immaculate, not a hair out of place in the smooth French pleat, blouse pristine white, dark green skirt and cardigan an exact match, shoes gleaming like polished chestnuts. She didn't look too pleased to see them: the brown eyes behind the horn-rimmed spectacles were hostile, resentful. 'I hope this won't take too long. I've got a lot to do today.'

'We weren't sure if you'd be in, as it's Sunday,' said Thanet.

She made no comment, simply led them into the office and sat down behind her desk, taking up the same pose as yesterday: knees together, feet side by side, hands folded in lap.

No doubt about it, thought Thanet, she would like life to be equally neat, well organised, under control. Maybe her hostility towards them stemmed from the fact that she didn't know how to deal with it when it became messy. And murder was invariably messy, in more ways than one.

'May we?' said Lineham, putting a hand on one of the other two chairs.

'If you must. As I said, I hope this won't take long.'

'We'll be as quick as we can.' Lineham swung the chair around to face her and Thanet moved the other one across to the window. This was Lineham's idea, Lineham's show.

'Nice computer system,' said Lineham. 'New, isn't it?'

Her eyebrows arched in surprise. 'Relatively, yes.'

'How long have you had it?'

'Three months or so.'

'Which firm did you buy it from?'

Her shoulders twitched impatiently. 'Look, is this relevant? I don't want to be rude, but . . .'

'If it wasn't relevant, Mrs Prote, I wouldn't be asking about it.'

She frowned. 'I really don't see how . . .'

Lineham sighed and said wearily, 'Mrs Prote. Do you want your employer's murderer to be found?'

'Well of course I do! What a ridiculous question!'

'Then perhaps you could be just a little more cooperative.'

'But I am being cooperative!'

'Are you? We obviously have different ideas of the meaning of the word. As far as we're concerned you weren't particularly cooperative yesterday and you're not being particularly cooperative today. First you say you've got a lot of work to do so you'd like this interview to be as brief as possible and then you prevaricate, thereby prolonging it.'

'I wasn't prevaricating!'

She glanced at Thanet, as if expecting him to back her up. He folded his arms and stared back at her, his face unresponsive, making it clear that he agreed with Lineham.

'I just don't see what computers have to do with Mr Randish's death.'

The point had been made. She was on the defensive now and Lineham recognised this. His tone was patient as he said, 'Mrs Prote, we are the ones who are investigating Mr Randish's death. Perhaps you'd allow us to judge what is or is not relevant.'

There was a brief silence, then Lineham went on. 'So, would you now answer my question: which firm did you buy it from?'

'Compu-Tech, in Sturrenden.'

'I haven't heard of them. They're a small firm?'

'Yes.'

'Were you pleased with the service they gave?'

'Very.'

'Was this the first computer system you've had here, or did you have a less sophisticated one before?'

'No, this is the first.'

'So I suppose the firm supplied you with someone to work beside you for the first day or two, while you got used to it?'

'Yes. It was one of the reasons why we chose that particular firm.'

'Was the person they sent a man or a woman?'

'A woman. Why?'

Lineham ignored the question.

'What was her name?'

'Elaine.'

Thanet could tell that Lineham was longing to flick a

triumphant glance at him. *Told you so!* But the sergeant restrained himself.

'Elaine what?'

'I've no idea. She just called herself Elaine, you know how these girls do.'

'A girl, you said. How old was she, would you say?'

Mrs Prote thought. 'Mid-twenties, perhaps?'

'But she looked younger?'

'Yes, on a first impression. She was small, slim, dark.'

Just Randish's type, according to his friend Mark Benton, thought Thanet. He could see Lineham thinking the same thing. And she matched Wakeham's description.

'Did she give Mr Randish tuition too?'

'Yes. It was part of the package. We both need — needed — to use the computer, if for different reasons.'

'How did Mr Randish get on with this Elaine?'

Mrs Prote was looking wary. 'All right.'

She didn't ask why, Thanet noted.

'Did he take any special interest in her, did you notice?'

'What do you mean?'

'To put it bluntly, did he fancy her?'

Her lips tightened. 'How would I know?'

'Mrs Prote, are you trying to tell me that you stayed here in this room with the pair of them for — how long? A day? Two days?' Lineham paused, waited pointedly for her answer.

'Two days,' she said reluctantly.

'And you didn't notice Mr Randish's attitude towards her?'

She was chewing the inside of her lip. She didn't reply.

Lineham sighed and sat back in his chair, folding his arms. 'I really don't know why you're making this such hard work,' he said.

'I just don't believe in idle gossip, Sergeant,' she said primly. 'Nor do I think one should speak ill of the dead.'

'Idle gossip!' said Lineham explosively. 'How *can* you sit there so self-righteously and say that? A man has been *murdered*, Mrs Prote. In my book that is a far worse crime, a far worse sin, if you like, than speaking ill of the dead. And no one could ever convince me otherwise.'

She stared at him, apparently silenced. Then she blinked. 'I hate this,' she said in a low voice, and took off her spectacles, as if this would help her to avoid seeing something she didn't want to look at. Without them she looked several years younger and vulnerable, as if her protective armour had been removed. 'I absolutely hate it.'

'I can understand that,' said Lineham. 'No one likes getting caught up in a murder investigation.'

'But don't you see?' she cried, with more feeling than she had shown so far, 'that's just a fine-sounding generalisation! "No one likes getting caught up in a murder investigation." It doesn't even begin to tell you what it *feels* like! It's horrible, as if everything is ... contaminated.' And she shuddered, crossing her arms and hugging herself as if to try to contain her revulsion.

He had never heard it put quite like that before, but Thanet knew she had summed up how people in her position felt. Their lives had been touched, however briefly, by the most evil of crimes, the taking of human life, and nothing would ever be quite the same again. They would go on living, carry on in much the same way as they always had, but there, lurking in the back of their minds, would always be the long shadow cast by murder.

He decided to step in. 'Mrs Prote, you must believe us when we say we do understand that. I'm sure you feel that we are poking and prying gratuitously, but we're not, I assure you. Sergeant Lineham is right. Murder is the worst crime in the book and we need every ounce of help we can get, from people like yourself, to try and clear the matter up. I can understand that you don't like going against the principles by which you normally live your life, but you have to accept that these are not normal circumstances and normal rules do not apply.'

While he was speaking she had put her spectacles back on, he noticed. When he had finished she nodded slowly. Then she sighed. 'I can see that. All right. I'll try.'

Lineham waited a moment, then said, 'So was Mr Randish attracted to her, do you think?'

She sighed again. 'Yes, he was. Very much so.' A faint flush crept up her neck. 'It was positively embarrassing at times.'

'Do you think he might have taken her out?'

'That's what you've been getting at, isn't it? You think they might have had an affair? To be honest, I just don't know. I never saw them together. And even if they did, I can't see how it would matter, now.'

'Do you *think* they did?' persisted Lineham.

'Well . . .' She stopped.

'What?'

She hesitated.

Old habits die hard, thought Thanet.

But she stuck to her decision to be open with them. 'Well, as I said, I just don't know. And it doesn't seem fair, to guess. But for what it's worth, I do believe he was the sort of man who did. Have affairs, I mean.'

'Why do you say that?'

Had he made a pass at Mrs Prote? Thanet wondered. No. Not his type.

'Occasionally I've seen him with other women. And it

was obvious, from the way he was behaving, that it had gone past friendship.'

'Did his wife know?'

'I've no idea.'

'Or his father-in-law?'

She shook her head. 'Sorry.'

She wrote the address of Compu-Tech down for them.

Outside they hesitated, and Lineham said, 'Do we still want to see Vintage? We've got all we need from Mrs Prote, haven't we?'

'There's just one point,' said Thanet.

'What?' said Lineham automatically. He was tucking away in his notebook the piece of paper which Mrs Prote had given him. 'That's funny. This address is in a residential area.'

'Mrs Prote said they were a small firm. Perhaps they work from home. Small firms often do. Good. That means we'll be able to go and see them today.'

'What were you saying about Vintage, sir?'

'Well, you remember when I asked him how Randish and Mr Landers got on together, he was a bit evasive?'

'Yes. Why?'

'Well, I'm wondering if he'd overheard something.'

'Some argument, you mean?'

'Well it's possible, isn't it? It doesn't sound as though Randish was all that discreet. If Mrs Prote saw him with other women, Landers could have, too. I'm sure he was lying when he said he didn't know if Randish was having an affair. It might have happened just once too often for his liking and he decided to tackle Randish about it.'

How would he feel himself, Thanet wondered, if Bridget were married and he discovered her husband was cheating on her? Furious, he imagined. Any father would. It cheapened what he held most dear. In his own case, if he hadn't been relieved that Alexander had broken it off he would be pretty angry with him now, for rejecting Bridget – as a matter of fact he still was, Thanet realised, for causing her to suffer like this.

'If only we didn't have to drag all this information out of people!' said Lineham. 'It makes the whole process so laborious.'

'What?' Thanet tore his attention away from Bridget's unhappy situation. 'Oh . . . I don't know, Mike. We grumble about it, yes, but just think how boring it would be if everybody told us everything we wanted to know straight off.'

'It'd certainly make our job easier, though, wouldn't it! Anyway, do we see Vintage, or not?'

'Might as well, while we're here.'

There was no sign of either Vintage or his temporary helper in the yard and they went back to the office to ask Mrs Prote where he might be.

'Probably cleaning out the vats, in that barn,' she said, pointing.

They walked across the yard. Thanet paused at the door and called out. 'Mr Vintage?'

The barn was apparently empty. Machinery hummed faintly and there was a swishing noise from somewhere. Along one wall there was a row of tall stainless-steel vats with circular doors in front like those on automatic washing machines, but larger. Two of the doors stood open and to Thanet's surprise a head now poked out of each, as if a giant tortoise had just woken up. One of them belonged to Vintage. He saw the look on their faces and grinned.

'We're cleaning the vats out. This is the only way to do the job properly.'

It was the first time he'd seen Vintage smile, Thanet realised. It made him look much younger.

Vintage climbed out and said, 'You carry on, Steve, won't be long.'

He was, Thanet thought, definitely looking better today. The dark circles were still there beneath his eyes but the dragging weariness which had permeated his every movement had gone and there was an air of buoyancy about him. It was amazing what a couple of good nights' sleep could do.

'What are they?' Lineham waved a hand at the tanks.

'Fermentation and storage vats.' Vintage went on explaining while Thanet began to edge unobtrusively towards the door. As he hoped, Vintage followed. He thought the winemaker might talk more freely if they couldn't be overheard – though just how much would be audible from inside one of those vats he had no idea. 'How's your wife today?' he asked, when Vintage had finished.

Vintage looked shamefaced. 'I owe you one for yesterday, Inspector. To be honest, when you started dishing out advice I was pretty angry. But I really needed someone to come along and give me a kick up the backside. Beth and I had a long talk last night and we've decided to hire a nanny, for however long it takes for her to come out of this. When my father comes back tomorrow I'll ask him for a loan. I'm pretty sure he'll help us out but if not I'll borrow from the bank. Beth's a lot happier already, now we've decided on a positive course of action. I think she'd more or less given up hope that things would ever improve.'

'Good.' Thanet couldn't help feeling a glow of satisfaction. It wasn't often that anyone handed out bouquets in his line of work.

'So,' said Vintage. 'What did you want to see me about?'

Despite what Thanet had said to Lineham, it was a relief to know that for once he wasn't going to have to work for the cooperation of a witness. 'When we were here yesterday I asked you how Mr Randish got on with his father-in-law. You weren't keen to talk about it. But since then we've learned that he wasn't exactly the most faithful of husbands and apparently didn't bother too much about being discreet. It doesn't take much imagination to work out that Mr Landers might well have found out and become pretty angry about the way his daughter was being treated. And that you were aware of this.'

Vintage thrust his hands in pockets and looked away, as if seeking guidance from somewhere. 'I heard them arguing,' he said eventually, with obvious reluctance. 'I went over to the laboratory one evening to ask Zak something and Mr Landers was there.'

Thanet felt a spurt of satisfaction. He was right. Landers had been lying. 'When was this?'

'A few days ago. Tuesday or Wednesday. Wednesday, I think.'

'What were they saying?'

'I didn't hear much. I'm not in the habit of eavesdropping. The door was open and I just caught a few words as I approached. When I heard what was going on I came away.'

'So what, exactly, did you hear?'

Vintage compressed his lips. 'Mr Landers was . . .' He stopped and his mouth now set in a stubborn line. He shook his head. 'It's no good, I can't tell you. You'll have to ask him yourself.'

'Was it that incriminating?'

'No! It's just that habits of a lifetime die hard. I know I said I owe you one, but I still don't think that gives you the right to ask me to go against the principles I live by.

And telling tales about someone I like and admire is one of them. If that makes me sound like an insufferable prig, then that's just too bad, it's how I feel. Anyway, I really can't believe that Mr Landers had anything to do with Zak's death.' He glanced at his watch. 'If you want to talk to him about it, he should be here in ten minutes or so. He said he'd be over about 12.30, to see how things were going.'

Thanet had no option but to let Vintage go.

'That'll teach me to think an interview is going to be plain sailing!' he said to Lineham as they returned to the car to wait for Landers. 'Anyway, what do you now think about your theory that Mrs Vintage's depression could be over Randish breaking off an affair with her?'

'I still haven't changed my mind,' said Lineham stubbornly. 'It's still possible, in my view. If he'd ditched her when he found out she was pregnant, he'd have been on the lookout for a replacement when this Elaine came along.'

'Hmm. I don't know. I feel we're only just beginning to scratch the surface of this case.'

'There's Landers, sir. He's early.'

Landers' Mercedes was pulling into the car park and they went to meet him.

THIRTEEN

The strain was beginning to tell on Landers, Thanet thought. His shoulders sagged beneath the well-cut tweed jacket and he looked as though he hadn't got much sleep last night: his eyelids drooped as if he were having difficulty in keeping them open. Anxiety on Alice's behalf? Thanet wondered. Or guilt?

He suggested they go across to the Randishes' house and Landers led the way without comment. The central heating had been left on and the house struck warm as they entered. Landers took them into the sitting room, where there was a faint, acrid smell of stale woodsmoke.

He took up the same slightly belligerent stance as last night in front of the cold woodstove. 'Well, what is it this time?'

Thanet wasn't going to allow him to take the initiative. 'Why did you lie to me yesterday, Mr Landers?'

'Lie? About what?' An unconvincing pretence at surprise.

'I asked you if you knew whether your son-in-law was having an affair. You said no.'

'What about it?'

'You were overheard having a row with him about precisely that.'

'Ah.'

Disappointingly, Landers did not seem over-concerned at having been caught out. 'Nobody likes having his dirty linen washed in public.'

'Don't try to minimise the importance of this, Mr Landers. We now know that you had two reasons for being very angry with your son-in-law. He was knocking your daughter about and being unfaithful to her as well.'

'You can be angry with someone without resorting to violence.'

'Without *intending* to resort to violence, yes. But if something triggers that anger off . . .'

'Such as?'

Thanet shrugged. 'I've no idea. It could have been a dozen things. You could have issued an ultimatum to him when you had that row with him on Wednesday, and found that he had ignored it.'

'Perhaps you saw him with this woman on Friday,' said Lineham, 'and decided to have another go at him.'

'Or maybe you noticed that fresh bruise on your daughter's arm when you came over to see her at her request on Friday evening,' said Thanet.

'Or perhaps,' said Lineham, 'she herself told you he'd been ill-treating her again.'

'And if you did go up to see him for any of these reasons after leaving her,' said Thanet, 'he may have reacted to what you were saying in a way which made you see red.'

'He could have laughed at you, for instance. Imagine how that would have made you feel, in the circumstances!'

'All right, all right,' said Landers irritably. 'You can stop the double act. I get the scenario. But it's all in your imagination. I told you, I left here after talking to Alice and went straight to the pub.'

'But you have absolutely no way of proving it,' said Thanet.

'And neither have you!'

'Yet,' said Thanet succinctly. 'But believe me, if that was what happened, Mr Landers, we'll find a way.'

'Think what you like,' snapped Landers, 'but you'll never prove it because it didn't happen.'

They left together and Landers strode angrily off in the direction of the pressing area.

'Well,' said Lineham gloomily. 'That didn't get us very far.'

Thanet grinned. 'Cheer up, Mike. Remember Bruce and the spider.'

'Very funny.'

'I think you need refuelling. We'll call in at the pub again, before paying Compu-Tech a visit.'

Three-quarters of an hour later, considerably refreshed, they were driving slowly through one of the older suburbs of Sturrenden, looking out for the premises of Compu-Tech at number 15A White Horse Lane. The houses here had been built in the 1930s when space was not at a premium and they were set well back from the road in generous gardens, some of which had recently been divided to provide new building plots. Thanet guessed by the address that this was what had happened with Compu-Tech. He would have thought that this was too far from the centre of town to run a successful business, but evidently he was wrong, perhaps because there were so many cowboys around in computers that reliability and efficiency were what people were looking for. Word-of-mouth recommendation was important and if all Compu-Tech's customers were as satisfied as Mrs Prote no doubt the word had soon got around.

He spotted a white signboard. 'I think that's it, Mike.'

Lineham slowed to check, then turned into the driveway.

Inside the gate the drive divided, one arm snaking around behind the substantial stockbroker-Tudor-style house to the right, the other turning sharp left into an attractive parking area of block paving laid in a herringbone pattern in front of a neat one-storey building.

'I suppose the bloke who lives in the house runs his business from here,' said Lineham. 'Looks as though he's doing all right.'

The place had a prosperous air. The parking area was embellished with terracotta pots filled with variegated ivy and there was not a dead leaf or a scrap of litter to be seen. Compu-Tech's premises were relatively new; paintwork sparkled, windows shone and despite yesterday's rain the ramp of non-slip tiles leading to the front door was unsullied.

Ramp?

Thanet looked about him with new eyes. There was a handrail alongside it, he noted, and the door was unusually wide. He pointed this out to Lineham. 'If the chap who runs the firm is handicapped, maybe that's why his office is here rather than in the town.'

'Could be,' said Lineham. 'In any case, is there any point in knocking here? Perhaps we ought to go over to the house instead.'

'We're just assuming the owner lives in the house. We'll try here first. If there's no reply, we'll go across.'

They knocked twice, with no response.

They were just turning away when they heard footsteps approaching along the side of the building and a moment later a young woman rounded the corner.

'Can I help you?'

She was absolutely beautiful, thought Thanet, tall and

slender with abundant black hair and dusky skin almost the colour of a ripe aubergine. She was wearing jeans and a brightly patterned sweater and on her hip she carried an enchanting little girl of about five. Four velvet-brown eyes stared at him as he explained who he was and presented his identification.

'We wanted to have a word with the owner of Compu-Tech, in connection with a case we're working on.'

'Is he in trouble?'

'No, not at all. We just want some information from him.'

'He's out to lunch, but he said he'd be back about a quarter past two. What time is it now?'

A Kentish accent, Thanet noted. Second generation immigrant background, then.

Lineham checked his watch. 'Five to.'

She hesitated, then said, 'I'm his housekeeper. You can come into my place and wait, if you like.'

Thanet accepted with alacrity. This was an unexpected bonus.

'The owner of Compu-Tech doesn't live in the big house, then?' he said as they trailed behind her to the far end of the long, low building. 'We rather wondered if we were knocking at the wrong door.'

She shook her head and flashed a smile at him over her shoulder, her teeth dazzlingly white and even. 'His parents live there. Giles – Mr Fester – built this place with the compensation money from his accident.'

'His accident?'

She had left her blue-painted front door standing ajar and they followed her through a tiny hall into a small square sitting room. The overwhelming impression was of colour, but of daring colour harmonies rather than of garishness. The carpet, which was scattered with toys, was neutral but the curtains were a kaleidoscope of pink, purple, and magenta with, here and there, touches of red which should have clashed but somehow didn't. There was very little furniture: one sturdy low coffee table with a portable television set on it, two armchairs with loose covers, one pink, one purple, and a child's wicker armchair. On the long blank wall opposite the window hung a sizeable appliqué picture of what Thanet immediately recognised as Sturrenden High Street. Fascinated, he went to look more closely at it. There it was, executed in a wealth of different fabrics – wool and cotton, velvet and taffeta, silk, brocade, and lace – and in a variety of embroidery stitches, down to the last picturesque detail: antique shops, church, pubs, market square and beyond, the silvery sheen of the river Sture, its tiny waves stitched in shiny metallic thread.

She had gone off to fetch a kitchen chair and when she came back he said, 'Did you do this?'

She nodded, smiling. 'Yes. It's my hobby.'

'It's amazing. How long did it take?'

'Several months, working in the evenings. I don't go out much.'

She wasn't wearing a wedding ring, Thanet noticed as they sat down. A single parent, then, whose life and choice of work would be dictated by the needs of her little girl. But it looked as though she had been lucky here. A council flat, often in a high-rise building, was as much as most young women in her position could hope for.

'It's very kind of you to allow us to wait here, Mrs . . .?'

'Miss,' she said, with a wry smile. 'Miss Patel. But call me Kari. And this' – she hugged her daughter, who had climbed on to her lap – 'is Jemima. Jem for short.'

Thanet smiled at the child. 'Hullo, Jem.'

'You were saying your employer – Mr Fester, was it?' said Lineham.

'Mr Fester, yes.'

'You were saying he'd had an accident.'

Her smile faded. 'Yes. A bad one. I didn't know him then, of course, this was seven or eight years ago, I believe, but he was in a car crash and he's been in a wheelchair ever since. He's paralysed from the waist down. He's an amazing man, when you think what he's achieved in spite of his handicap.'

The warmth with which she spoke of him made Thanet wonder if she felt more than admiration for her employer. 'Yes. The clients we talked to spoke very highly of his firm.'

'It has a very good reputation in the area. But then, he's got a real talent for his work, or so I'm told. I don't understand much about computers myself.'

'What does he do, exactly?'

Apparently deciding that the two strangers offered no threat Jem slipped off her mother's lap and knelt on the floor by a weird and wonderful creation in Lego bricks. She scooped up some more bricks and automatically her mother held out cupped hands to receive them, then began to hand them one by one to her daughter as she used them. It was obviously a well-worn routine.

'Anything to do with computers,' said Kari, watching Jem. 'He's an agent for some of the well-known makes and he's written a couple of very successful word-processing programmes. But the thing he enjoys most is inventing computer programmes to suit clients' special needs. And then he dabbles in computer games as well.'

'Wow,' said Lineham, obviously impressed. 'He must be a genius!'

She laughed. 'Not far off it, I imagine.'

'And you presumably look after this place for him and cook his meals?'

'Yes. I clean, tidy, wash, cook. He can do most of those things for himself but he prefers to spend his time on other things. Like basketball, for instance.' She smiled at their surprise. 'Before his accident he was a great sports-man and it's lucky he found a sport he can still play. He's in the Kent team and spends a lot of time practising and working out in the gym in Sturrenden.'

'He certainly does sound pretty amazing,' said Thanet.

She smiled. 'I told you. He is. I was very lucky to get this job.' She dropped a caressing hand on to Jem's curls. 'It suits us down to the ground.'

'Is it a very big firm?' said Lineham.

'No. There's just Giles, a girl called Elaine, who's also qualified in computers, and a receptionist-cum-secretary.'

The way she said 'a girl called Elaine' gave her away. Thanet was sure now that he'd been right about her feelings for her employer. She was definitely jealous of Elaine, or at least resented her for some reason. Perhaps Fester was the man in Elaine's life?

Probing further he learned that Elaine lived in Sturren-den and had worked for Giles Fester for two years – and that it was Elaine he had taken out to lunch. She would be coming back here with him afterwards and would probably spend the afternoon with him. He glanced at Lineham. *Take over, Mike.* He wanted to think.

The reason why they had pursued this particular line of inquiry was because they had wondered if Randish's current mistress could lead them to a jealous husband or boyfriend lurking in the background, and it had obviously also occurred to Thanet that Elaine's employer could be the man they were seeking. When he had learnt that Giles

Fester was confined to a wheelchair he had dismissed this idea but Kari's reaction, coupled with the fact that the relationship between Elaine and Fester was obviously more than a working one, had made him think again. Fester seemed an unlikely candidate, true, but was he as unlikely as all that?

Lineham was asking if Fester and Elaine spent much of their time off together.

'A fair amount,' said Kari.

It was obvious that she did not like the turn the conversation had taken. Now she cocked her head in relief. 'I think that's them now.'

'Just one more question, Miss Patel,' said Lineham quickly as she jumped up, taking Jem by the hand.

'What?'

Already at the door she half turned, poised for flight.

He stood up. 'Was Mr Fester out on Friday night?'

Her expression hardened. 'I've no idea. I spent the evening with a girlfriend. Jem came with me.'

She turned and hurried on ahead, Jem running to keep up with her. Behind her back Thanet and Lineham exchanged rueful glances.

'Sorry,' Lineham murmured. 'Mucked that up, didn't I?'

Thanet shook his head. 'Don't worry about it. She wouldn't have told you anyway.'

'Perhaps not. Pretty keen on him, isn't she?'

They caught up with her at the parking area. With Jem settled on her hip again she was talking through the car window to the man in the driver's seat of a BMW with a disabled sticker in the back. He turned his head to watch them as they approached.

Kari turned away – reluctantly, Thanet thought, and went off down the side path again.

'Sorry to disturb you on a Sunday afternoon, sir,' said Thanet. He introduced himself and Lineham and smiled at the girl who was getting out of the passenger seat.

She smiled back at him. 'Elaine Wood.'

She looked familiar. Thanet had probably seen her around the town. It wasn't surprising that Wakeham had noticed her, he thought. She was eye-catching enough to attract any man's attention, though her regular, Barbie-doll features, fashionably tousled shoulder-length dark hair and immaculate make-up were too magazine-cover-ish for his own taste. But she was certainly Randish's type – small, slender and exuding femininity. She was wearing tight jeans and an expensive soft suede jacket in a pale mint green. And, no doubt about it, that smile had been tinged with nervousness. She knew why they had come.

'Have I done something I shouldn't?' said Fester with a grin.

Without waiting for an answer he swung open the car door, revealing the fact that he was sitting not in a conventional car seat but in a wheelchair.

Thanet's doubts over the safety of this arrangement were quickly dispelled. Fester leaned first to one side then the other and with a series of sharp tugs revealed that the wheelchair had been securely bolted to the floor. Thanet and Lineham watched fascinated as Fester then pressed a switch which caused a small platform to slide out beside the driver's door. In no time at all he had manoeuvred his electric wheelchair out on to the platform, activated concealed hydraulics which lowered the platform to the ground, wheeled himself off it and returned it to its original position.

'That's an ingenious arrangement you've got there, sir,' said Lineham in obvious admiration.

Fester laughed. 'We had some teething troubles, but I think we've got them cracked.'

He was a handsome young man of about thirty with a mop of curly hair and a luxuriant beard. He was wearing chestnut-coloured corduroy trousers and a thick white Aran sweater. His shoulders were broad and his arms powerful. His parents must have been heartbroken when an accident had put him in a wheelchair for the rest of his life, thought Thanet.

'Did you design it yourself?' said Lineham.

Fester was enjoying the sergeant's interest. 'Yes, I did, as a matter of fact.'

'You ought to patent it. You'd make a fortune.'

'I'm afraid you'd need a small fortune, to buy one! I don't think the DHSS would be too keen on it as a standard modification.'

Swinging around, Fester set off up the ramp to the front door, followed by Elaine. Inside they passed through a reception area and along a short corridor with two office doors opening off to the left. At the far end was another door and Fester took a plastic key-card from his pocket and inserted it into a slit beside it. The door clicked open. 'Extra security,' he said with a smile.

They followed him in and found themselves in an open-plan hall/living room/kitchen with a wide door at the far side leading probably to a bedroom and en suite bathroom, Thanet thought. The kitchen area had been designed with low work-surfaces and the living area was comfortable, attractive and obstacle-free, with colourful floor-length curtains in a masculine, geometric design of black, red and grey, and black leather settee and arm-chairs on an off-white carpet. One wall was covered in bookshelves from floor to ceiling and there was an expensive CD system with racks of CDs alongside.

Fester waved a hand. 'Do sit down, Inspector, Sergeant. I'm most intrigued by your visit. Would you like some tea or coffee?'

Thanet refused and he and Lineham sat down. Elaine remained standing.

'I expect you want to talk to Mr Fester privately,' she said.

Thanet smiled at her. 'Oh no, not at all. In fact, the only reason why we came here was to try to find out where you lived. We thought that as your employer Mr Fester would know.'

'Me?' she said nervously. She glanced apprehensively at Fester.

She's been two-timing him, Thanet thought. The question was, had Fester known?

'So please, Miss Wood, sit down, won't you?'

FOURTEEN

Elaine sat down in one of the armchairs, the black leather accentuating the darkness of her hair and eyes, the soft luxurious paleness of her suede jacket. She had recovered her composure and looked relaxed, knees folded sideways, one hand in her lap, the other lying carelessly along the arm of the chair. It was a studied pose – too studied to be natural, Thanet thought. In his experience even the most innocent members of the public were tense and nervous when interviewed by the police for the first time. What did she have to hide? he wondered. If she had concealed her relationship with Randish from Fester, perhaps she was still hoping that she could bluff her way out of this.

Thanet reminded himself not to fall into the familiar trap of equating glamour with lack of intellect. Elaine Wood was a trained computer expert, an intelligent woman. It would be best to establish at the outset that they were aware of her connection with Randish.

'As you, Miss Wood, have no doubt realised, we are investigating the murder of Mr Randish, the owner of Sturrenden Vineyard.'

'A terrible business,' said Fester. 'We were talking about it over lunch. But . . .'

Thanet acknowledged the comment with a nod before going on. 'Miss Wood, I must confess I was somewhat taken aback by your reaction just now, when I said we'd come here to try and trace you through your employer. A number of witnesses have confirmed that you were going out with Mr Randish and it seems that you didn't exactly try to hide the fact. You must surely have been expecting us to interview you.'

She flicked a glance at Fester, who raised his eyebrows at her. But Thanet was sure that his surprise was feigned, not genuine.

She gave a resigned sigh. 'Half expecting it, I suppose you might say.'

'You seem surprised, Mr Fester.'

'Why shouldn't I be?'

'You didn't know about this relationship?'

'I resent that word, Inspector,' said Elaine. 'You make it sound much more serious than it was.'

'Did you know about it, Mr Fester?' Thanet persisted.

'No. Miss Wood's private life is her own affair.'

'Except that it does seem to overlap with yours.'

'Why should that concern you?'

'I should have thought it was fairly obvious.'

'Not in the least.'

'Then think about it, sir.' Thanet turned back to Elaine. 'When did you last see Mr Randish, Miss Wood?'

'On Tuesday.'

'Where did you go?'

'We went out for a pub lunch, at the Barley Mow on the Cranbrook Road.'

'I suppose it must have been difficult for you to meet in the evenings lately, it was the busiest time of year for him. Did you see anyone you know?' Thanet was thinking of Landers. If Landers had seen them having lunch together on Tuesday that would account for his having had a row with Zak about it on Wednesday.

'No.'

'Anyone Mr Randish knew?'

'Not to my knowledge. But I really haven't the faintest idea whether we did or not. He must have known loads of people I didn't. He grew up in the area.'

'And you didn't?'

'No. I was brought up in Sussex.'

'So you never met Mr Randish until you went out to the vineyard to work with him on the new computer system?'

'No.'

'You knew he was married?'

'Naturally. I could hardly fail to know, considering his wife and family live on the premises.'

Thanet wasn't here to question her morals. 'You don't seem exactly heartbroken that he's dead.'

'Why should I be? I was upset when I heard the news, of course I was, I'd be upset if I heard anyone I knew had been murdered – wouldn't you? But don't get it wrong, Inspector. It wasn't exactly the love affair of a lifetime. Zak was attractive, yes, fun to be with, and he gave me a good time. But that's all.'

'That may be true. But it might not have looked that way to other people . . . to Mr Fester here, for instance.'

'What do you mean?' she said.

'Well, as I was pointing out a moment ago, you do go out with him as well.'

'So?' said Fester.

'Don't pretend that you don't understand, sir. The fact is that a man has been murdered. We don't yet know why, but as I'm sure you're aware, there are a limited number of motives for a crime like this. And one of them is jealousy.'

'Jealousy!' Fester gave an ironic laugh. 'How you can look at me, look at this' – his gesture encompassed the wheelchair, his useless legs – 'and talk about a crime of passion, I just don't know.'

'Don't treat me like an idiot! Do you think I don't know that someone in your situation is as capable of experiencing powerful emotion as the next man?'

'Not much point in having feelings if you can't do anything about them, though, is there, Inspector?'

Fester's tone was flippant, but Thanet's question had gone home, he could tell. 'Maybe,' said Thanet softly, 'that very fact would make the situation even more explosive.'

'How can you talk to Giles like that?' interrupted Elaine. 'With him being . . . as he is?'

'Strangely enough, Elaine,' said Fester, 'I don't actually mind. In an odd way the inspector is actually paying me a compliment.'

'A compliment! You call accusing you of murder a compliment!'

'Yes. He's ignoring the fact that I'm a cripple and treating me just like anyone else. It's practically a unique experience for me. All the same, Inspector, you're still wrong.'

'Giles and I are just good friends,' said Elaine. 'I know the phrase is a bit of a joke, but in this case it's true. We just enjoy each other's company, that's all.'

Thanet caught the flicker of pain in Fester's eyes. That may be true on your side, Miss Wood, he thought, but it's far from being true on his. And don't pretend you're not aware of it, either. 'Let's go back to Friday night,' he said to her. 'What did you do?'

'Believe it or not, I stayed in. Watched television, had a bath, washed my hair, went to bed early. Very boring, I'm afraid.'

She was hiding something. 'There's something else, isn't there? Something you're not telling me.'

'I assure you I'm telling you the truth, Inspector. That was what I did – stayed in, all by myself, and had a thoroughly domestic evening.'

'I'm not querying the truth of what you're saying, simply questioning that you've told me all there is to tell.' She had darted a quick, uneasy look at Fester, Thanet noticed. And Fester was listening intently, eyes narrowed.

Thanet tried to think. What if Fester had asked her out on Friday evening and she had put him off, ostensibly because she wanted to have a quiet evening at home, but in fact because she had arranged to meet Randish? She would now be reluctant to admit it in front of Fester because she wouldn't want to be caught out in a lie. All the same, it would be interesting to see her reaction. 'You had a date with Mr Randish, didn't you?'

The quickly suppressed glint of surprise in her eyes and her too-swift denial confirmed his guess. Thanet suspected that Fester's thought processes had paralleled his own and that he too had seen through her reaction – his hands had clenched on his knees and a fleeting expression of disillusionment had crossed his face, vanishing so quickly that Thanet might have missed it if he hadn't been watching him so closely. Had Elaine seen it, he wondered? There was no doubt about it, her composure had slipped. Her tension showed in the painted fingernails tapping against the arm of the chair. She saw him looking and hastily put her hand in her lap, folding it into the other. He decided it was worth pursuing the subject a little longer. 'What time had he arranged to come, Miss Wood? Late in the evening, perhaps, as he was so busy?'

'I told you, Inspector, you're barking up the wrong tree.'

She had no intention of retracting, that was obvious.

Thanet gave her a sceptical look, making sure she knew he didn't believe her. 'Do you live in a house, a flat?'

'A flat.'

'Where?'

'Landway House in Beecham Road.'

Thanet knew it, a new block of flats on the site of a former warehouse near the river. 'Did you see or speak to anyone on Friday evening?'

She shook her head. 'Not that I can remember, unfortunately.'

He turned to Fester. 'And what about you, Mr Fester? What were you doing on Friday evening?'

Fester smiled. 'You'll think us a very dull pair, I'm afraid, Inspector. I, too, spent the evening at home, watched television etc., etc. Though I didn't wash my hair, I must admit.'

He was being flippant again – too flippant, for a man who had just been informed he could consider himself a murder suspect. And he was watching Thanet's reaction too closely. It was obvious, however, that he wasn't going to change his story without good reason either. Thanet decided to leave it for the moment. He caught the brief flash of relief in Elaine's expression as he stood up. Simple relief because the interview was over, he wondered, or was she hiding something else? Perhaps there was a question which she had expected but which he had failed to ask? He hesitated a moment, racking his brains, but it was no good. No doubt about it, they'd have to look into this further, come back later.

He said so to Lineham, outside.

'They were both lying in their teeth, if you ask me,' said the sergeant as they got into the car. 'I bet she'd given him the brush-off for Friday evening because she

165

had a date with Randish, and didn't want to lose face by admitting it. Where now, sir?'

'Back to the office, I think. Mmm. I'm not sure there wasn't more to it than that. But yes, I agree, that's what I thought. Though according to what Vintage said about the workload at the vineyard, I wouldn't have thought Randish would have had much time for his love life during harvest.'

Lineham started the car and pulled out. 'Perhaps she was getting fed up with never seeing him in the evenings, made a fuss about it, and to shut her up he agreed to take her out for a quick drink or something.'

'Possible, I suppose. Though in that case you'd think she'd have rung his office to find out why he hadn't turned up.'

'Perhaps she did, before Vintage discovered the body at 9.30, and got no reply.'

'True.'

'But Fester is a different matter, in my opinion. I mean, if you'd told me I'd ever suspect a bloke in a wheelchair of committing this murder I'd have thought you were joking. Now, I'm not so sure.'

'He's certainly pretty taken with the delectable Miss Wood,' said Thanet.

'Who wouldn't be! Just think what it must be like to be in his position, working with a girl you really fancy, day in and day out, and to feel you can't make a real play for her because it wouldn't be fair on her to ask her to marry a cripple.'

'Able-bodied people do marry handicapped partners, Mike.'

'I know that. But you have to be a pretty special person to take on someone handicapped to that degree. And Elaine, well, she just didn't strike me as the type.'

'I agree. Underneath that porcelain exterior I'd say she

was pretty tough and calculating. Ambitious, probably, too.'

'Yes. But she is most definitely the sort of girl a bloke might go crazy over. And if Fester had had a pretty clear field until Randish came along . . .'

'Quite.'

'And he's pretty remarkable isn't he? I mean, look at what he's made of his life despite his handicap. You can't help admiring him. Honestly, sir, I really do hope he's not the one we're after. But to be realistic, it's obvious that he's the type who really goes for what he wants and usually gets it. And if what he wants is Elaine . . .'

'I agree. There's another point that occurred to me too, Mike. The actual method of the murder ties in uncomfortably close with the limitations Fester's condition imposes on him.'

'What do you mean?'

'Well, if you actually try to visualise what happened in that laboratory, you begin to realise that there are certain things we already know about this murderer.'

'Such as?'

They had arrived back at Headquarters. There were various things to attend to and they waited until they were back in Thanet's office before taking up the conversation where they had broken off.

'What were you saying about the murderer, sir?'

'Well, I think we can assume, for a start, that this was an unpremeditated murder. Right?'

'Right.'

'An accidental murder, even?'

'I'd go along with that.'

'That what happened was that someone who was very angry with Randish went along to have it out with him and the whole thing got out of hand.'

Lineham was nodding.

'Well, have you given any thought as to what that person must be like?'

'Not really. There's been so much to take in . . .'

'Well think about it now.' Thanet was longing to smoke. Of its own volition his hand emerged from his pocket holding his pipe. Becoming aware of this he shoved it back in again. He was addicted and he knew it. Part of him was ashamed of the fact but the far larger part was realistic: if he smoked he was a happy man and functioned well; if he didn't he was just plain miserable and his work went to pieces. But he had come to appreciate that it was misery for Lineham if he lit up in his presence, so he really made a big effort these days to be considerate about this.

Lineham noticed. He occasionally had pangs of conscience about Thanet's self-imposed restraint. 'Go on, sir, light up if it'll help you to think.'

'Thanks.' Thanet took out his pipe and pouch with alacrity. 'You can open the door and the window if you like.' He couldn't help smiling to himself. Sometimes he and Lineham functioned like an old married couple. He had occasionally had to work with a substitute and it was never the same. He and Mike were on the same wavelength and that was all there was to it. They were so used to each other that their communication was frequently unspoken: all it needed was a glance, a nod, a shake of the head. He watched indulgently as Lineham half opened the window and propped the door ajar with a box file. Cool air filtered into the room and the papers on Thanet's desk stirred in the draught. He finished filling his pipe and lit up before speaking again.

'As I was saying, Mike, just think about it. Imagine for the sake of argument that the murderer is a man. Now, in normal circumstances – leaving aside your armed criminal, that is – if a man has a row with another man and one of them loses his temper, what is the most likely thing for him to do?'

'Go for him. Sock him on the jaw, probably.'

The improvised ventilation system, though somewhat uncomfortable, was effective. The through draught was whisking the clouds of smoke away, out of the open window. 'Quite. But in this case?'

'He chucked something at him.'

'So what does that tell us about him?'

'Either that he was afraid of what he would do if he lost control of himself, or that he was afraid of Randish.'

'Physically, you mean?'

'Yes. Randish was a big man and pretty fit. So our murderer was much smaller, perhaps. Or . . . I see what you mean about Fester. Yes. He wouldn't have gone for Randish in the usual way but he's very adept at manoeuvring himself about in that wheelchair. Also, all that basketball must have given him pretty powerful arms and shoulders.'

'There's a further possibility, too, Mike.'

'What? Oh, yes. That it could have been a woman, you mean.'

'Exactly.'

'So where does that get us?'

Thanet struck another match. His pipe wasn't drawing properly yet. 'Think of our suspects, Mike, in the light of what we've been saying. Take Landers first.'

'Too big.'

'Vintage.'

'He's fairly slight. Possible.'

'Reg Mason?'

'Ditto.'

'And Fester, of course, as we said. Then there are the women. Alice Randish, her mother . . .'

'I didn't know we were considering Mrs Landers, but I suppose you're right. Are we counting Elaine Wood, too?'

'Why not? The more the merrier, it seems to me.'

'So what we were saying doesn't get us very far, does it? Except for Landers they're all still in the running. Do we definitely count him out, now?'

'Certainly not, Mike. We were only theorising. It was considering Fester as a suspect that set me off. No, what we really need now is some hard evidence.'

'Not much prospect of that at the moment, is there? D'you want me to get a house-to-house going, see if we can find anyone who might have seen Fester go out that night?'

'Yes. Ditto Elaine.' Thanet was silent, puffing steadily and gazing up absent-mindedly at the sinuous movements of the smoke swirling away into the gathering dusk. 'You know, Mike, I can't help feeling that there's something we've overlooked.'

'Something we heard when we were interviewing Fester and Elaine, you mean?'

'I don't know. But there is something, I'm sure.'

'Take your own advice, sir. Stop thinking about it and you'll remember.'

Thanet grinned. 'It's easier to give advice than to take it.'

FIFTEEN

As he opened the front door Thanet sniffed appreciatively. A delicious aroma was wafting along the hall to greet him. The kitchen door was ajar and he could hear voices and laughter. All the way home he had been thinking about the case and trying to recall what it was that had triggered off his uneasy feeling of having missed something, but now he could feel the cares rolling off his shoulders. He put his head into the kitchen. 'That smells good.' He kissed them both, in turn. Bridget looked a lot more relaxed, he was thankful to see, their morning disagreement apparently forgotten.

'Supper in ten minutes,' said Joan.

It was good to have his family united around the table for once, thought Thanet as they all sat down. It was a rare experience these days. Bridget was not usually here, of course, and Ben seemed to snatch his meals between activities, often eating earlier or later than his parents. It was also a great pleasure to see Bridget and Ben behaving like adults — most of the time, anyway. The childish squabbles of old seemed to be a thing of the past, civilised conversation the order of the day.

The savoury smell had emanated from an elaborate fish risotto and they all tucked in enthusiastically.

'Great!' said Ben, after the first mouthful. 'How's Jonathan?'

'He's recovered consciousness, I'm glad to say, and he's been moved out of intensive care.'

Joan had obviously heard the news before and she glanced at Thanet. 'That must be a tremendous relief for his mother, mustn't it?'

'It certainly must,' said Thanet. 'Did you see her?' he asked Bridget.

'Yes. D'you know, she still hasn't been home since Friday night! She's been sitting beside his bed ever since!'

'I can understand that,' said Thanet. 'If you or Ben were in a coma . . .'

'Don't!' said Joan with a shudder. 'It doesn't bear thinking about. Anyway, it's wonderful that Jonathan's come round. Sometimes you hear of these motorcycle accident victims being in a coma for months.'

She hadn't looked at Ben and Thanet didn't think the remark had been directed at him, but Ben obviously didn't see it that way. 'All right, Mum! No need to rub it in. I've got the message.'

'He's still very dazed, though,' said Bridget. 'He doesn't remember a thing about Friday evening.'

'That's not unusual after an accident,' said Thanet. 'In fact, some people never do remember the circumstances surrounding it.'

'Yes, but I'm not just talking about the accident itself. The worst thing is, he doesn't even remember that Karen is dead.'

'Oh, no!' said Joan. 'You didn't tell me that.'

'Poor Mrs Redman,' said Bridget. 'She's absolutely dreading breaking the news to him all over again.'

'I can imagine,' said Thanet. 'You went in to the hospital yourself, I gather.'

'Yes. I didn't stay long, though, there wasn't much point. Jonathan wasn't up to talking and Mrs Redman was so tired I thought she'd fall asleep where she was.'

'She could go home and get some rest now, though, couldn't she?'

'Yes, she could, but she wants to wait a bit longer first. Jonathan's all she has left now, and I don't think she could bear to leave him.'

'Bridget's been playing the good Samaritan,' said Joan with a smile. 'She took Jonathan's clothes home, fetched various things he and Mrs Redman needed, fed the cat . . .'

'I thought there was something different about you this evening,' said Ben to his sister. 'It's the halo.'

'Don't tell me the cat hadn't been fed since Friday!' said Thanet.

'Oh no. Mrs Phillips, their neighbour, had been looking after him,' said Bridget.

No doubt about it, thought Thanet, all this buzzing about had done Bridget good. Far better for her to be actively engaged in something than moping around at home.

All in all she seemed to have had a busy day. Conversation turned to her visit to the Mallards this morning and then to the joint trip she and Joan had made out to Thaxden, to have tea with Joan's mother.

After they had cleared away the first course and stacked the dishes in the dishwasher Bridget brought in the dessert.

'Oh boy!' said Ben, his eyes lighting up at the sight of the raspberry pavlova she had made. 'I can put up with this treatment as long as you like!'

'You'd better make the most of it,' she said. 'I'm going back tomorrow evening.'

'So soon!' said Thanet. 'And I've hardly seen you.'
He'd been afraid this might happen, which was why he'd
made a special effort to get home early this evening.

'And not likely to, with a murder case going on,' said
Bridget. 'Don't worry, Dad, I do understand. Anyway, I
was wondering if you could give me a lift to the station.
Mum's got a meeting. It doesn't matter if you can't, I'll
walk.'

'Of course I will, if I can.'

His back gave him trouble all evening and it was again
a relief to get into bed and allow tense muscles to relax.
He closed his eyes and at once, with the distraction of
what was happening around him shut out, started worrying again about what it was he couldn't remember. What
was the precise moment at which he had become aware
of it? Joan's voice broke into his thoughts.

'Luke?'

It was obvious from her tone that she'd tried to catch
his attention before. He opened his eyes.

She was taking off her dressing gown. 'Ah, so you are
still awake.'

'I was thinking.'

'So was I. About that poor woman.'

'Mrs Redman, you mean?'

'Yes.' She switched off the overhead light and slid into
bed beside him. He put his arm around her and she
snuggled into his shoulder with a sigh of contentment.
'We're so lucky.'

'I know.'

'When I think of what she must have been through . . .
D'you know what Bridget told me today?'

'What?'

'She's known for years, apparently – Bridget, I mean.
But she's never said anything before, she promised

Karen ... But now Karen's dead I suppose she feels released from that promise ... Well, I don't know. Perhaps she doesn't. Perhaps it was because she's still so upset about Karen ... And she knows I won't talk about it to anyone else. Except you, of course.'

'Darling,' said Thanet. 'Come to the point. What did Bridget tell you?'

'It really shook me, I can tell you. And as you know, I'm not easily shaken.'

In her work as a probation officer Joan saw plenty of the seamy side of life.

'I suppose it's because it happened to one of Bridget's friends ...'

'Joan!'

'All right! Well, as you know, Karen has been anorexic for years. Ever since she was twelve, in fact. What I didn't know until today was why.' Joan pulled away a little and twisted her head to watch Thanet's reaction. 'When she was twelve she had a baby.'

'At twelve!'

Joan nodded. 'At the time, no one knew about it. Bridget didn't know Karen at the time, it was the summer before they both started at Sturrenden High. But that autumn Bridget and Karen became friends and she stuck to her faithfully through the bad times, as you know, always visited her when she was hospitalised. It was during one of those periods, when the girls were about seventeen and Karen was at a very low ebb, that she told Bridget about the baby.'

'She actually had the baby?'

'Yes. It was adopted. But apparently Karen was five months' pregnant before her mother realised! Incredible, isn't it? I mean, I've read about such cases, even about girls actually having the baby without their mothers' knowledge, but it is difficult to comprehend. Though I suppose it's less surprising in that household than it would be in most. I gather nudity was considered so taboo that even when the children were tiny they never shared baths or saw each other naked. Anyway, by the time her mother found out it was too late for Karen to have an abortion and even if it hadn't been I gather her parents would never have allowed it, it would have been against their principles. So they sent her away to some home for unmarried mothers and put out a story that she was visiting relations. Her absence covered the period of the long summer holidays, apparently, so no one was ever the wiser. The whole thing came as a terrible shock to Karen. She'd no idea she was going to have a baby. You wouldn't believe it could still happen in this day and age, but Bridget says that Karen's mother was so inhibited about sex that she never talked to her about it and Karen was unbelievably ignorant, she only knew what she'd picked up at school. She'd only had one period, a very slight one, and she'd heard that periods were often irregular to begin with, so when she didn't have any more she didn't think anything of it. But she did notice she'd begun to put on weight, so without telling anyone she began to diet.'

'And that was how her anorexia started.'

'Yes. The dieting, of course, was one reason why no one noticed she was pregnant. But naturally she found that no matter how little she ate, she was still getting fatter.'

'But she realised why that was, surely? When she did find out she was pregnant?'

Joan was shaking her head. 'Intellectually yes, she knew that was why she was putting on weight. But emotionally, by then she was powerless to stop herself believing otherwise.'

'But later on, then, after she'd had the baby, when things got back to normal . . .?'

'That was the tragedy. They never did get back to normal. By then the idea that she was overweight was so entrenched in her mind that she simply couldn't shake it off.'

'Poor kid. And the baby's father?'

Joan was nodding. 'Yes. I can see you've guessed, after what the children were saying about him yesterday. Bridget is pretty certain it was Karen's father. Though Karen never actually admitted it. Perhaps she was too ashamed. It would fit in with the continuing anorexia, though, wouldn't it – I mean with the theory that for various reasons the anorexic is reluctant to grow up.'

'What theory is that?' Thanet didn't know much about anorexia.

'That for whatever reason, she wants to "deny her womanhood", as the jargon puts it. One of the results of starving yourself is that you stop having periods; not having periods means you're not becoming a woman. Not eating is therefore how you achieve the desired result. That's the idea, anyway.'

'And it was all hushed up, he got away with it.' In Thanet's work he saw all too often the results of such abuse, the lifetime of suffering to which the innocent victims were frequently condemned. He'd had a case not so long ago in which the murder victim had been in that position, a talented artist whose death had been the direct result of such childhood torture. In that instance the abuser had finally been brought to justice, but Redman, perhaps equally guilty of his daughter's death, had died unpunished for his sins.

'If he really was responsible then yes, I'm afraid so.'

Joan was quickly asleep but Thanet lay awake for

some time, staring into the darkness and thinking back over the hectic activity of the last couple of days. It was always the same at the beginning of a case. There was so much to do, see, assimilate, that it was essential to stand back from time to time and try to make a cool, detached assessment of the situation. It was easy to get so bogged down in personalities, cross-currents and speculation that it was impossible to see what was really going on. Especially when, as now, he was beating his brains out trying to remember something. He clenched his hands in frustration under the bedclothes and then told himself not to be so stupid. There was no point in getting worked up about it. He would remember, sooner or later, and Lineham was right: he ought to put it clean out of his mind, forget about it, and let his subconscious get to work. Perhaps, by morning, the miracle would have happened and he would wake up to find that all had become clear.

Unfortunately, this was not the case. The alarm went off as usual at 6.45 and he staggered half awake into the bathroom, aware that the knowledge was still eluding him. He hadn't got to sleep until the early hours and he felt tired and depressed. Why do I do this job? he asked himself. Why do I beat my brains out, like this? Why not choose something less demanding, where I don't have to struggle and fight every inch of the way? His temper was not improved by the fact that he cut himself shaving. When he went downstairs Joan took one look at his face and said, 'Oh dear. Like that, is it?'

'Like what?' he snapped.

'Never mind. Here, have some cereal. You'll feel better after you've had something to eat.'

'I've come to a decision.'

'Oh?'

'I think I've reached a mid-life crisis. I'm going to

apply to be a postman. Just think what it must be like to do a job where people are actually pleased to see you when you knock on their doors!'

She came to sit down with him, a rare event in the morning, and buttered a slice of toast. 'I gather the case isn't going too well? I'm sorry, there seemed to be so much to talk about that I didn't even ask last night.'

'No, no, it's going along much as usual.'

'But?'

Thanet shook his head. 'Nothing, really.'

Joan looked sceptical.

'Oh all right. It's just that I'm trying to remember something, and can't. It's so frustrating! And don't say "put it out of your mind and you'll remember." I've tried that and it didn't work.'

'Then there's absolutely nothing you can do about it, is there?' she said calmly.

Toast popped up and she went to fetch it, poured him some coffee. She obviously thought he needed pampering, he thought wryly, usually he did these things for himself in the mornings. And she was right. It was ridiculous to allow himself to be thrown by something beyond his control. He felt himself begin to relax. He watched the Flora melt on his toast and spread the marmalade with a lavish hand. It was grapefruit marmalade, he realised, his favourite, and an expensive brand usually reserved for a weekend treat. He grinned, then began to laugh.

'What's the matter?' she said, an answering smile spreading across her face.

He held up the marmalade. 'You're treating me like a spoilt child – and, let's face it, you're absolutely right, I'm behaving like one.' He leaned across to kiss her. 'Sorry, love!'

'We're all entitled to be bad tempered occasionally.

Just remember that, the next time I start behaving like a bear with a sore head.'

'I will! Promise!'

The letterbox clattered.

'Post's early this morning,' said Joan, and went out into the hall, returning a few moments later. She flipped through the letters and put two beside Thanet's plate.

He glanced at them. One was an electricity bill, by the look of it, the other was his own handwriting. Some tickets he'd sent away for, probably. Nothing interesting, then, and they could both wait until later.

So why did he have this uncomfortable sensation in his head?

He glanced at Joan, who was reading one of her letters, and took another bite of toast, staring at the handwritten envelope. There *was* something. What was it?

Suddenly it came to him.

He stopped chewing and stared unseeing into space. Perhaps it hadn't been so important after all. No, it really would be too much of a coincidence, if ... But then, coincidences happened in real life which would never be believed in fiction, and there was at least one fact to back up the idea. And if he was right ...

Joan became aware of his immobility. 'Luke? What's the matter?'

He looked at her, a broad smile spreading slowly across his face, and kissed her again. 'You're a gem.'

She raised her eyebrows. 'Why, precisely? I mean, it's a great boost to the morale when your husband starts showering you with kisses and paying you lavish compliments at 7.30 on a Monday morning, but it would be nice to know what I've done to deserve it.'

'You made me switch off, stop trying to remember. And, of course ... bingo!'

Joan laughed. 'I can't believe it worked as quickly as that. It certainly doesn't in my experience.'

'Magic!' said Thanet. It was the handwritten envelope which had really done the trick, of course, but he wasn't going to spoil things by mentioning that.

'So come on, tell. What was it?'

He shook his head. 'Just a small thing. And I can't make up my mind if it really was important, or not. Let me think about it a bit more first. Anyway, I haven't told you enough about the case yet for you to understand its significance, if it has any.'

Thanet had always talked to Joan about his work. It was so demanding both on him and on their marriage that he felt it was essential she didn't feel excluded. She had always appreciated this, he knew – and on more than one occasion had helped him to see his way to a solution.

'I know. There's been so little time, with Bridget being here. We'll try to talk tonight, shall we? Oh, no, I've got that meeting. Still, with any luck it won't go on too late.'

'See you then,' said Thanet. Quickly he cleared away the dishes, stacked them in the dishwasher and felt for his pipe. He was eager to get to work and discuss his idea with Lineham.

Outside the day matched his new mood, bright and breezy. Puffy white clouds chased each other across the sky and there was an invigorating freshness in the air, more like March or April than late October. He hoped that Lineham hadn't chosen this morning of all mornings to come in later than usual.

He gave Pater, the Station Officer, a brisk greeting.

'Everybody seems to be looking cheerful this morning,' said Pater. 'Must be the weather.'

Thanet paused. 'Who's "everybody"?'

'The Super, for one.'

'Really?'

The two men looked at each other, aware of what this might mean. Pater lowered his voice. 'Good news about Mrs Draco, d'you think, sir?'

'Let's keep our fingers crossed.'

Thanet took the stairs two at a time. Lineham, he was relieved to see, was already at his desk, frowning over a report. 'Heard anything about Angharad Draco, Mike? Pater says the Super seems in a good mood this morning.'

'So I understand. I haven't actually seen him myself. But it sounds promising.'

'No doubt we'll find out at the morning meeting.' Thanet sat down.

'Any particular reason why you're looking so pleased with yourself, sir?'

'Could be. You know I said last night that I was sure there was something we'd overlooked?'

'Yes. Have you remembered what it was?'

Thanet nodded, smiling.

'And?' Lineham leaned forward eagerly as Thanet began to talk.

SIXTEEN

'It was simply a matter of making a connection,' said Thanet.

'Between . . .?'

'You remember those letters we came across, in the locked drawer of Randish's desk?'

'The love letters, you mean?'

'Yes. Specifically, the ones from Randish's wife. They were addressed to him care of his landlady, if you remember.'

'Yes, I do.'

'Do you by any chance remember her name?'

Lineham thought, deep frown lines creasing his forehead. 'It was short, I remember that, but . . . No, I can't.'

'It was Wood,' said Thanet.

Lineham stared at him. 'Are you suggesting there's some connection between her and Elaine Wood? Be a bit of a coincidence, wouldn't it?'

'Yes it would, agreed. But Elaine did tell us she'd been brought up in Sussex, and Plumpton's in Sussex.'

'But what connection? Randish's landlady couldn't be Elaine Wood's mother, surely?'

'Well, it's not out of the question, is it? It's only, what, fifteen or sixteen years ago. Mrs Wood could have had

Elaine in her late teens and only have been in her early thirties at the time. And some young men enjoy having affairs with older women. But no, I don't think so. Don't you remember Mark Benton told us that Randish had a particularly torrid affair with his landlady's daughter?'

'Yes, I do. So what you're suggesting is that this Mrs Wood was Elaine's grandmother?'

'Yes.'

'It's a bit far-fetched, isn't it? Wood's a very common name.'

'Maybe. But there's another thing, too. When I first saw Elaine I thought she looked familiar. I decided at the time that it must be because I'd seen her around, in the town, but now I wonder if it could be because she resembled one of the young women in that batch of photographs of Randish's girlfriends.'

'It could simply be because, as we know, Randish always seemed to go for the same physical type. You could equally well say that Elaine looked familiar because she looks like Alice Randish. Which she does, except that one is dark and the other's fair.'

That was true. Perhaps Lineham was right. The whole thing was too tenuous.

'Anyway, I'm not sure what you're suggesting, sir. Say you're right about all this. If Elaine's name is Wood and her grandmother's name was Wood, that means her mother must have been unmarried. Elaine can't be Randish's daughter, she's too old, she must have been, what, ten or eleven at the time.'

'I know. I agree, her mother must have been single.'

'Well, say all this is true. Say Elaine did know Zak when she was a child. Say she recognised him when she went out to the vineyard to install the computer system. So what?'

'So then he gets himself murdered, that's what!'

Lineham was shaking his head. 'I still think it's all too far-fetched. All right, we both know coincidences happen . . .'

'Not that much of a coincidence, Mike. People do run across each other by chance, years after they first met.'

'But they don't necessarily murder each other!'

Thanet was becoming exasperated. Lineham was only expressing many of the doubts he felt himself but the more the sergeant argued the more he found himself defending the theory. 'But they might! If there was good reason! In any case, there's only one way to find out.'

'Go to Plumpton, you mean?'

'Yes. It'll only take us an hour to an hour and a half.'

Lineham's face showed clearly that he thought this would be a waste of time.

Thanet sighed. 'Go on, Mike. You might as well say what you're really thinking.'

'Well, it's just that I think we ought to be trying to find out a lot more about some of the other suspects. We've hardly given a thought so far to Alice Randish or her father, for instance, let alone the most likely one of all, Reg Mason.'

'Did you have any specific action in mind?'

'Well, no, but we haven't really put our minds to it, have we?'

'True, but there's no rush, is there? We'd only be gone for a few hours. None of them is going to run away, they'll still be waiting when we get back.'

Lineham said nothing, just set his lips, stubbornly.

'Oh come on, Mike, admit it. These hunches of mine often turn out to be worth following up.'

'True,' Lineham said grudgingly.

'And it's not as though we'd be neglecting something

we really ought to be doing, is it? There are no promising leads we urgently need to follow up.'

'There was one thing. This came in this morning.' Lineham picked up a report and handed it to Thanet. 'Fester said he didn't go out on Friday night.'

Thanet scanned it quickly. A woman who lived opposite Giles Fester reported seeing him leave the house and drive away at around 7.15 that evening.

'So he was lying. Interesting,' said Thanet. 'I agree, we'll have to see him again. Well, if you're really keen to do that, we can split up. I'll go to Plumpton, take someone else with me, Wakeham perhaps . . .' Thanet knew Lineham wouldn't like this suggestion and he was right. The sergeant immediately capitulated.

'No, no, Fester isn't going anywhere either, after all. We can see him later.'

'True. If we leave for Plumpton straight after the morning meeting we can be back by early afternoon.' Thanet glanced at his watch and jumped up. 'And talking about the morning meeting . . . If the Super is on form again he'll expect us to be there on the dot.'

As Thanet hurried down the stairs he felt thoroughly disgruntled. He was annoyed with Lineham and annoyed with himself for being annoyed. The truth was that despite his own doubts he had really been hoping that Lineham would fall upon this idea with enthusiasm. He knew he was being unreasonable. Both he and Lineham were used to the other playing the devil's advocate, it was a useful way of seeing if a theory held water. But this time, for some reason, it had got under his skin. Perhaps it was because underneath, despite all the arguments against it, he just *felt* he was right. There was something about Elaine that had left him feeling uneasy and he wasn't sure why. He remembered now his impression that she had been relieved at the end of the interview, that there was a question he should have asked, and hadn't. Now he wondered: was it relief that her previous connection with Zak — if there was one — hadn't come out?

For his own satisfaction he had to know and a trip to Plumpton was the only answer.

He decided not to mention any of this at the meeting in case it came to nothing. After all, even if he were right and there was a connection between Elaine and Randish's former landlady, it might have absolutely nothing to do with Randish's murder.

At the bottom of the stairs he ran into Inspector Peter Boon of the uniformed branch, his long-time friend and colleague.

'Thirty seconds to go!' said Boon with a grin.

They hurried along the corridor to the door of Draco's office and as Thanet knocked Boon stood ostentatiously gazing at his watch whispering a count-down. 'Fifteen, fourteen, thirteen, twelve . . .'

'Come in!'

Thanet and Boon grinned at each other. It was a relief to hear something of the old vigour back in Draco's voice. 'Sounds in good form today,' said Thanet.

Draco glanced at the clock and waved a hand at them. 'Sit down, sit down.'

Chief Inspector Tody was of course already there, clipboard at the ready.

One look at Draco was enough to tell Thanet that the news about Angharad must indeed be good. Her husband's appearance had over the last two years acted as a barometer of her progress. Draco was a fiery little Welshman of barely regulation height, with dark Celtic eyes, sallow skin and wiry black hair which in his livelier moments seemed almost to crackle with electricity. During the first year of his wife's illness Draco had lost all his bounce and restless vigour, his eyes had dulled and even his hair had become limp and lifeless. During the second year there had been a slow, almost imperceptible improvement and today the transformation was complete. Draco's shirt collar was crisp, his tie tightly knotted, his trouser creases sharp as a knife, his shoes burnished to a gloss which even a sergeant major on parade would have found difficult to criticise.

Thanet was amused to find himself straightening his tie and running a hand over his hair.

'Right,' said Draco. 'Let's get on with it.'

The murder was still the most important investigation in hand at the moment and in view of Draco's previous absence, Thanet's report was lengthy and detailed. Draco listened intently and at the end peppered him with questions.

'Right,' he said eventually. 'You seem to be doing a pretty good job, as usual, Thanet. If there are problems or queries, of course, you know where to find me.'

'Yes, sir.' Draco's praise was so rarely given that it invariably produced a warm glow in the recipient. Thanet was amused to notice that he himself was no exception and Boon's ironic twinkle showed that he too was aware of what they privately called 'The Draco Effect'.

Draco squared up the piece of paper on which he had been making notes in the dead centre of his immaculately tidy desk. 'Right, gentlemen, I think that's about all for today . . .'

This was the signal for them all to rise and they were doing so when he said, 'Except . . .'

They subsided, each of them optimistic that Draco was now going to give them the news they were hoping to hear. Briefly, Thanet's mind flashed back to a similar scene two years ago, but then Draco's demeanour had been lack-lustre, his voice dull with despair.

I had hoped it wouldn't come to this, but ... I'm afraid, however, that it looks as though I am going to have to make somewhat heavier demands than usual upon you ...

And then had come the bad news.

Now, Draco's voice was full of barely suppressed joy, his Welsh accent more noticeable than usual. 'As you know, my wife has just had another test, as she has every two months over the last two years. What you may not have realised was that this was an especially important one, the last of that series. From now on, the interval between tests will be greater. And so far, the prognosis is good. She is still in remission. We've got a long way to go yet, but we seem to have cleared the first and most important hurdle.'

The other three all started to speak at once.

'That's great news, sir ...'

'Wonderful news, sir ...'

'That's terrific, sir ...'

Draco was beaming, his face split almost in two by an enormous, delighted grin. 'Thank you, thank you ... I haven't said anything until now about her progress because I had an almost superstitious dread that if I did something would go wrong. And I must emphasise that even now we are far from out of the wood ...'

According to Mallard, by at least three more years, thought Thanet.

'But I felt that I owed it to you all to tell you what was going on.' Draco paused, picked up an elastic band and began to fiddle with it, winding it around his fingers. 'I have never actually said so before, but I want you all to know just how much I appreciate your support over the last two years. You've often had to carry my workload as well as your own, and it can't have been easy. But not once, by word or gesture, have any of you complained.'

Thanet saw to his horror that Draco the fierce, Draco the fiery, the Welsh Dragon as they had called him behind his back when he first arrived, was on the verge of tears. He sent up a silent prayer: *Don't let him cry!* And then reproached himself. Why shouldn't men cry, if they wished? No one could ever, under any circumstances, call Draco unmanly, and certainly none of the three men here this morning would think any the worse of him for it.

But Draco was mastering his emotion. He shook out an immaculately laundered white handkerchief, which would have been a superb advertisement for any washing powder, and blew his nose loudly. 'Angharad has especially asked me thank you too on her behalf. She says that it has helped her enormously to have me there when she needed me, and she knows I couldn't have done that without you.'

'We were glad to be able to help, sir,' said Tody.

Thanet and Boon were nodding.

'Yes, maybe,' said Draco with a twinkle. 'But this business isn't over yet, remember. I hope you can still say that in a couple of years' time.'

'I'm sure we shall, sir. And allow me to say . . .'

Tody was overdoing it as usual, thought Thanet.

'. . . and I'm sure I speak on behalf of everyone in your sub-division, how delighted we are. Please give your wife our good wishes for her continued progress.'

'Thank you, Tody. All being well, of course' – Draco stood up and the others followed suit – 'the demands upon you should now diminish somewhat.'

'Great!' said Boon, outside. 'We'd better go and spread the good news.'

'I don't think we'll need to do much spreading,' said Thanet.

And it was true. By the curious osmosis endemic to small communities, the news seemed to have permeated the entire building already. It showed in the tone of voice of snatches of conversation, in a burst of laughter here and there, in a general liveliness which seemed to pervade even the corridors. There was no doubt about it, the influence of the man at the top was crucial to an establishment of this size, thought Thanet. Like a school whose tone is set by the headmaster, so much depended on the superintendent of a sub-divisional headquarters. Thanet would never have believed, when Draco first burst upon them in all his missionary fervour, that he could ever have felt like this about the man. And even now, of course, he had to admit that despite the affection and respect he felt for him, there were times when Draco drove him up the wall.

He gave Lineham the good news and they set off for Plumpton, calling briefly at the vineyard on the way to pick up the address of Randish's former landlady. Curious to see if his memory was playing tricks on him, Thanet also collected the cardboard box of photographs. Back in the car he put it on his lap and began to shuffle through them. It didn't take him long to find the one he wanted. 'Got it. Yes, this is the one I was thinking of, definitely.' Though he had to admit that the resemblance wasn't as striking as he remembered. The girl was smiling into the camera, leaning against a five-barred gate, wearing jeans and a T-shirt. Her hair was tied back in a pony-tail and she didn't look a day over twenty. If Thanet was right, she had at that time a daughter of ten or eleven and must have been least twenty-four or twenty-five, minimum. Was it possible that he was wrong after all, and this was a wild-goose chase? Well, if so, at least he would be satisfied that he had found out for certain.

He waited until they were on a straight stretch of road empty of traffic and held the photograph up so that Lineham could risk a quick glance at it.

'I can't really tell, without a proper look,' said Lineham.

'Take my word for it. The resemblance is there,' said Thanet, aware that he was trying to convince himself as much as his sergeant. Because, glancing through the other photographs, he also had to admit that Lineham's suggestion was equally feasible and it could simply be that Elaine was the same physical type. The girls were, without exception, small and slight, their height often betrayed by the scale of their surroundings. The one who perhaps was Elaine's mother, for example, couldn't have been more than five feet tall; the top rung of the five-barred gate was just below her shoulder.

Slipping that one photograph into his wallet Thanet sat back to enjoy the drive. It was, he thought, one of the loveliest in the south-east. Via Cranbrook, Hawkhurst, Etchingham and Burwash the road ran through beautiful rolling countryside which at this time of year was a glorious patchwork of autumn colour.

'Louise would love this,' said Lineham as they came into the pretty village of Burwash, with its tree-lined pavements and picturesque old houses.

'Bateman's is only a little way further on,' said Thanet. 'Rudyard Kipling's house. We had a family outing down this way once, there's lots to see.'

'We're hoping to do more of that sort of thing when the children are bigger. They're a bit young yet.'

Soon after Ringmer they passed the Glyndebourne turning and the bare sweeping curves of the South Downs reared up on their left.

Most of the way the sun had been shining but as they drove down the long hill into Lewes Thanet noticed a heavy bank of cloud ahead. The bursts of sunshine became shorter and shorter and at less frequent intervals.

'Looks as though the heavens are going to open,' said Lineham.

'I hope not. I haven't got my raincoat.' In his hurry to get to work this morning Thanet had forgotten it.

'There's an old anorak you can borrow in the boot, if the worst comes to the worst.'

'Thanks. Turn right, up the High Street, and right again, at the top.'

Lineham concentrated while he negotiated the heavy traffic through the centre of the old town then said, 'Actually, sir, I was thinking. We really should have rung, first. If she's out we'll have a wasted journey.'

'I thought of that. But even if she is out I thought we could make some inquiries, talk to neighbours.' The truth was that he hadn't wanted there to be a reason for not going. He wanted to fill in another blank in Randish's life, see the place where he had spent a number of years, talk to more people who had known him.

'She might have moved away.'

'True.'

'Or even be dead.'

'In the normal way of things, the odds are that she isn't. I worked it out and she's probably in her mid sixties.'

Soon afterwards Plumpton was signposted.

'Turn left here,' said Thanet. 'It's only a couple of miles, now. I don't suppose it's a very big village. We shouldn't have too much difficulty in finding the house.'

A rash assumption, he soon realised. Not long afterwards they came to a sign saying Plumpton half a mile. They passed a pub, then the Agricultural College on the right. Then came a couple of houses, then open countryside again. Lineham slowed down. 'Is that it?'

'Looks like it.'

Plumpton, they discovered, was a very scattered community with no proper centre and after asking directions they got lost twice before eventually managing to find Jasmine Cottage, which was not as picturesque as its name. It was Victorian and semi-detached, built of ugly red brick, with a square bay window to the left of the front door.

As they got out of the car it started to rain, huge coin-sized drops which spotted the road surface.

'I'd better borrow that anorak, Mike.'

Thanet raised his eyebrows at the garment Lineham produced. It was not just old but distinctly tatty, with stains down the front and a long tear in one sleeve.

'Sorry, sir, it looks even worse than I remembered. I keep it to use in emergencies – you know, for changing tyres in the rain and so on.'

'It looks like it!'

'Borrow my raincoat,' said Lineham magnanimously, beginning to take it off.

'No, no. Give me the anorak, quickly.' The rain was coming down steadily now. 'I'll just put it over my head.'

The front gate was broken, propped open with a brick, and the garden was neglected: the lawn was shaggy, the narrow flower borders choked with weeds. The long new season's growth of a rambler rose beside the door had not been tied in and thorns clutched at Thanet's sleeve as he rang the bell.

'Did it work?' said Lineham. 'I didn't hear anything.' He turned his collar up against the increasing downpour.

Thanet lifted the letter-box flap and banged it a few times. The sound reverberated through the house but there was still no response. The front door of the cottage next door opened and a woman came out, peering suspiciously at them from beneath an umbrella with two broken spokes.

'What d'you want?' She was middle-aged and grossly overweight, her legs and ankles so swollen that the flesh hung over the sides of her shoes.

Lineham stepped away from the shelter of the house, hunching down into his collar. 'We wanted to talk to Mrs Wood.' He fished his warrant card out of his pocket and held it up.

She reached across the dilapidated picket fence which divided the two gardens, took it from him and peered at it. 'Just a minute.' She waddled off indoors.

Lineham shrugged at Thanet. 'Looks as though Mrs Wood still lives here, anyway.' The rain was tipping down now and for shelter the two men huddled as close to the house wall as they could get – an unwise move, for a moment later without warning a blocked gutter above them overflowed, and water cascaded down upon them.

As they jumped back Thanet noticed that the net curtain at the bay window behind Lineham was moving. A small round blob had appeared at the bottom and one corner of the curtain was being raised a few inches. 'Look behind you, Mike!' he hissed.

Lineham turned, but the curtain had dropped and there was nothing to see. 'What?'

The blob had been the end of a walking stick, Thanet guessed. Which meant that Mrs Wood was probably immobilised and couldn't reach the curtain any other way. Hence the care being taken by her neighbour.

The woman had come out again. 'You can't be too

careful these days!' she said as she handed Lineham's card back.

'Quite right!' said Thanet.

Mrs Wood, it appeared, was bedridden with severe arthritis. The key to the front door was kept under an upturned flower pot nearby, so that regular visitors could get in.

'Not exactly the most original hiding place,' said Lineham as he retrieved it. 'It'd be the first place a burglar would look, especially if he knew a key was left out.'

They let themselves in and stood, dripping, on the doormat just inside. The house struck chill and the narrow hall was gloomy, with dark red floor tiles and brown paintwork on doors and banisters. Ahead, a passageway beside the staircase led to another door.

Thanet shivered. 'Better take our coats off.'

They draped them over an old-fashioned hall-stand to the right of the door.

'It's freezing in here!' said Lineham. 'And my feet are soaking.'

'Stop grumbling, Mike. Look at me!' The anorak had afforded little protection. Thanet's trouser legs and feet were also wet and he had an uneasy feeling that the water had run down and soaked the bottom of the back of his jacket, too.

He raised his voice and called, 'Mrs Wood?' then knocked at the door on the left, confident that that was where he would find her.

SEVENTEEN

Thanet put his head around the door. 'May we come in, Mrs Wood? Don't be alarmed, it's the police. We showed our identification to your neighbour and she told us where to find the key.'

'Come on in.'

The figure in the bed by the window was so thin and frail that she barely made a hump in the bedclothes. He must surely have been wrong in his estimate of her age, thought Thanet. This woman was in her seventies. She must have borne her daughter much later than he had guessed. Her straight white hair had been cut short by an inexpert hand and her skin was so pale as to be almost translucent. Her hands were pitifully swollen and gnarled with disease. On top of the bedspread lay a lightweight aluminium walking stick and beside the bed was a cluttered bedside table, a walking frame and a commode. The room was large and had evidently once been a sitting room, but the temperature in here didn't seem to be much higher than it was in the hall; a solitary bar glowed on the electric fire which had been put in the middle of the floor, facing the bed. A portable television was running and an advertisement was urging viewers to book now for a winter sunshine holiday.

Mrs Wood invited them to sit down. A couple of chairs had been placed near the bed, for visitors.

When they were settled, Thanet said, 'I don't know if you've heard, but a former lodger of yours died the other day . . .'

An extraordinary change came over Mrs Wood's face. Her eyes glittered and a tide of red, startling against the colourless hair and washed-out nightgown, flowed up towards her hairline.

If her physical condition had allowed it she would have clenched her hands into fists, Thanet thought, watching the misshapen fingers curl. There *was* something, then. His scalp prickled with excitement.

The colour had ebbed as swiftly as it had appeared, leaving her skin more devoid of colour than ever. 'Zak Randish, you mean,' she said. 'Oh yes, I heard about that all right. Murdered, wasn't he.' And she smiled, a small, cold, satisfied smile.

There was somehow something shocking about this pathetic old lady displaying such vindictiveness, thought Thanet, though why that should be he wasn't quite sure. 'I wonder,' he said, 'would it be possible to turn the television off for a while?'

The remote control was to hand and after a couple of abortive attempts, Mrs Wood managed to stab the correct button. 'It's no more than he deserved, I'm sure,' she announced loudly into the ensuing silence.

While they waited for her to turn the set off Thanet had noticed that on the bedside table, with their backs to him, were a couple of photographs. Would one of them be of Elaine? he wondered. How could he get a look at them? 'You obviously didn't like him,' he said, half his attention on the photographs and aware that this was an understatement if ever there was one.

'I hated him!' she said vehemently. 'He killed my daughter!'

She wasn't even looking at them to gauge the effect of this announcement but was gazing fiercely into space, focused upon some inner vision that had nothing to do with their presence here. Thanet and Lineham raised eyebrows at each other and shrugged. Neither of them believed she had meant it literally. Then she seemed to become aware of her surroundings again and her eyes wandered over the bed, her pathetic hands, the single-bar electric fire and finally Thanet and Lineham. 'I wouldn't be stuck here like this now, all alone, if it wasn't for him. I'd still have my Jill to look after me.'

'How is that?' said Thanet. He recognised the signs. People who lived alone, especially those who were elderly and incapacitated, were almost invariably eager to talk, usually about whatever it was that they spent their time brooding upon – their health, a grievance, their memories. Once launched, the occasional question here and there was all that was necessary to prompt them into further elaboration. He sensed Lineham beside him going into what he thought of as the sergeant's invisible mode; over the years, when Lineham judged that a witness was about to open up, he had developed the knack of fading into the background. Still as a statue, only the occasional blink betrayed the fact that he was alert and absorbing everything that was going on. Whenever Thanet was stuck with an inexperienced officer who fidgeted, coughed, scribbled ostentatiously and generally distracted the witness he thought longingly of this trick of Lineham's and wished that it was part of standard training procedure.

Her tale was much what he expected. A boyfriend had 'taken advantage' of Jill when she was fifteen and had dropped her flat when he heard she was pregnant. Not long before that a neighbour had had an abortion that had gone wrong and been desperately ill, so Jill had refused even to consider having one. Around that time her father died and she and her mother had had to think of some means of earning money. They had decided to take in students from the nearby agricultural college. A number of local people did this, and it would mean that Jill could stay at home and look after the baby when it arrived. In fact, later on, when Linny went to school, Jill got a job in a shop in Lewes.

Thanet pricked up his ears, wished again that he could take a look at those photographs. This was the first time the child's name had been mentioned, its gender even hinted at. Linny sounded like a girl's name and could well be an abbreviation of Elaine. He would ask later if necessary. The old lady was well launched and he didn't want to interrupt the flow.

All went well until Zak arrived, at the beginning of the third and final year of his course. During his first year he had been in college residential accommodation; during his second he had been living on the farm on which he had been doing his year's practical experience. Until then Jill, wary of men after that early, disastrous experience, had not taken much interest in the opposite sex, but reading between the lines Thanet gathered that one look at Zak had changed all that. According to Mrs Wood, of course, it was Zak who had made all the running.

'Promised to marry her, he did,' she said bitterly.

Wishful thinking, thought Thanet. In view of Zak's long-term plans for the future he very much doubted Randish had ever had any such intention. Alice Randish, with her father's spreading acres, would be a much more enticing proposition.

'She couldn't believe it when, after he left, she didn't

hear a single word from him. She waited and waited, wrote him time and time again, but never a word from him did she hear. She was beside herself. It was awful to see her watching and waiting for the postman every day, I got so that I'd wake up in the mornings feeling sick to think of her disappointment when there was no letter for her yet again. In the end she said to me, "There's nothing for it, Mum, I'll just have to go and see him. Perhaps he's ill, perhaps he's broken his arm and can't write . . ." And perhaps pigs might fly, I thought to myself. I didn't say so, of course, it wouldn't have done any good, but I saw from the first what he was like, with his smarmy ways. A real ladies' man, that's what. If he ever got married I bet his wife had a terrible time of it. Anyway, I did try to persuade Jill not to go. I guessed it would end badly. But she wouldn't listen, go she would. So she went. And I never saw her again.'

'What happened?' said Thanet, startled into a direct question.

'She crashed the car on the way home, on that big hill the other side of Etchingham. She was killed instantly, they said.'

'Are you suggesting it wasn't an accident?'

'No one knows.' Mrs Wood was shaking her head, the tears coming to her eyes. 'No one will ever know.' She groped blindly for a box of tissues on her bedside table and Thanet handed them to her. Clumsily she pulled one out, dabbed the tears away. 'Thanks. But it makes no difference, don't you see? Whether it was a genuine accident or whether she . . . she did it on purpose, it was him what killed her. If it was an accident, it was because she was so upset after seeing him. She was a good driver, careful . . .'

Even the best of drivers can have accidents, Thanet

knew, but he could see that there was no point in saying so. Mrs Wood's ideas were too deeply entrenched for a brief conversation with a stranger to alter them even slightly. And after all, it was quite likely that she was right. Even if Jill Wood had not intended to kill herself, her concentration may well have been poor after a final rejection by Zak. 'I expect your granddaughter was a comfort to you,' he said, pleased that his patience had been rewarded and he had at last been able to introduce the subject which had brought them here.

And as he had hoped her response confirmed that the child had been a girl.

'She was only ten! What can you expect from a child of that age, especially when she's so upset herself? Still, you're right. She was a comfort. Until she went away to college, that is. Mind, I wouldn't have wanted to hold her back. She's done very well.' Mrs Wood began to grope for one of the photographs. 'That's her, there.'

Thanet leaned forward with alacrity to help her. As he turned the photograph around a thrill of triumph shot through him. There was no doubt about it, this was Elaine Wood, a little younger, perhaps, but instantly recognisable. He held it out for Lineham to see. 'She's a beautiful girl.'

Mrs Wood fumbled for the other photograph. 'And that's her mother.'

Further confirmation. This was definitely the girl he had thought might be Elaine's mother. 'They're very alike.' He passed the second photograph to Lineham, who held them side by side to compare the two young women. 'I suppose your granddaughter is very much the same age now as your daughter was when that was taken.'

'Yes, she is. She's doing very well. Works with them new-fangled computer things.'

'How did she get on with Mr Randish when he was here?'

'Oh, all right. He went out of his way to worm himself into her good books, so she wouldn't make things difficult for him with her mum. And, of course, she'd never had a father, so she did tend to make a beeline for the men. But after Jill died I made sure Linny knew it was all his fault Oh yes, I made sure of that all right.'

'Does she come to see you often?'

'Whenever she can get away. It's difficult for her, she doesn't work locally. She works in . . .' Mrs Wood broke off, stared first at Thanet, then at Lineham, then at Thanet again. At first welcoming the distraction of visitors and then becoming engrossed in her story, until this moment she had not really questioned the reason for their presence. Now, perhaps, she had sensed danger for the first time. 'Where . . . Where did you say you were from?'

'From Sturrenden. We are investigating Mr Randish's murder.'

'Why have you come to see me?'

She had talked so freely until now that Thanet was certain she had no idea that her granddaughter had been involved with Randish. If he told her, he would perhaps cause her a great deal of unnecessary distress. If it turned out that Elaine had in fact killed Zak then that distress would be unavoidable. Meanwhile it would be best to keep her in ignorance. 'Naturally,' he said, 'we are trying to talk to everyone who knew him.'

He stood up and watched her relax a little at the thought that they were leaving. 'It's a pity your granddaughter doesn't live nearer. She might have been able to help you more.' Why wasn't Elaine doing more for her grandmother, anyway? With her qualifications there would surely have been plenty of jobs available in Lewes or Brighton. Not that it was any of his business, but still . . .

The old lady had sensed his unspoken criticism and was shaking her head. 'I'm here because I want to be. I always said I didn't want to go into a nursing home, I'd die in my own bed. And that's what I'm going to do.'

'It must be very difficult for you.'

'I manage.' She waved a hand. 'People come. I get meals on wheels, and the district nurse comes in to bath me.' She scowled at Thanet. 'I wouldn't want Linny ruining her life for my sake. You're only young once, and you should be free to enjoy it.'

Outside Thanet was thankful to see that it had stopped raining.

Lineham said, 'You got into her bad books there, sir. Daring to hint at criticism of her precious Linny.'

'I did it on purpose, to distract her, as I've no doubt you realised, Mike. Anyway, I don't know about you, but my feet have gone numb.'

'Mine too.'

'Early lunch, I think. I wonder if that pub back there has a fire. What was it called?'

'The Half Moon.'

'That's right. Let's go and find out.'

They were in luck. As soon as they stepped through the door a blissful warmth enveloped them. The Half Moon had not one fire but two, a woodstove at one end, near the dartboard and billiard table, and an open fire at the other. Best of all, there was an empty table near the latter.

'What d'you think that means?' Lineham nodded at the

smoke-blackened concrete lintel over the fire, on which some words had been chiselled.

WOOD FEEDS FIRE WORDS IRE.

'Ire means anger, doesn't it?' said Thanet.

'Ah. I see. Life would be pretty boring if we all took a vow of silence, though, wouldn't it?' Lineham stretched out his feet to the welcoming warmth. 'Wish I could take my socks off!'

'I don't think you'd be too popular with the landlord!'

They contented themselves with eating something hot – home-made moussaka – and allowing the heat to soak into their bones. Afterwards, Thanet sat back and lit his pipe, watching his wet trousers steaming gently. 'That's better.' He waited until his pipe was drawing properly and then said, 'Well, Mike?'

'OK, sir, so I owe you an apology. You were right. But I'll tell you this. Although I didn't like Elaine Wood and, frankly, I wasn't too keen on her grandmother, either, I do hope she's not our murderer. She's all the old lady's got.'

'I think it must be advancing years that are turning you soft, Mike. First you say you hope it wasn't Fester, now you say you hope it wasn't Elaine. Are there any other candidates you'd like to put out of the running?'

'Oh, all right, sir. So I'm going soft. You may not be saying so, but by your past record I bet you feel exactly the same underneath.'

Thanet laughed. 'Touché. But in any case, you have to admit now that Elaine does have a motive.'

'A real classic, isn't it: revenge for the death of her mother. Yes. I'm sure old Mrs Wood would have missed no opportunity over the years to make sure Elaine had got the message. And Elaine would have recognised Randish the minute she saw him, don't you think? Between their twenties and their thirties people don't change all that much.'

'She might have realised who he was before that, Mike, if she'd heard his name before she went out to the vineyard, which is quite likely. It's pretty unusual, after all.'

'So she might have been on her guard. The question is, would he have recognised her?'

'She would have changed a lot, between ten and twenty-five. If he did, it would be because of her resemblance to her mother.'

'As you pointed out, sir, she is very much the same age as her mother was when Randish knew her.'

'Quite.'

'Her surname might have rung a bell, too.'

'If he heard it, Mike. You know how informal people are these days. She was probably only referred to as Elaine. And that wouldn't have meant anything to him if he only knew her as Linny.'

'Perhaps he did recognise her, sir. Perhaps it added spice to the situation, as far as he was concerned.'

'Possibly, yes. In any case, if either of them did recognise the other, I wonder if they let the other person know. Quite an intriguing situation, really. What d'you think?'

Lineham considered. 'I'd say that he might have, but she probably wouldn't have.'

Thanet tapped his pipe out on the ashtray. 'Come on, let's go and find out.'

EIGHTEEN

On the way back to Sturrenden the weather was at its most capricious: periods of brilliant sunshine followed by heavy outbursts of rain. On one occasion visibility became so poor that Lineham pulled in to the side of the road until the worst was over.

The heater was on in the car but both men were still uncomfortably aware of damp feet, and Thanet decided that before going to Compu-Tech to interview Elaine and question Fester about the lie he had told it would be sensible to go home and change. He would collect his raincoat, as well.

They called at Thanet's house first, Lineham electing to wait in the car. In the hall Thanet almost fell over a pair of discarded trainers lying in the middle of the floor – Bridget's, presumably. He picked them up to move them out of the way. It looked as though she had been caught in a downpour too. They were sodden, the patterned soles caked with mud and embedded with pieces of gravel and even a splinter of glass. What on earth had she been up to?

'Dad! What are you doing home? For a minute I thought we had burglars!'

Bridget had appeared at the top of the stairs, a towel wound around her head.

'We got soaked, like you.' Thanet waggled the trainers at her.

'Oh, sorry. I was going to put them in the kitchen to dry as soon as I'd changed. I wasn't expecting anyone else home for hours yet.'

'I'll put them on the mat by the back door.' Thanet did so, first picking out the fragment of glass in case Bridget didn't notice it and cut herself. He dropped it in the waste bin, then hurried upstairs.

A minute or two later she appeared at his bedroom door as he was pulling on some dry trousers. 'Got time for a cup of coffee?'

'No, sorry, love, Mike's waiting in the car outside and we're on our way to an interview. It's just that I knew I'd be in trouble with your mother if I spent the rest of the day with wet feet.' Thanet was tugging on fresh socks as he spoke.

'Quite right, too,' said Bridget with a grin.

Thanet slipped on some dry shoes and wiggled his toes. They felt blissfully cosseted and comfortable. 'That's better!'

Bridget followed him as far as the top of the stairs. 'Still all right for tonight?' she called down after him.

'So far.' Thanet raised a hand in farewell. 'The 8.05, you said?'

'That's right.' Her ''bye' floated after him as he closed the door.

After a brief halt at Lineham's house they set off again.

'Think we ought to call in at the office?' said Lineham.

Thanet shook his head. He was eager now to get to Compu-Tech.

'Which of them are we going to talk to first?'

'Fester, I think. It shouldn't take long. Frankly, I don't think we're going to get anywhere with him.'

'Why not?'

'I think he'll simply continue to deny that he went out that night. He'll realise it's the witness's word against his and challenge us to prove he's lying. And of course, we won't be able to. End of story.'

'There must be something we can do, to get him to admit it.'

Thanet shook his head. 'I don't see how, at this stage. Unless . . .'

'What?'

'Hold on a minute, Mike. I'm thinking.'

Perhaps it would be better to interview them together. Then, if Fester saw that Elaine was in difficulties he might be driven to indiscretion himself in order to bail her out. But it was going to be difficult enough anyway to get Elaine to talk freely and if Fester were present she would be even less likely to open up. 'No, that won't work.'

'What?'

Thanet explained.

'I see what you mean.'

'No, we'll have to see them separately, do the best we can.'

At Compu-Tech Kari was sweeping up sodden leaves in the paved parking area and shovelling them into a wheelbarrow. The sky was still heavily overcast and in the dreary grey light she was a welcome splash of colour in bright red wellies and anorak. Her flowing hair was tied up into a pony-tail which swung as she worked. She paused as they got out of the car, leaning on the handle of her broom. 'It's a never-ending job at this time of the year.'

'I didn't know you were the gardener as well.'

She grinned and gestured at the ivy-filled terracotta

pots. 'If you can call looking after those being the gardener, then yes, I suppose I am. But I do like to keep the place tidy.'

Kari had called herself lucky the other day, thought Thanet, but it was not all one-sided. Fester was lucky too. He had struck gold here.

There was a silver Peugeot 205 parked next to Fester's BMW.

'His and hers,' said Lineham in a low voice as they walked up the ramp to the door. 'I bet that's Elaine Wood's. Just the car I'd have expected her to choose.'

'Could belong to a client. She might be out on a job.'

Lineham shook his head. 'It'll be hers.'

Privately, Thanet agreed with him. At first, however, it looked as though the sergeant was wrong. The office was empty except for a receptionist typing busily.

'Can I help you?' She was young and pretty, with beautifully cut very short black hair and a wide smile.

To Thanet's relief Fester and Elaine were both in. They were in Fester's office and the receptionist rang through. A moment later Elaine emerged. Not surprisingly, she didn't look too pleased to see them and Thanet did not miss the glint of relief in her eyes when he asked to speak to Fester.

Fester's office was strictly functional, the walls bare of the certificates, diplomas and photographs considered obligatory by so many. It was predictably uncluttered, the only furniture being four low armchairs grouped around a coffee table on one side of the room and on the other an interesting desk, custom-made by the look of it. It had been built on a shallow curve and ingeniously designed without legs at the two front corners, to allow easy access to Fester's wheelchair. Not surprisingly in view of the nature of Fester's business, there seemed to be a lot of sophisticated electronic equipment. This, presumably, was where he did a great deal of his creative thinking.

Fester rolled forward to greet them. Here, at the very heart of the success he had forged out of disaster, he looked confident and assured, in expensive casual trousers of a silky grey-green fabric with a slight sheen to it and a roll-neck cashmere sweater of exactly the same shade. 'Another interrogation, Inspector?' A joke, his smile said.

'Yes, as a matter of fact.' The armchairs were, Thanet noted, lower than Fester's wheelchair and not wishing to feel at a disadvantage he strolled across to the window and leaned against the sill.

'I can't persuade you to sit down? No?' Fester's smile had faded and as if to reassert his authority in his own domain he wheeled himself behind his desk and picked up a slim gold pen which had been lying on the open file in front of him. He began to slide it to and fro through his fingers. 'How can I help you, then?'

He had addressed his question to Thanet and looked slightly surprised when it was Lineham who moved forward to position himself squarely in front of him and, using the confrontational opening upon which he and Thanet had agreed, said, 'You lied to us the other day, sir. And we'd like to know why.'

Fester's eyes narrowed. 'What do you mean?'

Lineham did his best but as Thanet had predicted Fester flatly denied that he had been out that evening. The neighbour was mistaken, he claimed, had probably confused Friday with Thursday, when he had indeed gone out, to the gym in Sturrenden.

Nothing would shake him so Thanet asked if they could borrow his office to interview Elaine again.

With an ill grace he agreed, and used his intercom to ask the receptionist to send her in. 'I hope this won't take too long, Inspector. It's very inconvenient. I do have work to do, you know.'

'I realise that, sir. We'll be as quick as we can, I assure you.'

Fester left the room looking distinctly put out and Thanet noticed that instead of turning right towards the main office he turned left towards his living quarters.

A moment later Elaine came in and they all sat down. As they did so there was an almost inaudible click from the direction of the desk. Thanet was nearest to it and he glanced at the others to see if they had heard it. Evidently not. Lineham was fishing a pen out of his pocket and Elaine was settling herself in her chair. Earlier on Thanet's position by the window had given him a clear view of Fester's equipment and now the curve of the desk still allowed him an angled view of part of it. A red light on the intercom had come on, a different one from that which had lit up earlier when Fester spoke to the receptionist in the outer office.

Thanet realised what had happened. Despite the remarkable way in which he coped with his handicap Fester's mobility was still restricted and he had installed an elaborate intercom system which enabled him no doubt to communicate with any part of his establishment either from here or from the flat next door. Fester was, Thanet was convinced, in love with Elaine and no doubt part of his bad temper of a moment ago had been due to the fact that he was being excluded from this interview and wouldn't know what was going on. This was why he had turned left to his living quarters when he went out of the office just now. He must have realised almost at once that if he was quick about it he could listen in if he wished, and had hurried next door to switch the intercom on.

Thanet was pleased. With any luck now, his own problem was solved: Elaine would talk as freely as they could persuade her to, without being inhibited by Fester's presence, and Fester could possibly be provoked into playing the knight in shining armour and giving himself away on Elaine's behalf. It would make the interview rather complicated but Thanet enjoyed a challenge. He would see what he could do.

He became aware that Elaine had said something and that she and Lineham were both watching him expectantly. 'Sorry, I was thinking. Now then, Miss Wood, I feel we ought to tell you that we are rather better informed than we were last time we interviewed you.'

'Oh?' Her eyes were wary. She had managed to combine the glamour-girl look – immaculate make-up, carefully contrived casual hairstyle – with an air of efficiency. Her hyacinth blue suit and crisp white blouse with matching blue coin-sized spots were both stylish and businesslike.

'Did Mr Randish recognise you, when he first met you again, a few months ago?'

A flash of alarm, quickly suppressed. 'Recognise me?' she said, carefully.

'Oh come, Miss Wood, don't pretend you don't understand what I mean. But to spell it out, I'll tell you that we have just returned from Plumpton, where we had a very interesting conversation with your grandmother.'

She stared at him. Then, unexpectedly, he saw a spark of amusement in her eyes. Her lips curved in a wry smile. 'Ah,' she said.

He waited, interested to see what she would come up with next.

'You have been busy, haven't you, Inspector.'

'Evidently.' His tone was dry.

She crossed her legs, nylon whispering against nylon. 'So, what of it? It's all ancient history now. I don't see how something that happened fifteen years ago can possibly have any bearing on Zak Randish's death.'

'Don't you? I find that very difficult to believe. But let's go back a little. When did you first realise who he was?'

'As soon as I heard his name, naturally. I wasn't certain, of course, not until I saw him. But it is a very unusual name. I've never come across it at any other time, before or since.'

'That would have been when?'

'About four months ago. Tracey – our receptionist – told me that a Mr Randish had rung to enquire about a computer system and she'd told him I'd ring back.'

'You, not Mr Fester?'

'No. I handle sales and installation.' She glanced at the desk with its bank of equipment. 'Giles does the more creative stuff.'

'How did you feel, when you realised who Mr Randish might be?'

'It was a bit of a shock, naturally.'

'Did you mention that you might have met him before, either to Tracey or to Mr Fester?'

'No, of course not. It would have meant giving explanations, and I wasn't prepared to do that.'

Thanet wondered what Fester was making of all this. By now his curiosity must be at boiling point. 'And when you saw him, you knew at once that it was the same man?'

'Yes. He seemed scarcely to have changed at all.'

'Which brings me back to my original question. Did he recognise you?'

She shook her head. 'I was only ten when I knew him.

It doesn't take too much imagination to see that I must have changed a great deal since then. I did wonder if my name would ring a bell but nobody ever called me Elaine at home and Wood is a very common surname, you only have to look in the directory.'

'You are very like your mother, though.'

'Not sufficiently like, apparently.'

'So did you tell him who you were?'

'No.'

'Why not?'

'Because it would have been too awkward, of course! I knew I'd have to spend a couple of days in his office while he and that po-faced manager of his got the hang of the computer and I just thought it would be much easier if I said nothing.'

'Did he ever find out?'

'No!'

'No,' echoed Thanet softly. 'But not telling him led to a further complication, didn't it? You found he was attracted to you.'

She put up one hand to toss back her hair in a coquettish gesture. 'I'm used to that. I can handle it.'

'But you responded, all the same.'

She lifted her shoulders. 'Why not?'

'Why not, Miss Wood? Because according to your grandmother he was responsible for your mother's death, that's why not!'

'We don't know that, do we?'

'No, we don't *know* that. But what we do know is that he treated her very shabbily indeed, giving her good reason to believe he was going to marry her and then walking out on her and never contacting her again. I would have thought he'd be the last man on earth you'd choose to go out with, in the circumstances.'

'I told you! That was all ancient history!' But her composure was slipping, he was glad to see. If he could just make her say what she had really thought, really felt . . .

'Ah, but it wasn't really ancient history at all, was it? It could have been, I agree, if your grandmother had let it rest, but she didn't, did she? She couldn't. In her eyes, Randish killed your mother and that was all there was to it – and she told us, in no uncertain terms, that she had made sure you knew it. So are you really asking me to believe that when you met him again you were able to put all that aside and not only forgive him but actually enjoy going out with him?'

He was deliberately goading her, watching her closely for the signs that her control was about to snap, and now he was rewarded.

'All right!' she said, clutching at her head with both hands and jumping up. 'All right, all right, all right!'

Her agitation took her to the window where she stood with her back to them, leaning on the sill with both hands, arms rigid, head down and shoulders hunched in tension. After a few moments she lifted her head and took a couple of long, steadying breaths. They saw her shoulders relax before she turned. 'You're quite right, of course. It was impossible to forgive him. How could I? My grandmother probably told you that my mother was the only parent I ever had.'

'So why did you agree to go out with him?'

'To make him pay, of course.' Her tone was flat, weary. She returned to her chair. 'I could never bring her back, but I could make him suffer what she suffered.'

There had been no sound from the next room and Thanet wondered how Fester was taking all these revelations. 'Suffer how, exactly?' he said.

Her eyes gleamed with malice as in reply she smoothed

her skirt over her thighs and then ran the fingertips of one hand caressingly over one shapely, silky knee. 'I should have thought that was obvious, Inspector.'

Her smile mocked not only Thanet but Lineham, Randish, all men. How can you look at me and ask that question? it said. You are but putty in the hands of a woman like me.

'Spell it out for me,' Thanet said, face and voice carefully neutral. He saw Lineham shift uncomfortably and knew that the sergeant was sharing his distaste.

'Very well. It's quite simple, really. I intended to do everything in my power to make him fall for me.' Her tone was light, almost playful, but now it suddenly changed, became venomous. 'And then, when he had, to leave him flat, as he left her.'

Thanet again thought of Fester, listening next door, and couldn't help feeling sorry for him. Any illusions he had had about Elaine must be crumbling fast. 'I see. And I assume that you would claim he died before you were able to finish carrying out your plan.'

'Unfortunately, yes.' There was a wry glint in her eyes as she said, 'I must confess that I wish whoever killed him had waited just a little longer.'

Thanet caught Lineham's eye and knew what he was thinking. *Charming!*

'So let's go back now to Friday. You weren't telling the truth, were you, when you denied having arranged to meet Mr Randish that evening?'

'No.' She sighed. 'That was because Giles was there, of course. He didn't know I was going out with Zak. It won't have escaped you that he's rather keen on me and with him in his condition, well, let's just say I don't like to upset him if I can help it.'

Thanet flinched inwardly, thinking of Fester listening

next door. The mixture of indulgence and condescension in her tone must have made him wince.

'So when he asked me to go out with him on Friday I refused, told him there were various things I'd planned to do at home that evening.'

'What time did you and Mr Randish arrange to meet?'

'He said he couldn't give me a specific time, it all depended on when he could get away. And then he'd probably only be able to stay for half an hour or so. To be honest, I was pretty fed up about it. It meant I'd have to waste the evening hanging about waiting for him to turn up, unable to settle down to anything else. But he was dead keen, so I had to go along with it. He'd been so busy with the harvest lately that he'd hardly seen me. In the event, of course, he didn't turn up at all.'

'So what did you do?'

'Nothing. Why should I? I couldn't have cared less – except that, as I say, it meant a wasted evening.'

'You didn't try ringing the vineyard?'

'No.'

'And you didn't go out there?' A pointless question really, but it had to be asked. Thanet was convinced that Elaine had been telling the truth. Her idea of revenge rang true in the light of what he now knew of her character.

'No!'

'So you say.' Thanet was still conscious of their unseen listener, though in view of what Fester had heard it was highly unlikely that he would be as anxious to jump to Elaine's defence as he might have been half an hour ago.

She remained unruffled. 'So I say. And you'll never be able to prove otherwise because what I've told you is the truth.'

'Well,' said Thanet, rising, 'we shall see.'

Elaine stood up. 'That's all? I can go?'

'For the moment, yes.' Out of the corner of his eye he saw the light on the intercom go off and heard the click for which he had been listening.

He saw at once that Elaine had heard it too. She had been turning towards the door but now she froze and her eyes went towards the desk.

From where she stood, Thanet realised, she couldn't see the face of the intercom panel, so she wouldn't know whether it had just been switched on or off, whether the click meant that Fester had overheard the entire interview or had just switched on because he was about to speak. She waited a moment, presumably to see if he was going to, and when he didn't calmly walked to the desk and leaned forward for an unobstructed view of the panel.

She had to know whether or not Fester had been listening, Thanet realised, couldn't have left this room without knowing.

She registered the absence of lights and straightened up, stood for a moment thinking, then with set face crossed the room and opened the door.

Fester must have moved fast. He was outside, waiting.

Thanet wished that he could see their faces as they looked at each other in the light of their new knowledge. He felt sorry for Fester, and guilty over the pain he must have caused him. On the other hand it was not he but Fester who by eavesdropping had brought about this situation and it was perhaps just as well that the man's illusions about Elaine should have been destroyed. Nothing but heartache would have awaited him along that road. Perhaps now he would be free to look for a more worthwhile relationship. Remembering Kari, Thanet thought that Fester might not have to look far.

Lineham was looking puzzled. 'What's going on?' he whispered.

Thanet shook his head. 'Tell you later,' he murmured as Elaine moved away in the direction of the main office and Fester rolled forward into the doorway, blocking their path. 'Could I have another word, Inspector?'

'By all means.'

This time, by unspoken mutual agreement, they arranged themselves around the low table.

Fester gave Thanet a searching look. 'Am I right in thinking you know what I did just now?'

Thanet nodded. 'I heard the click at the beginning of the interview. And from where I was sitting I could see the light come on. But I'd better just explain to Sergeant Lineham. He wasn't as well placed.' Briefly, Thanet did so, watching Lineham take in all the implications.

'I assure you I don't make a habit of it,' said Fester, 'and I can't pretend I'm proud of myself. Quite the opposite, in fact.' He gave a wry smile. 'I suppose I deserved all I got. They say that eavesdroppers never hear anything good about themselves, don't they?'

'You didn't hear anything bad.'

'It depends what you mean by "bad". Nothing derogatory, no, but it was a bit of an eye-opener, as I'm sure you realised.'

'If it's any consolation, you're not the first to be taken in by an attractive woman, and you won't be the last. And Miss Wood does seem to be something of an expert. Look how she deceived Mr Randish.'

Fester gave a shamefaced grin. 'Thanks. Anyway, I think I owe you an explanation. Before, I was prepared to lie. Now, I'm not. Not that I have any great revelation to put before you, don't think that. I'm not about to confess and hold out my wrists for the handcuffs.'

'I didn't think you were,' said Thanet smiling. 'In fact, I think I can guess what you're going to tell me. So, to save you the humiliation of actually doing so, let me see if I'm right. On Friday evening, suspecting that Miss Wood was not telling you the truth – that in fact she had a date with someone else, you decided to keep an eye on her. Am I right?'

Fester gave a resigned nod.

'You couldn't own up the last time we spoke to you because she was present and you didn't want her to know you'd been watching her.'

'Yes. I left here about 7.15 as your witness claimed, drove to the car park behind Elaine's block of flats and parked where I could see both her garage and the entrance to the flats. I stayed there until around ten, then came home.'

'So you'll be able to tell us for certain whether or not she went out that night,' said Lineham.

'Quite,' said Fester. 'And she didn't.'

'You're sure of that, sir?'

'Positive.'

That seemed to be that. There was nothing more to be learned here.

Back in the car Lineham said, 'If he's telling the truth, they're both in the clear. And you believe him, don't you?'

Thanet nodded. 'Don't you?'

'Yes,' said Lineham reluctantly. 'So where does that leave us?'

Thanet sighed. 'Back at square one, I'm afraid.'

NINETEEN

They drove in silence for a few minutes and then Thanet banged his knee with a clenched fist in frustration. 'What a waste of time!'

'Not at all,' said Lineham. 'We've done some eliminating, if nothing else.'

Small consolation.

Silence again. Thanet was sunk in gloom. He'd thought he was so clever, with his ingenious theory of revenge for past wounds! He was only thankful that he'd said nothing of all this at the morning meeting. He could imagine Draco's reaction now.

Yes, well I'm not surprised. We have to keep our feet on the ground, you know, Thanet, not allow ourselves to be carried away. Perhaps it would be as well to remember in future that good police work is always based on fact, not fancy.

Thanet realised that he was close to grinding his teeth. Had he been doing so? He glanced at Lineham, but the sergeant was concentrating on his driving. Thanet gazed moodily out of the window. Even the weather was being perverse; now that they were equipped for rain, the sun had come out and the roads were already almost dry.

Lineham pulled up to allow a stream of schoolchildren to cross the road. The lollipop lady, as the traffic controllers on such crossings are invariably called, smiled her thanks at him as she waved him on. The school day must be over already. Thanet glanced at his watch. Yes, it was half past three. He groaned. What a waste of time, he thought again.

'Come on, sir. Cheer up. You were right, after all.'

'About what?'

'About the connection between Elaine and Randish's former landlady. Honestly, I don't know what you're looking so gloomy about.'

'Hurt pride, I suppose, Mike, if the truth be told. It's always a blow when it turns out that you're not as clever as you thought you were. Serves me right.'

'Well, if you ask me you're over-reacting. I don't know what you expected. That Elaine would say, "Yes, it's a fair cop, guv. I done it because of what he did to my mum"?'

Thanet gave a shamefaced grin. 'If I'm absolutely honest then yes, I suppose I did rather hope for something like that. I certainly thought I'd cracked it. As it is, well, I suppose I should just be thankful my hunch proved right. I could have been way off beam, after all. We could have found that Elaine had absolutely no connection whatsoever with old Mrs Wood.'

'Exactly.'

'Not that it gets us very far to find out that she did. I suppose that's why I'm so angry with myself. I feel I've been self-indulgent, and wasted the best part of a day. I just wanted to prove that my theory was right and to hell with everything else.'

'What else, for example?'

'Well . . .' Thanet thought, but couldn't come up with anything.

'Exactly. You could only say you've wasted the time if we could have been usefully employed elsewhere and as you said yourself this morning there wasn't really anything else to follow up – apart from the fact that Fester had been lying about not having gone out that night, and we've dealt with that anyway.'

Lineham was not only right, but in view of his reluctance to go to Plumpton today, was being very generous. Thanet glanced across at the sergeant's familiar profile and experienced a surge of gratitude and affection. 'Thanks, Mike. What would I do without you?'

Lineham went pink. 'I dare say you'd survive, sir,' he said.

They had arrived. Back in the office they checked on messages and information that had come in while they were away.

'Nothing in the least bit promising,' said Lineham despondently.

'Never mind.' Thanet was brisk, spirits restored. 'It's obviously time to do a rethink. After all, it's not as though we haven't got any suspects. If anything we've got too many.'

Lineham sat back, stretching out his legs and folding his arms across his chest. 'So who would you put your money on, sir? Reg Mason?'

'I'm not sure.'

'He's the one who Randish was hurting most, after all. From the way Mrs Mason reacted the other night it's obvious that she can't put up with too much stress. If you ask me, Mason might well have ended up losing his wife as well as his home. But now, well, I should think it quite likely that Mrs Randish will at least pay off the original sum agreed for the work done and Mason's problems will be over.'

'It's true that he probably benefits most in the short term.'

'And a man in his position is bound to have a pretty short fuse. Let's face it, he had motive, means, opportunity, the lot. He really does fit the bill.'

'Maybe. But what about Landers? He was pretty browned off with the way Randish was treating Alice, wouldn't you say? I know how I'd feel if I discovered Bridget's husband was not only knocking her about but regularly being unfaithful too. It's all very well for him to protest that he couldn't have killed Randish because Alice would be heartbroken to lose her husband. I should think he could pretty easily convince himself that she'd get over it in time, wouldn't you?'

'Are you saying you think Landers went up to the lab that night deliberately to kill Randish? I thought we'd agreed that this murder was unpremeditated.'

'No, I'm not. But he's obviously fond of Reg Mason. It's much more likely that after hearing about the repossession and despite his decision to offer Reg a cottage if the worst came to the worst, he went up to the winery to make one last attempt to persuade Randish to pay up at least a part of the disputed sum. Randish could have been dismissive or rude or just plain insulting, and all Landers' grievances against him could suddenly have rolled together and erupted.'

'But you said you thought Randish must have been killed by someone much weaker or smaller than he was, because of the way it happened. If Landers lost his temper with Randish he wouldn't have started throwing things at him, surely, he'd have gone for him.'

'True. Unless, as you suggested yourself, whoever killed Randish – let's just assume it was Landers – was so angry with him that he was afraid that if he started a fight he might completely lose control.'

'And lost it anyway, you mean?'

'Perhaps. Yes.'

'It's possible, granted. But personally, if we're going to discount Reg Mason, I'd go for Vintage. If anyone's living on a knife edge, it's him, and he had the best opportunity of anybody. He had the whole evening at his disposal.'

'True. But you could say the same of Alice Randish. She not only fits the bill perfectly as far as motive, means and opportunity are concerned but statistically she's the most likely suspect. In fact, the more I think about it, Mike, the more I wonder if we've been pretty remiss in not looking at her more closely.'

Lineham considered the idea. 'If Randish had been unfaithful once too often . . . Maybe she found out about Elaine. Maybe her father told her, hoping to disillusion her! Yes! What if Landers hoped that by telling her about Elaine she could be persuaded to divorce Randish? Landers would just love to have her and the children under his control again, wouldn't he? Actually, sir, if you think about it, that's an added motive for him, don't you think?'

'Yes. I hadn't thought of that.'

'What if he told her about Elaine that evening, when he came over to see her about Reg Mason? And then, after he'd gone, she felt she had to know, she had to find out if it was true. She couldn't bear the prospect of waiting until her husband came back, he was always so late at harvest time, so she decided to go up to the winery and tackle him then and there. And suppose he admitted it but refused to stop seeing Elaine – or worse, laughed at Alice, asked her what she proposed to do about it . . . Those are exactly the circumstances in which she might have lost her temper, picked up the nearest thing to hand to throw at him and then, having started, found she couldn't stop.'

Thanet was nodding. He could see it all too clearly. 'There's just one snag, though, isn't there? If Alice did do it, why did she insist on going back up to the winery with Vintage, to look at the body? And would she have been sick if she'd seen it before?'

'Maybe she didn't realise he was dead. Maybe she threw everything she could lay her hands on at him and then turned and ran just before he went through the window?'

'She'd have heard the crash, surely,' said Thanet. 'And gone back to investigate?'

They were both silent for a while, thinking, then Thanet stirred. 'Well, all this speculation isn't getting us very far. In fact, I don't suppose we are going to get much further unless we can come up with some concrete evidence. Still, we ought to go through the motions, so . . .'

'Don't tell me,' said Lineham, pulling a face. 'We ought to go through the files.'

They both hated this stage in a case, when there was no obvious way forward. Equally, they both knew how valuable it could be to stand back and take a fresh look at what had already come in. Details which may have seemed unimportant when they first emerged could later on, in the light of new information, prove significant. And as their knowledge of the people involved in the case became more extensive, discrepancies in behaviour initially dismissed as irrelevant could stand out as being worthy of further scrutiny.

The phone rang and Lineham snatched it up eagerly. 'Yes? I see. Right, Sister. Yes, of course. Certainly. We'll come along right away.'

He put the phone down, beaming. 'Saved by the bell.'

'Sister?' said Thanet.

'Sister Benedict. No she's not a nun. She's the sister in charge of the ward where Randish's nephew is recuperating after that motorcycle accident.'

'Jonathan Redman.'

Lineham's eyebrows went up. 'I didn't know you knew his surname.'

'It's a long story. I forgot to mention this before, it didn't seem relevant. But to be brief, he and his twin sister – the girl who died – are friends of Bridget's. She's been to visit him in hospital.'

'Well, apparently he's asking to see you.'

'Me, specifically?'

'Well, the detective in charge of the Randish case.'

'I wonder why.'

As they hurried down the stairs like schoolboys excused from a particularly tedious piece of homework, Thanet told Lineham the little he knew about the boy.

'And Bridget says he doesn't remember anything about the accident?'

'When she saw him yesterday he hadn't even remembered his sister was dead. Bridget said his mother was dreading breaking the news to him all over again.'

'Poor kid. I can imagine. So perhaps his memory has come back. Perhaps, before he had the accident that night, he'd been driving along the road past the vineyard and saw something significant – someone leaving, whatever . . .'

'We'll soon find out. But I shouldn't get too excited, Mike. I don't suppose it's anything very important.'

'Anything's better than nothing,' said Lineham.

In the hospital Lineham set off briskly along the corridors with the air of someone who knows where he is going. He had become familiar with the sprawling, labyrinthine mass of Sturrenden General Hospital in the days

228

when Louise had been working here full-time. Thanet trailed along behind.

Sister Benedict was evidently on the look-out for them; the moment they set foot in the entrance to the ward she appeared and asked them to step into her office. She was young and pretty, with a shining cap of hair the colour of burnished copper, a sight to gladden the heart of any sick person, Thanet felt. Her manner was brisk, businesslike, but there was no doubt about her concern for her patient.

'You might as well know that I don't think this is at all a good idea,' she said sternly. 'Jonathan had a really nasty motorcycle accident a couple of days ago and was unconscious for the first twenty-four hours. He didn't come out of intensive care until yesterday, so I really do not want him upset.'

'I do understand,' said Thanet. 'I know a bit about him, as a matter of fact. He's a friend of my daughter's and she's been in to visit him.'

'The pretty girl with fair hair?'

Thanet nodded, with the small inner glow of satisfaction he always experienced when anyone paid Bridget a compliment.

'Well, you'll know what I'm talking about, then. But he seems so determined to speak to the police I didn't think he'd settle until he had.'

'What does he want to see us about, do you know?'

She shook her head.

'When did he start asking for us?'

'After his mother left, about an hour ago.'

'She's been here all day?'

'No. I understand she didn't leave his side for the first forty-eight hours. Then last night we managed to persuade her to go home and try to get some rest. I don't think she did, though. Poor woman, she's having a terrible time ... There's this awful murder, for a start and then ... But, of course, you'd know about her daughter, Karen, Jonathan's twin?'

'Yes, Karen and my daughter have been good friends for years.'

'You'd know that Jonathan and his sister were very close, then. He was with her when she died, apparently, and his mother thinks that it was because he was so upset, afterwards, that he was driving carelessly and had the accident. Your daughter may have told you that he has partial amnesia, which is quite common, of course, after an accident, but the awful thing is that in this case it also extended to the period just before, and he had forgotten that his sister was dead. His mother was absolutely dreading breaking the news to him again.'

'You're using the past tense. I gather he's now been told?'

'She told him this afternoon. She came back late this morning and we had to tell her that as he was feeling so much better, Jonathan was urging us to put him in a wheelchair and let him go and visit his sister. In fact, that's the reason he's still in bed. We felt that the minute we allowed him up it would be difficult to keep on finding excuses for not letting him do so. But that situation couldn't be allowed to go on indefinitely, obviously, and although we very much sympathised with Mrs Redman we felt we had to make this clear to her. We did offer to break the news of Karen's death to Jonathan for her, but she said no, she'd rather do it herself.'

'So how did he take it?'

Sister Benedict lifted her hands in a gesture of surprise. 'Astonishingly well, I gather. She said he just went very quiet, seemed to go off into a trance. Patients never fail to surprise us. You can simply never tell how how they're going to react. Anyway, she was a lot happier when she went off just now – if you can use that word, in her present circumstances.'

'And how does he seem now?'

'Quiet. But then, he's been quiet all along.' She gave a rueful smile. 'But not docile, mind. As I said, he was absolutely determined to see you.'

'Did his mother also tell him about his uncle's death, or did he hear about it in some other way – radio, television, newspaper?'

'He hasn't been out of bed yet,' said Sister Benedict, 'and the television is in the day room. And he's not been feeling well enough to read or listen to the radio on the head phones. After a crack on the head like that you need rest and quiet. No, I think she must have told him. We did discuss whether he should be told or not and although she was reluctant to do so, she did realise he might otherwise hear about it in the media. I don't think she was too worried about breaking the news to him, actually. I got the impression he wasn't particularly close to his uncle. It was telling him about his sister's death that was worrying her much more.'

While they had been talking she had relaxed but now the stern look with which she had met them returned. 'I'll take you in to see him now but please remember what I said. I really do not want him upset. As I say, if he hadn't been so insistent I would have refused to ring you, made him wait until tomorrow.'

'We'll do our best, Sister, I promise.'

She led them right down the ward to the far left-hand corner. Thanet always hated walking the length of a hospital ward. He never knew whether to smile to right and left, acknowledging those patients who were conscious as if he were visiting royalty, or to ignore them. At least on this occasion, with Sister Benedict marching purposefully ahead, he didn't have to scrutinise each one in search of a familiar face. Which was probably just as well. He may have met Jonathan Redman in the past, amongst all the other young people Bridget brought home, but he didn't think he'd know him when he saw him.

But he was wrong. Sister Benedict had stopped and the face on the pillows before them was at least vaguely familiar. Although Karen and Jonathan had been non-identical twins there was still a strong resemblance. And it was obvious that the lad had recognised him.

Thanet had been prepared, obviously, for Jonathan to look ill, but he was still shocked by what he saw. Jonathan's face was paper-white, his head was still swathed in bandages and his hands lay limply on the bedcover. Like Karen he had always been slight in build and his body seemed scarcely to mound the blankets.

Sister Benedict glanced from one to the other. 'Well, here are your policemen, Jonathan. No need to introduce you, I see. I'll leave you to it.'

With a last, warning look at Thanet she swept the curtains around the bed, creating a false illusion of privacy, and left.

Thanet and Lineham seated themselves on the stools provided for visitors.

'Well then, Jonathan,' said Thanet smiling. 'What's all this about?'

TWENTY

'But before you tell me,' Thanet went on, 'let me say how very sorry Mrs Thanet and I were to hear about Karen.'

Jonathan pressed his lips together and turned his head away. Thanet was dismayed to see tears roll down the boy's cheeks. Jonathan looked so young, he thought, more like sixteen than twenty, and desperately vulnerable. Perhaps he shouldn't have mentioned Karen? But how could he have spent some time talking to the lad without saying a word about her? He watched helplessly as Jonathan wiped the tears away and mumbled an apology. With three people in it the tiny enclosed world of the curtained cubicle suddenly seemed claustrophobically small and on impulse Thanet leaned across and murmured in Lineham's ear. Jonathan might feel more comfortable alone with someone he knew. Discreetly, Lineham withdrew.

'Thanks, Mr Thanet.' But despite the expression of gratitude Jonathan didn't look any more at ease.

Thanet decided it would be best to press on, let the boy get off his chest whatever it was that was worrying him. Conscious of the fact that there was another patient in a bed only a few feet away, he moved his stool closer to Jonathan and said in a low voice, 'So, why did you ask to see the police?'

'You are in charge of my uncle's case?'

'Yes.' Jonathan wasn't merely uneasy, Thanet realised, he was very much afraid, and in the split second before the boy spoke again he experienced a tremor of premonition.

'I wanted to tell you I killed him.'

Thanet felt as though he had run into a brick wall that had materialised from nowhere. He stared at Jonathan, astounded.

Jonathan's fingers clutched convulsively at the bedclothes and his tone was despairing as he said, 'This may sound crazy, but I didn't remember anything about it until a couple of hours ago, when Mum told me about . . . about the murder.'

In a blinding flash of comprehension Thanet suddenly saw it all. 'It was Karen, wasn't it? She told you, before she died?'

There was no need for him to spell it out. They were both on the same wavelength. Jonathan nodded, eyes full of misery. 'So you know about the baby.'

'Yes.' Thanet was uncomfortably aware that he knew only because of a confidence between Bridget and her mother.

'I suppose Bridget told you. I expect she thought it didn't matter, now Karen is dead.' There was no condemnation in Jonathan's voice. He just sounded inexpressibly weary, defeated.

Still, Thanet felt bound to defend his daughter. 'I wouldn't put it like that. She's known for years and has never said a word. I think it's only because she was so upset about Karen that she told her mother now. And naturally, my wife told me. We had no idea who the father was, of course.'

'Neither did we. Karen never would tell us, I don't

know why. To be honest, I suspected ... I feel awful about it now, but ... Oh, God ...' He put up a hand, rubbed his forehead as if to ease the pain of knowing. 'In the beginning Mum tried to get it out of her, but ... I didn't know much about it at the time, of course. In fact, I don't think anyone ever actually spelled it out to me, that my sister was having a baby. Mum finds it difficult to talk about things like that. But later, when Karen's anorexia got worse – did you know the theory was that the pregnancy triggered off the anorexia?'

'Yes, I did.'

After a halting start Jonathan was now well launched into his story. It was, no doubt, the first time he had ever talked about this to anyone outside the family and it would probably be an immense relief to him to get it off his chest. All Thanet now had to do was lend a sympathetic ear and make the occasional appropriate response.

'Well later, when this came out, I was much older of course, and Dad was dead. Mum didn't have anyone else to talk to, and she was so sick with worry about Karen she just had to talk to someone, so she talked to me. And she told me that at the time it was almost as if, all along, Karen would never really accept that she was actually having a baby. Mum said it was impossible to talk to her about it. She wouldn't even acknowledge your question, she'd just ignore it, change the subject. In the end Mum gave up. And afterwards, after the baby was born, I think all we wanted to do was forget about it as quickly as possible, put the whole thing behind us. I think we might even have managed to pretend it had never happened if it hadn't been for Karen's anorexia. But on Friday ... On Friday, I think she knew, knew she was going to die. And I think I knew it, too. And I couldn't bear the thought that I would never, ever know who'd done this to her. So

I pressed her to tell me. I'd never done that before and I suppose she could see how important it was to me. So she told me.'

Jonathan shook his head, slowly, as if even the slightest movement hurt. 'I still don't understand why she never told anyone before. You'd think she'd have wanted people to know, wanted him punished. I can only think it must have been because she knew how upset Mum would be. Mum thought the sun shone out of Uncle Zak, still does – did. I don't think they had much of a life with their parents and this made a pretty strong bond between them. I know she did all she could to encourage him to get a decent education. From things she's said I suspect that while he was away at college she regularly used to send him money from the little she earned, and I think she always felt she'd contributed to his success. And I must admit he's always been decent to her. He's helped us out ever since Dad died . . . Looking back, I suppose that was conscience money,' he added bitterly.

Brisk footsteps tapped their way down the ward and Sister Benedict put her head around the curtain. 'Everything all right?' She gave Jonathan a penetrating look and, apparently satisfied by his appearance and their reassurances, left them alone again.

'The really awful thing,' said Jonathan into the ensuing silence, 'is that I was there when it happened – oh, not present of course, I don't mean that. But around, somewhere.'

'When he . . .' Thanet found he couldn't say 'raped'. Not to this grieving boy and not in these circumstances. He resorted to the common euphemism. 'When he abused her, you mean?'

'Yes. For the last hour or two, ever since Mum told me Karen had died – I'd forgotten, can you believe that? Forgotten, that my twin sister was dead!'

'The mind plays odd tricks,' said Thanet. 'Sometimes we "forget" what we don't want to remember. And as I'm sure they've told you, amnesia of varying degrees is very common in cases of head injury.'

'Well anyway, ever since she told me, and it all came back to me in a rush – what Karen had said, and what I'd done afterwards – I've been lying here struggling to block out those last pictures of what happened to Uncle Zak by trying to remember. It was when we were twelve. Mum had to go into hospital for some minor op ... She was only away for a couple of days, and for some reason Dad couldn't look after us – I think he was away on business or something. Anyway, Uncle Zak took us out to stay with him and Auntie Alice, at the vineyard. That was when it happened, apparently. It was just that once.' Jonathan gave Thanet a miserable glance and shook his head. 'It doesn't bear thinking about, does it? A few minutes' pleasure and he'd signed Karen's death warrant.'

It sounded melodramatic but it was the simple truth, thought Thanet. 'Look, Jonathan, you're not trying to say you feel responsible, are you? That you should have protected Karen, prevented it happening? Because that simply isn't true.'

'Isn't it?'

'No! A boy of twelve can't be his sister's self-appointed guardian twenty-four hours of the day, every day, year after year. Because we're not just talking about the time you spent at the vineyard. Karen was equally vulnerable at any time, before or since.'

Jonathan said nothing.

'You really must not torture yourself like this,' said Thanet.

Still Jonathan remained silent. But he must have been

considering what Thanet had said because eventually he sighed, plucked at a loose thread on his pyjama cuff and said, 'I suppose you're right.'

'I am,' said Thanet, with all the certainty he could muster.

'Anyway,' said Jonathan with a sudden spurt of energy, 'that doesn't alter the fact that he thought he'd got away with it, the filthy pig! God, how he must have squirmed, when he learnt Karen was pregnant – as I assume he must have – in case she gave him away! But as time went on and nothing happened he must have felt more and more safe. And all the while, Karen was slowly dying . . . When she told me, on Friday, all this seemed to sort of explode in my head. I didn't show it, of course. I didn't want to upset her. She died soon afterwards.' Jonathan bit his lip to stop it trembling. 'And when she did . . . I couldn't bear to stay there, in the same room, and look at her. All I could think of was having it out with him, telling him what I thought of him, *making* him understand what he'd done to her . . .' Jonathan shook his head in wonderment. 'I assume I must have got on my motorbike and driven out to the vineyard, but I don't remember a thing about that. The next thing I remember is barging into his laboratory.'

Even though he knew what he was going to hear Thanet was conscious that his breathing had become shallow, his pulse had speeded up. Now, at last, he was approaching the heart of the mystery.

'He was standing at the bench, doing something with test tubes. I wanted to go for him but I made myself stop. I wanted him to *know* what he'd done.'

'Jonathan! What the hell do you mean, bursting in here like –'

'Shut up! She's dead, you bastard, and you killed her!'

'What do you mean? Who's dead? What are you talking . . .?'

'Karen! Karen's dead! Oh, what a relief that must be for you! Now no one will ever know!'

'Know what? Really, Jonathan, you –'

'Don't "really, Jonathan" me! I'll spell it out for you, shall I? I've come straight from the hospital, where my sister Karen has just died. And before she died she told me that it was you – you, who raped her when she was a kid of twelve – only a few years older than Fiona. How would you feel if Fiona has a baby when she's twelve because some filthy pervert couldn't keep his hands off her? Yes, that got to you, didn't it?'

'Jonathan. Calm down. I'm sorry to hear about Karen . . .'

'Are you? Are you sorry? Like hell you are!'

'I repeat, I'm sorry to hear about Karen. But I really cannot see how that makes me responsible for her death.'

'Oh you can't, can't you? Well that's because you haven't been living with her for the past eight years, seen her dying by inches because when she was pregnant with your bastard she got it into her head for once and for all that she was too bloody fat!'

'Fat!'

'And he thought that was *funny!*' Jonathan shook his head in despair. 'Funny! When it was thinking she was too fat that killed her! The bastard grinned! He actually grinned! And that did it. I went for him.'

David and Goliath, thought Thanet. He could visualise it all too vividly: the slight figure hurling itself in fury against the tall, well-muscled Zak Randish.

239

'But he was so much stronger than me. He just put up his hands, got hold of my forearms and held me off. Oh God, it was so humiliating . . .'

'*Jonathan. Calm down and back off, will you?*'
'*Let me go. Let me go, you pervert!*'
'*All right, I will.*'

'And he just sort of threw me back against the wall. I fell over and as I got up I noticed some full bottles of wine lined up on the floor under one of the benches. I grabbed one and, without thinking, threw it at him. He ducked and I missed. The bottle smashed through the window behind him and . . . I don't know how to describe what happened next. It was as if the sound of breaking glass triggered off something in my head, as if I actually felt something snap in my brain . . . Honest, Mr Thanet, I'm not trying to make excuses, just trying to tell you how it was.'

'I know that, Jonathan.'

The boy shook his head. 'I suppose I just went berserk. I just chucked everything I could lay my hands on at him. I didn't mean to kill him, I just, well, I suppose I just wanted to get that awful . . . rage out of my system. I can't tell you exactly what made him lose his balance and go over backwards, but he did. One moment he was standing there and the next he'd crashed through the window. The blood . . . It was horrible. And then he just sort of slid down into a sitting position. There was blood everywhere, and it was really gushing out, pouring down his neck and front . . . He . . .'

'All right, Jonathan. No need to go on. I get the picture.'

'I couldn't move. It was as if I was paralysed or something. It seemed only a matter of seconds before he slumped sideways and I could see he was dead. So I ran.'

And you were so distraught that on the way back you had the accident, thought Thanet. Once again he wondered if it had been the site of Jonathan's accident he had passed on the way to the station to meet Bridget, Jonathan on the stretcher he had seen being loaded into the ambulance.

'Jonathan,' he said, 'I have to ask you this, because others will do so. Why didn't you ring for an ambulance?'

'But he was dead! There was no point!'

'Did you check?'

'No, but it was obvious.'

'What do you mean?'

Jonathan frowned, remembering, and trying to work it out. 'It was his eyes,' he said at last. 'If people are just unconscious they have their eyes shut. His sort of . . . glazed over, and stayed open.'

'Yes, I see. All the same, it might have been a good idea, just in case.' A fatuous statement, really. Jonathan had obviously been incapable of rational thought.

'I suppose so. Oh God, what a mess. I don't know how Mum's going to react. What on earth am I going to say to her?'

'She'll have to know. And know why you did it, too. Or perhaps you've already told her it was your uncle who was responsible for Karen's pregnancy?'

Jonathan shook his head. 'When it all came back to me I was too shocked to tell her anything, in case I said the wrong thing. Does she *have* to know it was him?'

'Oh come on, Jonathan,' said Thanet gently. 'How else are you going to explain what happened? In any case, she's bound to find out eventually.'

'It'll come out in Court, you mean. Oh God, I don't think I can face it. Unless . . .' He looked up, his eyes gleaming.

'Unless what?' By the way Jonathan was looking at him Thanet had a feeling something tricky was about to come up.

'I don't suppose . . . No, I can't ask you.'

Thanet refrained from asking 'What?' He thought he could guess.

Jonathan waited a moment and when Thanet didn't respond said desperately, 'Have you told anyone else about Karen and the baby?'

'Of course not!'

'Well, no one else knows. If you didn't tell anyone, I wouldn't have to either, would I? I mean, I could just say I did it because I was angry with Uncle Zak.'

'About what?'

Jonathan waved a hand. 'I'd think of something.'

'No. Sorry, Jonathan, I couldn't agree to that.'

'But why not? Bridget told Mrs Thanet in confidence, didn't she? And Mrs Thanet told you. If you tell anyone else Bridget will be furious with you.'

'I know,' said Thanet grimly. 'But the fact is that I simply cannot withhold evidence which has come into my possession. And if Bridget realises, and I would make sure she did, that knowing *why* you killed your uncle would probably have a profound effect upon the kind of sentence you're likely to get, I think she'll probably forgive me. I really am sorry, Jonathan, but I can't do it. In any case, as far as your mother's concerned, just remember you're all she has left now. I think you'll find it's more important to her to understand why you did this than to preserve your uncle's reputation.'

'Do you think so?'

'I do. And what's more, in the circumstances, I think Karen would, too.'

'But I promised her I wouldn't tell anyone, ever!'

242

'Circumstances have changed, you must see that. Do you think she'd want you to spend years and years in prison?'

'I will anyway, surely.'

'Your chances will be improved, if the jury can be given good reason why you lost control as you did. It's no good, Jonathan. You really can't keep quiet about this.'

Jonathan remained silent, lips set in a stubborn line.

'Look,' said Thanet, with an inward sigh. 'Would it help if I told your mother for you? At least then you will, strictly speaking, have kept your word.'

It was a compromise, a less than satisfactory solution, but Jonathan seized on the suggestion eagerly. 'Would you? Would you really?'

What have I let myself in for? thought Thanet as he walked back down the ward. I must be mad.

Lineham was sitting on a chair outside Sister Benedict's office. She must have been watching out for Thanet through the glass panel which gave her a view of what was going on in her ward, because she came out as he approached. 'How is he?' she said.

Lineham stood up, joining them as Thanet said, 'Happier in his mind, I think. Would you excuse me just for a moment, Sister?'

He felt he owed it to Lineham to break the news to him first. When he did so, the sergeant looked as stunned as he himself had initially felt.

'And you believed him?'

'Yes, Mike, I did. Look, I'll explain it all to you in a minute, but I have to square things with sister, first.'

Sister Benedict, too, reacted with incredulity and once again Thanet had to explain that he was taking the confession seriously. 'I'm afraid we shall have to cause you a certain amount of disruption. I know he's not going anywhere at the moment but I shall have to put someone on guard here and of course we shall have to take a formal statement. He'll need to see his solicitor, too.'

After the initial shock Sister Benedict had made a swift recovery. 'From what you're saying, I assume I can take it that he is no danger either to my staff or my patients?'

'Absolutely not. I can guarantee it.'

'Right. Well, in that case, one of the side wards is vacant. We'll put him in there.'

'An excellent idea.'

She put her office at their disposal and arrangements were swiftly made.

'Right,' said Lineham, as they left. 'I can't wait to hear this.'

'I'll tell you on the way.'

'Where to?'

'To see Jonathan's mother. And believe me, I'm not looking forward to it.'

TWENTY-ONE

Thanet decided that it would be best to sit in the car in the hospital car park to talk. Explanations would be complicated and he wanted Lineham's undivided attention. Lineham listened in silence and when Thanet had finished said, 'Poor kid.'

'Jonathan, you mean? Or Karen?'

'Both of them.'

'Well, I never thought the day would dawn, but at last it has!'

'What day?'

'The day when you were actually sorry for someone who has committed a murder!'

Lineham looked sheepish. 'Well, these are rather unusual circumstances, sir.'

'Murders frequently are committed in unusual circumstances. No, Mike, there's no doubt about it. What I said the other day is true. You are definitely going soft in your old age.'

At thirty-four Lineham was able to smile at the idea.

Thanet sobered. 'Unfortunately, so am I, if in a rather different way.'

'What do you mean?'

'Because the idea that Jonathan could have done it never even entered my head!'

'But how could you possibly have known?'

'Well, I don't see how *you* could have worked it out, certainly – and don't look like that, Mike! I'm not in the habit of insulting you, am I? I'm about to explain why! The point is that in order to have done so you really did need one or two essential pieces of information – or rather, three, to be precise: that Karen had had a baby when she was twelve; that no one ever knew who the father was; and that it was her pregnancy which triggered off the anorexia that killed her. You had none of them, but I had them all.'

'Even if you did, I don't see how you could have guessed.'

'Not guessed. Worked it out. Yes I could! Think about it. The clues were all there.' Thanet began to tick them off on his fingers as he spoke. 'Landers told us that Alice Randish had been particularly fond of Karen ever since the twins came to stay at the vineyard for a few days when their mother was in hospital, and *that it was just before Fiona was born.*'

'Why is that so significant?'

'For two reasons. One, Fiona is eight. Now, I knew that Karen was twenty, because she is the same age as Bridget. And I later learnt that Karen was twelve when she had the baby.'

'So you could have worked out that it was around the time when they went to stay at the vineyard that Karen became pregnant – and therefore, that Randish might have been responsible.'

'Exactly.'

'And the second reason?'

'Because if it was just before Fiona was born, Randish

might well have been suffering from sexual frustration. And he was always a man who needed women.'

'And Karen just happened to be around at the time, you mean?'

'Quite.'

'Nasty.'

'He was a pretty nasty character, by all accounts. And that in itself was important, too. Only a nasty character would have taken advantage of his twelve-year-old niece.'

'Go on.'

'Landers also told us that Karen seemed to get on better with Alice Randish than with her uncle.'

'Nothing unusual about that. Everyone's got relations they like better than others.'

'You're missing the point, Mike. The point is that the fact has significance only if you take other factors into consideration.'

'So, what other factors?'

'A major one was Randish's taste in women.'

'Small, slight, you mean.'

'Invariably, yes.'

'I see what you're getting at. As Karen would have been. Not quite the same thing, though, is it? A twelve-year-old girl?'

'Perhaps not. But has it occurred to you that possibly that was where Randish's taste truly lay? That he picked his women because physically they were the nearest thing to pubescent?'

'That's a thought, sir. Do you think he might have tried it on with Elaine Wood? She was ten at the time. Perhaps that's another reason why she was so determined to get her own back on him.'

'Possibly. If so, I don't suppose we'll ever know. And of course I could be doing him an injustice in suggesting it.'

'He must have got the fright of his life when he heard Karen was pregnant. Perhaps that's what has kept him on the straight and narrow ever since.'

'So far as we know. Quite. Anyway, the other thing that ought to have put me on to Jonathan, of course, was the coincidence of two deaths and a major accident in one family within the space of only a couple of hours. Just think what the odds must be against it! There *seemed* to be no connection between them but I really should have realised that there must be – or at the very least have considered that there might be. If I had, all these other things would have begun to fall into place. I just assumed that Jonathan had had an accident because he was so upset after being with his sister when she died. But if I'd checked the time at which he left the hospital along with the time of his accident, I might have begun to wonder if he hadn't been upset for another reason, such as witnessing or even committing a murder.'

'There seemed to be such a tenuous connection . . .'

'But the connection was there, that's the point. And knowing all these other facts, I should have spotted that it was more important than we assumed. In fact, I ought to know by now that you shouldn't assume anything, in this game, ever.'

'I think you're being unduly hard on yourself.'

'I haven't finished yet! There's one other, further point, which came up only this afternoon. It was just a small thing, but it should have given me cause to think . . . You remember when we called in at my house, for me to change? Well, Bridget was there. She'd got soaked too, and I nearly fell over her trainers. She'd left them on the mat in the hall, so I picked them up. They were in an awful state – caked with mud. And there was a fragment of glass embedded in the sole of one of them.'

'So? I don't see what you're getting at.'

'Glass, Mike! Think!'

'I'm beginning to feel distinctly dim, sir. I can't see any possible connection between Bridget's trainers and Jonathan's guilt.'

'No, you're not being dim, Mike. I'm not being fair to you. Once again, I'm in possession of the facts and you're not. Will it make a difference if I tell you this? When Bridget went to visit Jonathan yesterday she discovered that Mrs Redman hadn't left Jonathan's bedside since she first arrived at the hospital after the accident. There were various things that needed to be done, so Bridget volunteered to do them – and this included taking Jonathan's clothes home. The clothes he was wearing on the night of the murder.'

'I see ... You're saying that Jonathan might have picked up some splinters of glass either in the soles of his shoes or elsewhere in his clothes and that when Bridget was handling his things, some of them might have fallen out and she trod in them?'

'Possibly, Mike, yes. Oh, I do realise that she could have picked that bit of glass up anywhere, that it could be pure coincidence. But you saw what a state the laboratory was in. Glass must have been flying about all over the place. Anyway, forensic might be able to verify – provided I can rescue the piece of glass from our kitchen waste bin. I actually put it there myself! In any case, whether that was what happened or whether she picked it up somewhere else, by chance, it was one more thing which should at least have given me pause for thought, a nudge in the right direction. No, Mike, there's no doubt about it. I've been shamefully slow on the uptake.'

'Well, I still think you're being too hard on yourself. And in any case, we'd no doubt have got there in the end.'

'When forensic identified Jonathan's fingerprints on pieces of glass picked up in the laboratory, you mean? I'd like to think so, yes – if it would ever have occurred to us to take his prints in the first place, to compare them..'

'It would have,' said Lineham confidently. 'You'd have added two and two together sooner or later. I'm sure of it.'

'I wish I agreed with you.'

'If you don't mind me saying so, sir, I think what's really bugging you is that Jonathan got in first with his confession and beat you to it.'

'Ouch. You're probably right. And if you are it'll do me good to be brought down a peg or two.' Thanet grinned. 'The trouble with you, Mike, is that you know me too well.' He glanced at his watch. 'Anyway, we'd better make a move. I want to get this over with.' He gave Lineham Mrs Redman's address.

'I assume we're going to see her to break the news of Jonathan's confession,' said Lineham as he started the car.

'There's a bit more to it than that, I'm afraid.'

Thanet explained his agreement with Jonathan and Lineham groaned. 'Great! Honestly, sir, you do land yourself in it, don't you?'

The Redmans lived on a big council estate on the far side of town. It was five o'clock and despite the much vaunted one-way system which had been installed some years ago, the roads were clogged with home-going traffic. Patiently, Lineham settled down to work his way through the endless sets of traffic lights.

Although he wasn't looking forward to the interview, by the time they arrived Thanet found that he was feeling increasingly curious about Mrs Redman. So far she had been a shadowy figure, ever-present but always in the background, out of sight. He had met her a couple of times briefly, years ago, at school functions, but she was very quiet and they had scarcely exchanged more than a few words.

She had certainly had more than her share of misfortune, he thought: an unhappy childhood with a 'drunken brute' of a father, a difficult marriage with a rigid, unyielding man who had given both Bridget and Ben 'the creeps', and then all the pain of seeing a daughter who was no more than a child bear a child herself as the result of rape and thereafter spend the remaining years of her short life in and out of hospital under the cloud of anorexia. Then, to cap it all, had come the events of the last few days.

And he, Thanet, was about to deliver the *coup de grâce* – no, not a *coup de grâce*, because he wouldn't be putting Mrs Redman out of her misery but increasing it tenfold. What on earth had he been thinking of, actually to volunteer for a task like this? he asked himself as the car slid smoothly to a stop outside her house. He glanced at Lineham, who pulled a face. 'Good luck, sir. I'd rather you than me. Do you want me to come in with you?'

Thanet shook his head. 'It'll be easier alone.'

The sky had become overcast again and lights had been switched on in some of the houses. The Redmans' house and garden were well cared for but all the curtains had been drawn and the place looked deserted, forlorn, as if the life had bled slowly out of it and all that was left was an empty shell.

Thanet told himself not to be fanciful. He walked briskly up the concrete path, noting the regimented rows of newly planted wallflowers, and knocked at the front door. There was no reply. He knocked again, stepped back, scanned the house, glanced over his shoulder at Lineham, who gave an exaggerated shrug. He knocked once more, still with no response. He was about to give up, walk away, when there was a sound from above. The curtain had been pulled aside and the window opened a crack. A face peered out. 'Yes?'

'Mrs Redman? It's Inspector Thanet, Bridget's father. Could I have a word?'

'I'll be right down.' The window closed.

She had no doubt been having a rest, thought Thanet, feeling guilty at having disturbed her. The past few days must have been exhausting beyond belief. He shifted his weight from one foot to the other as he waited, thinking that breaking bad news to people was the part of his job he hated most, and how this time was even worse because he knew everybody involved.

He didn't have to wait long. In a few moments the door opened. She had put on a plaid woollen dressing gown which was so long it touched the floor and looked as though it might once have belonged to her husband. She was still tying the twisted two-coloured cord at her waist. 'Is it Jonathan?' Her face was knotted with anxiety, as if she were bracing herself for the worst. She was, as he remembered, a little wisp of a woman who scarcely reached his shoulder. Unless she had married or had children very late indeed she must be about the same age as he and Joan, but she looked many years older. Long-term suffering and anxiety had left their mark, scoring deep furrows between her eyes and draining away any vitality she might once have possessed.

'Jonathan's fine,' said Thanet. 'I've just left him, as a matter of fact. But I do need to talk to you.'

She peered back at him anxiously, over her shoulder, as she led him into the room at the front of the house, switching the light on as she went in. With daylight still seeping in around the edges of the drawn curtains the artificial light cast a sickly glow over the sparsely furnished room. Randish's so-called generosity to his sister's family certainly didn't show in here, thought Thanet, noting the scuffed carpet and worn loose covers. The room, though shabby, showed evidence of care – it was scrupulously clean and someone, Jonathan perhaps, had recently given the walls a coat of emulsion paint. There was a small twelve-inch television set on a table in the corner. Evidently, since Mr Redman's death, some of the household rules had been relaxed.

She sat down on the very edge of a chair, tucking the dressing gown around her legs as if even a glimpse of ankle would be improper. 'Is it about the accident?'

'No, it's not.' Thanet took a deep breath. There was no way that this was going to be easy. Nothing could cushion the blow. He hesitated, seeking the right words. 'I'm afraid it's rather more serious than that.'

'It's about my brother, then? About his . . . death.' The last word was barely audible.

'Yes, it is. And I'm sorry. You've had a lot to bear these last few days, Mrs Redman. My wife and I were so upset to hear about Karen.'

She stared at him and he saw she was fighting to hold back the tears. The prospect of what he was about to do appalled him, but it had to be done. Perhaps in the circumstances it was not a good idea to be too sympathetic. Deliberately, he made his tone brisk. 'Yes, as I say, it does concern your brother. But I'm afraid, in connection with Mr Randish's death, it also concerns Jonathan.'

Surprise helped her to regain her self-control. 'How?'

Thanet put into words what he had been thinking a moment ago. 'Mrs Redman, there is no way I can soften this blow. But I was at the hospital because Jonathan asked to see me. Specifically, he asked to see the officer in charge of the investigation into your brother's death. Because he wanted to confess.'

She blinked, and it was a moment or two before her lips moved. 'Confess?' The word emerged as a whisper.

Thanet nodded.

'You mean ...' It was no more than a thread of sound.

'I'm sorry. Yes.' He had to spell it out, make sure that there was no misunderstanding. 'Jonathan has confessed to his uncle's murder.'

She was shaking her head. 'There must be some mistake. He wouldn't. He couldn't have.'

'There's no mistake, I'm afraid.'

Her head was still moving from side to side in rejection of what he was saying.

'Mrs Redman. Please. Listen. I have got to tell you.'

Suddenly she was still, intent. He waited a moment until he was certain she was concentrating and then said, 'This is what Jonathan has said. He told me that he went out to the vineyard on Friday night, that he had an argument with his uncle, that he lost his temper and started throwing things at him. Your brother slipped and crashed backwards through the window. That was how he died. Jonathan had no intention of causing his death, of course. He was so shocked that on the way back he had the accident. He must have been incapable of driving safely. I have to add that his account of the incident corresponds in every detail with what happened, details he couldn't possibly have known unless he had been there.'

She was staring at him, a fixed and desperate stare, as if every ounce of intelligence she possessed was being directed towards attempting to understand the incomprehensible. 'It can't be true. Why hasn't he told me? Why hasn't he said a word about it till now? And why, why should he have such a violent argument with his uncle in the first place?'

'If you think about it you'll realise why he hasn't said anything about this before. As you know, until this afternoon, he didn't even remember that Karen . . . what had happened to Karen. Not until you reminded him. But when you did, it all came back to him in a rush. He didn't say anything to you about his uncle then because it was such a shock to him to remember what he had done that at first he couldn't even begin to think straight.'

'But why? You still haven't explained why? I can't see any possible reason . . .' She had wound the loose ends of the waist cord around her hands so tightly in her agitation that her fingers were beginning to turn white. 'It must all be in his imagination. It's the blow on the head that's done it.' The idea drove her to her feet, twisting her hands to release them from the constricting cord. 'Yes. That's what it is.' She stood looking down at him, her eyes frantic, panting in her terror, agitation and anxiety to convince.

Thanet was cursing himself for not having had the commonsense to bring a policewoman with him. Was there no end to his blunders in this case? He stood up and grasped her hands. 'Please, Mrs Redman, sit down, and I'll explain.' Gently, Thanet coaxed her backwards into her chair. This time she sat well back, arms laid along the chair arms, fingers gripping the ends as if she needed to anchor herself to something solid.

Now came the crunch. 'The reason why Jonathan went rushing out to the vineyard on Friday evening was because before she died, Karen told him something.' He paused, hoping that she would now have an inkling of what he was going to say, but her expression didn't change.

'He told me he had never asked her before, but he sensed that she was slipping away and he felt he couldn't bear never to know who had ...' Thanet struggled to find the right words, conscious that even angels would find it difficult to tread such delicate ground without giving pain. 'Who had fathered her child. So he pressed her to tell him. And she did.'

He watched understanding dawn in her eyes. Slowly, her lips parted. 'Zak?' she whispered.

He nodded, thankful that it was over, done, but apprehensive now of her reaction.

Her eyes glazed and then she was frowning at her lap, gazing down as intently as if she would find there explanations of all that had so mystified her in the past. She was, Thanet realised, reinterpreting all that had happened, rewriting her family's history. Only the whiteness of the knuckles across her clenched fists betrayed how painful the readjustment was. He hadn't known what to expect — tears, hysterics, denials, perhaps — but not this silent suffering which was so painful to watch.

At last she looked up. 'What will happen to Jonathan now?'

He hadn't realised that he had been holding his breath and he released it in a long, slow sigh of relief that she had accepted the truth of what he had told her. He was relieved too that she was thinking now of Jonathan's future, of the living, not the dead, and thankful that she had not questioned how he had come by his intimate knowledge of Karen's past. Perhaps she simply assumed that Jonathan had told him, and he certainly wasn't going to disillusion her.

With any luck, the worst was over.

TWENTY-TWO

Bridget appeared in the hall as Thanet let himself into the house. She looked fresh and pretty in trim jeans and a dark green Dash sweatshirt with a colourful floral design on the front. She had twisted her newly washed hair up into a knot high on the back of her head. 'Hullo, Dad, you're earlier than I expected. Your supper's in the oven. I'll get it.'

She was still feeling low about Alexander, Thanet could tell, but the fact that she had made an effort over her appearance was a good sign, he felt. The girl who had arrived on Friday evening couldn't have cared less what she looked like. He hung up his coat. 'No, don't worry, I'm not hungry at the moment. I'll have it when I get back from the station. Ben in?'

Despite the heavy workload which was the inevitable result of the end of a case, Thanet had made a special effort to get home early in the hope of catching Bridget alone. Joan's car had gone, so he assumed she had left for her meeting.

'Doing his homework, upstairs.'

'Good. I want to talk to you.' Seeing her expression change, become wary, he realised she assumed he meant he wanted to discuss the situation with Alexander. 'About Jonathan,' he hastened to add.

Her eyebrows arched. 'About Jonathan?' She led the way into the sitting room and they both sat down, Thanet careful of his aching back, which was playing up again.

'Yes. I assume you haven't been in to see him this afternoon?' Thanet eased himself into a more comfortable position.

'No. I went in this morning. They seem to have endless visiting hours there. Why?'

'This afternoon, his mother broke the news of Karen's death to him. The shock seemed to act as some sort of trigger, and his memories of Friday night came flooding back.'

'That's great! I told him it would happen, sooner or later.'

'Yes. It's good in one way . . .'

'What do you mean?'

'This afternoon the sister in charge of his ward rang the office, saying that Jonathan wanted to speak to me – that is, to the officer in charge of the Randish case, which of course happened to be me.'

'Really? But why on earth . . .?'

'Just listen, love. So I went to the hospital. Where Jonathan told me that it was he who had killed his uncle.'

Bridget's eyes stretched wide. 'What?'

For the second time that day Thanet had to tell Jonathan's story, thankful that this time it wasn't such a traumatic experience for his audience. Bridget was shocked, yes, upset, but the news obviously didn't have the same emotional impact on her as it had on Mrs Redman. Her final reaction was the same as Lineham's.

'Poor Jonathan. And poor Mrs Redman, too. How is she taking it?'

'Very well, considering. It was an awful shock at first, of course.'

'Is anyone with her? I told you before, she just doesn't seem to have any friends. Perhaps I ought to go around, put off going back to London until tomorrow.'

'No, it's all right. Mrs Landers is with her – her brother's mother-in-law. She's a very nice woman, she'll look after her. She went to see her on Saturday, in the hospital, as soon as she heard about Jonathan's accident.'

'What will happen to Jonathan?'

'I imagine his legal representatives will persuade him to plead not guilty to murder but guilty of manslaughter, on the grounds of provocation and diminished responsibility.'

'Diminished responsibility, presumably, because the shock of his sister's death . . .'

'His *twin* sister's death . . .'

'. . . and of learning that his uncle was morally responsible for it, temporarily unhinged him.'

'That's right, yes.'

'And provocation?'

'Because, as I told you, when Jonathan tried to make his uncle understand why he was so angry with him, tried to explain precisely why he felt Randish was responsible for Karen's death, he laughed at him. That was really what made Jonathan snap, and in the circumstances it would certainly be considered provocation, I think.'

Bridget shivered. 'He must have been a horrible man.'

'Yes, he wasn't exactly an admirable character.'

'So what difference will it make, if the jury does find Jonathan guilty of manslaughter? He'll still go to prison, surely?'

'The difference is that the judge has much greater flexibility in sentencing. It's even possible that, if the judge is sympathetic, in the circumstances Jonathan might get away with a suspended sentence.'

'Oh I do hope so! After all they've been through ... It'll be bad enough as it is, having all their private family affairs broadcast in Court.'

'I know.'

'And then there's Mr Randish's family. Think how they're going to feel when all this comes out! He's got a wife, hasn't he?'

'And two young children, yes.' Thanet sighed. 'That's often the way with murder cases, I'm afraid. So many innocent people get hurt, and the effects go on and on for years.'

'I've often wondered how you feel when you have a case like this one, and the murderer turns out to be someone you really feel sorry for, someone who never intended to commit the crime in the first place.'

'That's a difficult one. There's no doubt you feel quite different if the murder was deliberate, or the result of mindless, wanton violence. But in cases like this ... Well, there is some satisfaction, I suppose, in having brought the thing to a conclusion. But in this particular instance I can't even claim to have done that. If Jonathan hadn't confessed he might never have been found out.'

'I don't believe that. You'd have got there in the end, I'm sure.' Once again, Bridget was echoing Lineham.

'Your faith is touching, love, but I'm afraid it's misplaced.'

'I don't believe that. Come on, Dad, admit it. When you're working on a case you're like a dog with a bone. You can't leave it alone. You go on worrying away at it, worrying away at it until you get there. I've lived with you nearly all my life, remember, and I've seen it happen over and over again!'

There was a sudden thunder of feet on the stairs: Ben in a hurry. The door burst open. 'Oh, hi, Dad, thought I heard you come home. Just nipping over to Tim's. Got a bit of a problem with my Maths. You off soon, Sis?'

'Any minute now,' said Bridget, smiling.

'See you, then.' He hesitated.

He probably wanted to offer comfort over Alexander, but didn't know how to do it, thought Thanet.

'Been nice to have you home,' Ben said awkwardly. And fled without waiting for a response.

There was a brief silence. It was obvious that Bridget, too, recognised what Ben had been trying to do. She flicked a glance at Thanet and gave an embarrassed laugh. 'Good to be appreciated.' Then she looked at her watch. 'Time to be off, Dad.'

Her green and orange squashy bag was already packed, waiting in the hall. Thanet picked it up and slung it over his shoulder. 'Of course,' he said as they walked to the car, 'it goes without saying that all this is in the strictest confidence. Only you've been so involved with Karen, in the past, and with Jonathan, over the last few days, that I felt I owed it to you to explain what happened.'

'I appreciate it, Dad. And, of course, I shan't say a word, to anyone.'

A few minutes later they were approaching the scene of Jonathan's accident. Earlier, curiosity had made Thanet check and yes, there was no doubt about it, it was Jonathan he had seen on that stretcher on Friday night, being loaded into the ambulance. He pointed the place out to Bridget.

'You actually saw the accident?'

'No, I arrived just afterwards. Naturally I had no idea who was involved. I'm afraid I was more concerned with being held up and not getting to the station in time to meet your train.'

It seemed a lifetime away. So much had happened in

those few short days. He had penetrated deep into the lives of those who on that Friday evening had still been strangers to him, equally unaware of his existence. For him the Randish case would one day be no more than an interesting memory, but for them the effects would, as he had said to Bridget, linger on, reverberating into the future. How was Jonathan going to live with the fact that he had killed a man? How was his mother going to come to terms with the fact that her much-loved brother had not only violated her young daughter but ultimately caused Karen's death and made her twin a murderer? Then there was Alice. She would find it very hard, having been so fond of Karen, but her passion for Zak had survived both physical abuse and repeated infidelities and eventually she would, he felt, forgive her dead husband his transgressions as she had forgiven him so many in the past. But what about the children, Fiona and Malcolm? Would their mother and grandparents always be able to keep from them the truth about their father's death?

'What's the matter, Dad?'

'Nothing in particular. Why?'

'You sighed. You're not worrying about me?'

It was the first time, since she had been so angry with him yesterday morning, that either of them had broached the subject. He was tempted to tell her the truth, that he had been thinking about the case, but he couldn't let the opportunity pass. Instead, he avoided a direct answer. 'I am concerned about you, naturally. We all are.'

He glanced at her, but it was difficult to make out her expression. Despite the occasional streetlamp the light in the car was dim. Then, briefly, the flare of passing headlights illuminated her face. She was, he realised with surprise, looking contrite.

'I've been wanting to say . . . I'm sorry I snapped at you yesterday morning,' she said.

'I hope you haven't been worrying about that! I'd forgotten all about it.' Not true, but he wasn't going to tell her that.

They had reached the station and he pulled into a parking place. Neither of them moved, unwilling now to leave unfinished business between them.

'I was thinking about it, afterwards,' said Bridget slowly. 'And I guess I was angry with you because I couldn't forgive you for being right about Alexander.'

Thanet knew how much that double admission must have cost her. But he was glad, too, that she had been able to make it. It was the first, important step back towards recovery. He put out his hand and touched hers, lightly. 'I'm sorry, love. I really mean that. I can't bear to see you unhappy.'

'I know.' Suddenly she was brisk again. 'It's all part of growing up, I suppose. But I must admit, it's a part I could do without.' She opened the door and got out.

Satisfied now that the healing process had begun, he followed suit.

They walked together on to the platform and waited for the train. It arrived on time and he saw her in, waved her off. He watched until its lights had vanished in the distance and then went back to the car. As he pulled away his mind moved ahead, to later on that evening when Joan would come home and he would be able to tell her all about the case.

Not for the first time he felt sorry for all those lonely, divorced or separated detectives in fiction.

As far as he was concerned, there was no substitute for having a wife to go home to.

SIX FEET UNDER

Dorothy Simpson

Curiosity killed the cat. Did it also kill Carrie?

At first Inspector Thanet doesn't know what to make of
the murder of the singularly unprepossessing middle-
aged spinster in a peaceful Kentish garden. He
considers her 'a most unlikely corpse'. But he soon
discovers that she not only had a few startling secrets of
her own but had been in an ideal position to ferret out
those of other people . . .

An alcoholic pianist, a wardrobe of disguises, forbidden
love affairs – strong and unexpected passions smoulder
beneath the surface tranquillity of life in Nettleton.
Thanet warms to the theme of blackmail but surprises
himself when he stumbles upon a rather more bizarre
and tragic explanation . . .

'A most valuable and accomplished mistress of the craft
of detective-story writing'
Gladys Mitchell

'Masterly . . . holds the reader's interest not merely on
every page but with pretty nearly every word'
Easter Daily Press

'Deft double-plotting'
Washington Post

DOOMED TO DIE

Dorothy Simpson

Perdita Master always sought solitude. Now her wish
has been granted – permanently and brutally. Her
body is found in the home of a prominent local
barrister – a chilling confirmation of her childhood fear
that she was doomed to die young.

But why? As Inspector Thanet and Sergeant Lineham
begin their investigations, it becomes apparent that the
clue to the murder lies in the beautiful artist's past.
Had she always been deeply unhappy, even before her
stormy marriage to the difficult, jealous Giles? And
what was the root of the turbulent emotions that she
could only express through her art? Whatever the
reason behind Perdita's untimely death, Inspector
Thanet soon realizes that he will have to read the
desperate mind of the victim, as well as that of the
murderer, to find the answer . . .

'A first-class detective story with well-rounded
characters and emotional problems which hold your
interest'
Annabel

'A subtle tale, dealing with people's dilemmas and
emotions. Simpson fans will be well-satisfied'
Yorkshire Post

'The deception is brought off with a conjurer's bravura'
Matthew Coady, *Guardian*

Other bestselling Warner titles available by mail:

☐ The Night She Died	Dorothy Simpson	£3.99
☐ Six Feet Under	Dorothy Simpson	£4.99
☐ Puppet for a Corpse	Dorothy Simpson	£4.99
☐ Last Seen Alive	Dorothy Simpson	£5.99
☐ Suspicious Death	Dorothy Simpson	£5.99
☐ Dead by Morning	Dorothy Simpson	£4.99
☐ Doomed to Die	Dorothy Simpson	£4.99
☐ Wake the Dead	Dorothy Simpson	£5.99
☐ A Day for Dying	Dorothy Simpson	£5.99

The prices shown above are correct at time of going to press, however the publishers reserve the right to increase prices on covers from those previously advertised, without further notice.

WARNER BOOKS

WARNER BOOKS

Cash Sales Department, P.O. Box 11, Falmouth, Cornwall, TR10 9EN
Tel: +44 (0) 1326 372400, Fax: +44 (0) 1326 374888
Email: books@barni.avel.co.uk.

POST AND PACKING:
Payments can be made as follows: cheque, postal order (payable to Warner Books) or by credit cards. Do not send cash or currency.

All U.K. Orders	**FREE OF CHARGE**
E.E.C. & Overseas	25% of order value

Name (Block Letters) _____

Address _____

_____

Post/zip code: _____

☐ Please keep me in touch with future Warner publications

☐ I enclose my remittance £_____

☐ I wish to pay by Visa/Access/Mastercard/Eurocard

Card Expiry Date

_____